Also by Reg Quist

JUST JOHN

REG QUIST

Published in the United States by Wolfpack Publishing, Las Vegas

CKN Christian Publishing
An Imprint of Wolfpack Publishing
5130 S. Fort Apache Road 215-380
Las Vegas, NV 89148

christiankindlenews.com

Paperback ISBN: 978-1-64734-663-8
eBook ISBN: 978-1-64734-662-1
Library of Congress Control Number: 2021935471

JUST JOHN

Chapter 1

The late evening sound was somewhere between a whisper and a light growl. But John heard the gleefully raspy voice clearly.

"There's them horses I told ya bout, Bronco. Seen them on the trail a bit ago. Ya got yer eye on em down there? Take a good look at that black. Now that there's an animal worth the taking. Worth some money, he is. The bay gelding ain't half bad neither."

A different voice chimed in.

"That ain't the only black that's worth some money, Elmer. That 'ol boy squint'n n' brush'n fire smoke away could bring us a fancy dollar. Most as much as the horses. Big boy like that? Fit for work'n? Will sell fast."

The first voice spoke up again.

"You think he stoled them horses Bronco? Ain't hardly no other way a feller like that could have two such fine animals hidden away."

Without waiting for an answer from Bronco, Elmer stood from his crouched position and started down the slight grade towards John. With the scattered forest and brush making its home on the hillside, plus the year's accumulation of dead grass and crinkled leaves on the ground, there was no hope of silence. John stood still, staring into the semi-darkness, wondering what to do next.

He was big and strong; strong enough to tackle and overcome most men. Most two men. But he knew that, as a slave, he could be in serious trouble if he showed aggression. All he could do was wait and see what happened. Still, he had clearly heard the talk of capture and selling. If there was any move in that direction, he would defend himself. He was bound by a promise to protect his owner's animals and he couldn't do that without protecting himself first.

A week and a half of careful, half scared to death riding, and searching out a way through country totally unfamiliar to him, had John hunkered down beside the small stream, hopefully hidden from sight. He felt he had chosen the spot well enough but no matter what, it was going to be a long night with little sleep. He preferred to camp in a village, visible to all. To hide away in the bush gave the impression of a slave runaway, attempting to remain hidden.

Two small, freshly caught trout were spitted on green sticks, suspended over a tiny fire.

His original plan was to douse the fire as soon as the fish were edible and to make as little noise as possible. He had the two horses on short tethers, just enough to allow for a bit of grazing, concealed as well as possible in the stream-side bush.

This was the first evening he had been unable to locate a village friendly enough to allow a traveling black man to seek sleep and shelter in the hay of the livery loft, or even in the straw of a somewhat clean horse stall. Although he was prepared to do what had to be done, his preference was to sleep in a church yard. He couldn't be accused of hiding if he was visible to anyone entering the church property. But when he knocked on the manse door a few hours ago, no one answered, so he moved on.

Although his horses needed rest, his request for livery and a bit of care, maybe a feed of oats for the animals, and a corner of the loft for himself, were met with inhospitable stares and a few unfriendly words. He had politely thanked the livery man, hoping to leave a good impression, and ridden on his way.

He recalled seeing a short trail into the forest, with a running stream below a slight grade, as he had approached the village. It might be the perfect, secluded spot. It was at least worth riding back that way for a look. Being close to the outskirts of the small village, he hoped to be safe enough.

That a black man was camped out alone, in possession of a valuable stallion, while riding a bay gelding, would raise suspicion in the minds of some of the folks who might come along. John was well aware of that possibility but he and the animals needed rest. Being turned away at the livery left him with little choice.

For the most part, John had journeyed on established roads. He eased through village after village, making no effort to be unseen, ignoring the questioning stares pointed his way. Having no knowledge of the countryside, he feared getting lost if he ventured away from the known and commonly traveled way. He knew nothing at all about wilderness travel.

John could neither read nor write but he could do sums and he knew directions. Tennessee was west of South Carolina. West of North Carolina too. He had no idea where South and North Carolina came together. He was simply following the main trail, as his owner had laid out the venture John was sent on. The trails he was riding were leading west, if a little north, as planned. He would be content with that for the time being.

The war was winding down to its final, inevitable conclusion. Territory seemed to be changing hands on a regular basis as small skirmishes broke out in unexpected places. Military forces, in either Blue or Gray, as well as renegades, could be expected almost anywhere. John rode light in the saddle, choosing rapid concealment as his defense at the first sign of trouble.

For a man with no experience beyond the farm he had spent all of his nearly twenty years of slavery on, he had managed the trip reasonably well. So far. But the road ahead, leading to his destination was long, leaving many miles yet to travel. Days? Weeks? He didn't know. The country beyond the home farm was a total mystery to him.

The bay gelding was a good, although common enough animal but the black stallion would be a prize in anyone's eyes. That John carried letters authorizing his travels would mean exactly nothing to a renegade or to a fleeing soldier who would rather ride than walk. And even with the end of the long war in sight, both armies still seemed to have a never-ending need for replacement animals. The toll taken on horses, in large and even smaller battles was cruel and heartbreaking. Most of the animals in the country had been commandeered by one army or the other. John was unaware of any of that. All he was doing was following the orders his owner laid out for him.

The camper had no clear idea of where he was. He had been shown a map before he set out, the first map he had ever seen. The pen scratches on the paper meant little to him. It might have helped if he could either read or write but that learning was held back from him. The State had mandated that no Blacks were to be educated. To do so carried a penalty no owner wished to contemplate.

His instructions were to somehow find his way from South Carolina to Central Tennessee and then to inquire for the Macintyre Horse Ranch. He had been adequately warned about the length of the trip but, even with that, he stood amazed at the distances. He had seldom been away from the farm he was born on. Driving a wagon to the small village for farm supplies had taught him nothing at all about the bigger world that held such mystery.

There were hills enough, as well as several running water sources, surrounding the Shady Acres Farm he slaved on, enough at least to add beauty and intrigue to the land. But the hills and streams he had crossed or ridden around in the past week made the farm country seem almost flat and dry by comparison. Before him, and on all sides, were green forested hills. Perhaps they were mountains. He had never seen a real mountain. As far as that went, he wasn't sure how big a hill had to be before it was considered a mountain.

When danger from uniformed troops forced him off the traveled road, he had lost hours and, perhaps, days, seeking out a way forward, and shallow enough crossings at all the many streams. Too much time was lost. He had hoped to cover more miles but he couldn't change the circumstances. Delivering the stallion would take as long as it took. That is, if he managed to hold onto the animal to complete the job assigned to him.

Even though his fire was small and the smoke nearly non-existent, John had worried about it being seen. He was about to scoop a bit of creek water with his one cooking pan to douse the flames when he heard the voices.

He stepped further into the bush with the two fish held in one powerful hand. He avoided looking up the hillside while he listened to the footsteps coming his way. He bit off a piece of the fish. And waited.

Chapter 2

"Well, well, looky here, Bronco. We cotched us a ol' boy with two stoled horses. Hid'n and figer'n to run off, I'm guess'n. Do we keep this feller and the horses both or do we make ourselves satisfied with just the two horses? Or maybe do we take the thieving slave and sell him off?"

"We don't do noth'n jest yet, Elmer.

Bronco stepped in front of his friend and looked closely at John.

"What'cha doin here boy?"

There was a bit of a pause as John searched for an answer, knowing that no answer would be good enough for these two.

"Where at did ya come by them there horses?"

Still, John held back.

"Ya got jest this here one chance ta speak up boy. Else it'l be the slave man from yonder town. He'll be giv'n y'all a free boat ride down the big river. Now, you could say that weren't neither right nor fair but say'n it ain't about ta change nothing, nor do ya no good."

John knew he could grab this man and wring his neck and the other one too but he would try telling the truth first. He saw no sign of a weapon on either man.

"Got me a job 'a work Boss. Deliver'n the black to the man what bought 'im. Horses ain't stoled. Jest tak'n a night's rest. We'll be off 'n down da road come mo'nin'. Be best if'n you was to jest let us be."

"Be best fer who boy? Best fer you I'm suppos'n. Ain't worried about you though. Ain't worried a'tall, far as that goes."

"Let's quit fool'n around Bronco. Tie this old boy up and let's get him up ta town. That there slave man is a travl'n fella. Mightn't be there come morn'n. We git some coin fer this here boy, we git some more fer the horses, we's gonna be sail'n, sitt'n pretty fer a month. Maybe longer."

John made up his mind he would not be taken to any slave catcher. With the end of the war and the end of legal slavery well within sight, the catchers were taking anyone they could grab with an eye to a quick sale. The market was no longer good, or really profitable, but there was enough market to keep a single slave man in a degree of financial comfort. There was still a small market among the few slave-owning holdouts that refused to accept the inevitable end.

Anything that would put a few coins in the pockets of Bronco and Elmer before it all came to an end would be welcome by the two thieving troublemakers. Selling the big slave would be a departure from what the two light-fingered scavengers usually did. More profitable too.

There was little chance of the slave catcher being caught with another man's property. It didn't take long to grab someone and start the wagon down the road. They could be three villages away before another morning greeted the land.

John would fight before he allowed that to happen.

"Let's just get er done, Bronco."

Hobart, the Shady Lane Farm overseer, where John and his family labored in the fields, enjoyed few things more than forcing two men into a fight. Fists, clubs, wrestling. It was all good entertainment to the enforcer. Especially as he made sure the other slaves were compelled to gather close to watch. Because of his size and strength, John had been singled out for combat on too many occasions. The only times he had ever lost was when he held back, rather than injure a smaller man.

Elmer reached for John's arm. He may have intended to tie him or perhaps, to turn him up the trail. Neither thing happened.

A single clout from John's fisted right hand had the man lying at his feet, unmoving. There was no broken nose or any sign of blood. The blow had hit Elmer on the side of the head, smashing his ear and doing damage at the edge of his left eye and his cheek bone. There was certain to be swelling showing and a colorful eye, within a few hours.

And he might have a little trouble hearing well. For a while anyway.

Bronco stood in amazement, looking down at his friend, unable to believe that a Black slave had really hit a white man. Foolishly, he looked for too long. John grabbed the man around the throat with his left hand and set himself to slapping him with his big right hand. Four resounding slaps, right to left and back again, left to right and then repeated, had Bronco's ears ringing and his eyes watering. Whatever fight had been in the cowardly bully was thoroughly dissipated.

Elmer groaned, rolled onto his side, and started to rise. John held Bronco firmly while he bent over and grabbed Elmer's shirt front. Taking a firm hold on a doubled portion of shirt, John lifted the still dazed Elmer to his feet. He shifted his grip, grabbing the man by the neck, as he had Bronco. Neither man was in a position to resist. Swinging the two men a bit away from each other, John hesitated, and then pulled them together with their heads clanging like dull bells. Both men soundlessly closed their eyes and faded from consciousness.

When John sensed the ability to resist was gone from the men, he let them slide to the ground, unconscious.

His actions brought immediate fear to him. He trembled just a bit, first thinking to run. But he knew the two thieves would seek out the sheriff. They would have a story conjured up that would put John as a runaway. Clearly, he couldn't outrun all the law nor a gathering of wrought-up villagers.

And once the story got around, there would be little chance of John being able to explain the truth.

Finally, hoping for something he couldn't rightly put into words, justice, perhaps, he picked up the stupefied Bronco and set him on the back of the well trained and gentled black stallion. He pushed Bronco's hands into the stallion's mane and said, "hold on". There was very little response, but he might have sensed a bit of finger tightening.

"Should be you wants ta stay breath'n Boss, you jest set there, and you don't go to caus'n Ol' John no more trouble."

He then quickly threw the saddle on the gelding, gathered up his few camp supplies and led the animal to where Elmer still lay inert. With seemingly no thought for Elmer's weight, John picked up the unconscious man and lay him face down, over the saddle. He tied the stallion's lead line to the saddle horn.

It was, perhaps, a long quarter mile into the village he had been turned away from. He would go back, hoping the church minister would be at home.

As he led off, Bronco was face down, onto the horse's neck. John could only hope the man could hold on, at least a little bit.

With the sun dropped behind the westward hills and only the dregs of evening light remaining to show the way, John took the lead on the gelding and started up the slope. He was back on the dirt trail into town within a couple of minutes. There was no one within sight on the road. In this early-to-bed land, most folks were home, milking a cow, splitting firewood by the light of a kerosene lantern, drawing water from a dug well or sitting down to dinner.

With the church sitting almost on the edge of the small village, John was soon back there. He turned the horses and their burdens into the yard and all the way to the rear, where the poor shack that passed as a home for the preacher sat. He was desperately hoping the village preacher would be home and that he would be a fair man.

Before John led the horses into the church yard, Bronco had raised his head a bit, just the once, looking around with bleary eyes. Everything seemed to be spinning in swift circles. Looking upward brought a stabbing headache. He squeezed his eyes tight, trying to hold off the pain.

He gave a brief thought to sliding off the horse. To making a run for it. Realizing he could barely hold his head up, let alone run, he slowly let his shoulders sag, and his chin drop back down until it was resting on his chest. He then folded back onto the animal's neck. Somehow, he had maintained a grip on the stallion's mane.

John wasn't sure the man was capable of running far but he watched him closely anyway. He had treated the fellow pretty roughly. It would take some time to recover.

Elmer had been stirring too but had made no effort to sit up.

John led his two horses through the side yard of the church and up to the door of the shack. There was lamplight showing through the single window that graced the front of the little building. John dropped the reins of the gelding, knowing the animal would stand until he returned. A quick knock on the door brought the scrape of what sounded like chair legs and then some shuffling footsteps. The door opened just a crack, letting out a slim wedge of lamplight.

"Who's there? What can I do for you?"

"Got a probl'm here Boss. Hop'n you could maybe help."

The door was cautiously swung wider but, still, no one was in sight. Finally, a head appeared around the edge, the eyes straining to see into the darkened yard. John sensed the man's reluctance to show himself. He figured what with the war and all, everyone was being cautious.

"Noth'n to fear out here Boss. Jest need'n some help. Need someone to read a letter and prove I ain't no thief. Nor no runaway."

Finally, a disheveled and cautious looking man, showing the gauntness so recognizable among those with long familiarity with short rations, appeared. He held a table lamp up before him.

"Who is it? asked a female voice from inside.

The minister ignored the question. He lifted the lamp up to John's face and then to the gelding. The light brought Elmer back, closer to reality. He twisted his head and squinted his eyes, looking towards the light. Disgustedly, the minister simply said, "Elmer". He stepped towards the black stallion. He kept his eyes firmly on John as he moved. Before the lamplight could identify him, Bronco

13

slipped from the horse on the offside. Within three or four staggering, hurried steps he was lost in the darkness of the surrounding bush.

Voicing further disgust, the minister said, "I expect that was Bronco."

With the evidence before him, the minister seemed to put the story together with no words from John. Moving back to the gelding, John reached up and grabbed the back of Elmer's shirt. With a slight tug, he slid the injured man to the ground.

As soon as Elmer's feet hit the ground John clamped a fist around the man's bicep, bringing forth a squeal of pain, and preventing him from running away.

"Tie your animals and come inside."

The order from the preacher didn't seem to leave much choice. John did as he was told, while the reluctant Elmer was prodded into the lamplit door by the much smaller pastor. John tied his horses and then slowly, respectfully, followed the other two men. Once inside, the door was closed. Wordlessly John and Elmer were directed to sit in two chairs that were backed against the wall of the small kitchen.

John had never been inside the home of a white before. He was distinctly uncomfortable. It wasn't until the preacher said, "Please take a seat", that he finally obeyed.

The preacher carefully studied John. He could easily see the black man's unease, perhaps it was even fear. His big hands were working his tattered hat into an unshapely roll. His lips were working on words that never quite became audible.

"Rev. Thaddeus Grimsley. What is your name?"

"I be John, Boss."

"Just John? No other name?"

"No Boss. No other name. Jest John. John be enough."

"Yes, well, it was certainly enough for the disciple that Jesus especially loved. All right, Just John, tell me the story."

John did, in just a few simple words. He thought to show the man his letters but was reluctant in front of Elmer. If someone were to waylay him and take his letters, he would have no proof at all about who he was or what job he was doing. Elmer and Bronco were just the type of men who would do that. It would be best if Elmer didn't know about them.

The minister turned to Elmer.

"We'll hear your story too Elmer but we'll wait just a bit."

Rev. Grimsley turned to his wife.

"Mrs. Grimsley, I hate to ask this of you in the dark of night, but I don't see another way. Could you please make your way to the sheriff's office? Ask Old Tom to come down here. You wait for him to escort you back. Tell him to hurry along. He can finish his checkers game another time."

Without a word, the woman slipped a badly worn shawl over her shoulders and ducked out the door. The three men sat in silence while they waited. Rev. Grimsley seemed to be studying each man carefully as he cast his eye from one to the other.

After a long, silent, twenty-minute wait, the door was pushed open. The three men straightened their slouching backs, sitting fully upright in their chairs while the sheriff and Mrs. Grimsley entered the old house.

"Evening Tom. We've got a situation here. You know Elmer, of course. His friend Bronco ran off and left Elmer holding the bag on this one. But I saw him doing the running, so we know he was part of the deal, whatever that deal may be."

Pointing across the small room he said, "This is John. Those two horses you saw outside are in John's possession. Elmer and Bronco decided to relieve John of the animals. I'm sure they meant to find a fast sale for them. And perhaps for John, as well. John objected.

"Rightly or wrongly, John has come to me as a fair arbiter in the matter, bringing men and horses along with him. So here they are. I have no real knowledge of what plans these two had for John himself. You might want to ask Elmer about that."

The sheriff looked first at John.

"Let's hear it, John."

Again, the frightened slave repeated the tale he had told Rev. Grimsley earlier. The story made no mention of how he came to have the horses, where he was from or where he was going. The sheriff put those questions to him.

"I tell you Boss, but best we be alone, just me and you and the preacher man."

"You don't wish to talk in front of ole Elmer here. Well, I can understand that. So, Elmer, what's your story?

Elmer had nothing to say. After waiting so long that Elmer's fidgeting was getting on everyone's nerves, the sheriff looked at the pathetic man.

"Get out of here Elmer. But don't you and Bronco think of running away. I'll be wanting to talk with you when I'm done here. You hang around close to the jailhouse, you hear? You don't want me to have to set out to find you. You understand what I'm saying?"

He nodded at the sheriff and then, with speed that defied Elmer's age and John's rough handling, he was gone. The slam of the door brought everyone's eyes back to John.

Wordlessly, the sheriff looked at the black man. John's eyes scanned the room as if to be certain that no one else was there. Finally, he reached into his shirt pocket, unfastened the crudely built safety pin that held it secure, and withdrew the three letters. From memory, he picked out the one that gave the reader the assurance that John was on a proper assignment from his owner. The letter included John's name, the owner's name, and the name of the purchaser of the black stallion. There were also instructions on how John was to be rewarded after the horse was delivered. Sheriff Tom slowly read the letter, looking up at John several times as he read. He then passed the letter to Rev. Grimsley.

The minister, knowing Mrs. Grimsley would want to know what the letter said, read it aloud. Mrs. Grimsley studied John with a fierce, although not unfriendly, scrutiny during the reading.

With the reading completed, the two white men looked at each other and then, as if they had practiced the move, swung their eyes back to the still frightened slave.

Tom motioned towards the other papers John held in his hand.

"What else have you got there, John?"

Reluctantly, John passed the letters to the sheriff, hoping they would be returned.

Following the preacher's example, Tom read both letters out loud. When he was finished reading, he slowly re-folded the three documents and returned them to John. He then passed an unspoken question towards Rev. Grimsley. The reverend was slow to answer, first glancing behind him, to his wife. It was Mrs. Grimsley who came up with the question.

"Did you know what these letters said, John."

"Yes'm Ma'am. I's remember what da Boss, Mr. Akins say."

"You can't read yourself?"

"No ma'am, I surely can't make out no writ'n."

Mrs. Grimsley ventured an opinion.

"How foolish of these slave owners to not teach their people to read and write and do sums. And the government to pass a law against educating the Blacks."

No one replied.

Rev. Grimsley looked first at Tom and then back to John.

"You have been on the road for nearly two weeks John. Have you had other trouble along the way?"

"Some people look'n, Boss but no bad trouble till today. I's stay in church yards all along de way. Be safe der. Until today an' no one be home to dis house. I come by earlier."

"Well, we're here now. There's a small corral out back with a gate that can be locked. I have no animals so there's grass growing in the corral for their forage. Mrs. Grimsley will put out a little something for your supper. You can bed down in the shed beside the horses. You'll be safe enough there. Don't leave in the morning until we have talked."

The Reverend turned to Sheriff Tom and asked, "You all right with that Tom?"

Tom answered by placing his hat back on his head, nodding and opening the door. The Reverend said, "If you should see Lefty, send him this way first thing in the morning."

Chapter 3

John lay in the dark shack listening to the horses ripping the green grass that would provide the nourishment and strength for another long day, provided the sheriff and the preacher man accepted his story. As he did most nights, he went over and over the strange happenings that had put him on unfamiliar roads, being trusted to deliver a valuable stallion to a purchaser hundreds of miles away. He knew it was an act of desperation by the plantation owner. A desperation brought on by war and other, mostly financial, circumstances.

What John didn't know, he imagined, being familiar with the thoughts and actions of his owner after a lifetime on the farm. He couldn't help putting the story together while he waited for sleep to overtake him. What he didn't know for an absolute fact he added in from his rather vivid imagination.

"Hobart", hollered Jedediah Akins. "Get our adult people gathered into the big shed. I'll be down to talk with them in one-half hour."

Akins, owner of a medium-sized farm in South Carolina, knew it was well past time to make a decision and to act on that decision. If he didn't do it soon, it would be too late. The evidence was overwhelming and he was nothing, if not realistic. Some who knew him might even call him cunning. Many of his farming neighbors were scattered to the winds. A few of them were dead and buried. Some of the beautiful homes were burned to the ground, their livestock stolen, the land growing into weeds. He was determined that Shady Acres Farm would survive and thrive. Somehow.

He wondered if the fact that his farm home was modest, compared to the grandeur of some of those around him, had held off the anger of the invaders. Or perhaps it was that the invaders had come and gone, forever on the move, sparing his home from the fire they so commonly used as a subduing weapon.

Hobart nodded at the order to assemble the slaves.

"Yes, Sir. I'll see to it, Sir."

When Akins entered the shed at the appointed time, there were eighteen black faces, including John's, staring at him, wondering what was about to happen. These gatherings usually meant discipline of some sort and often enough, a whipping.

Lately, it hadn't taken much to send the worried owner of the Shady Acres Farm into a fit of anger.

Or perhaps it was desperation. The war was not going well, from his point of view. It had become clear that major changes were underway, both political and economic. He could see no power, anywhere, that would stem the flow of change.

The Confederacy was still fighting, now broken into small, scattered remnants of their former glory. But it was over. Only desperation and pride remained. And, of course, the waiting deaths of too many more young men.

After pacing the floor for more days and nights than he wanted to think about, he had made a decision. Clearly, it was time to take action before it was forced upon him.

He would control his anger. And his badly damaged Southern pride. Successfully salvaging three generations of work that his family had put into the farm was more important than giving in to anger and despair. Salvaging the farm would come with its own rewards, including at least some regained pride. Perhaps a more silent pride than before but, still, Southern pride.

If he was to hold onto anything of his estate now was the time, before the forces that were sure to become victorious came riding down the long, tree-lined lane.

"Listen up, people. This is important. It's important to me and certainly, to you. I'm sure you have all heard at least some of the news. We have lost the war. Oh, it's not official yet but it soon will be. It may be a day, it may be a week, it may be a month. But it's over.

"You may think that is good news. You may even hope that I, and other slave holders, will be somehow punished. And I'm sure some of you will be silently smiling at the idea of being set free. But perhaps you haven't thought what that might mean. When you are free you will be able to walk off this farm and go wherever you wish, live any way you wish. Or any way you are able. But that won't be as easy as it sounds."

Never holding the Blacks in very high esteem, nor crediting their intelligence as anywhere near equaling his own, he spoke slowly, pausing often to give time for the slaves to absorb what he was saying.

"You know next to nothing of the world outside this farm. If you walk away, you will be joining thousands of other freed Blacks. You will find no work and little welcome, anywhere you go. How are you going to eat? Where will you find shelter? Most freed Blacks will end up back working on farms, doing what they have always done.

"So, I have an offer for you."

He paused and studied each face, one by one. Having decided that they were listening, he continued.

"Provided the Northern army doesn't take the farm from me and my family, I'm suggesting that you stay where you are and work as you always have. Working on Shady Acres Farm. The difference will be that you will be working for wages and you will be free to come and go as you wish. Free to spend your money as you wish.

"How big your wages will be, depends on conditions that are not yet clear. Much will change after the fighting stops. What market we will have for what we now grow is uncertain. At first, your wages might be small. But I can promise you a wage of some sort. And as conditions improve, you will be paid accordingly.

"You can stay in your present cabins. The farm has enough stored foods, hidden away from the armies, to keep us all fed for a while. We may be left eating potatoes or turnips, but we will eat, and not starve. And we still have our chickens.

"There will be a lot of hard work to get crops into the ground this spring. The army took all but two of our horses. The saddle animals as well as harness horses are gone. Took our cattle and hogs too, as you know.

"You have no reason to like me or my family. And I don't pretend to have any close feeling for most of you. My offer is not presented on the feelings of like or dislike. It is presented on need only. The farm needs workers. You need homes and a way to live. A safe way. You need to survive.

"Shady Acres Farm can provide those things. When conditions improve, you will be free to stay or go as you wish."

Again, he looked from face to face. As he thought of what he wanted to say next, he came close to choking up. Steeling himself, desperately not wanting to show weakness in front of his slaves, he said, "You know the war cost Mrs. Akins and I our only two sons. They were farmers at heart. Men who loved this land. But they will not be coming home to work it.

"I, too, love this land. As strange as this will sound to you, I will be working alongside those who decide to stay. I will be getting my hands as dirty as you get yours. To survive the next couple of years will take great strength and more work than we can probably foresee. But that work, with a cabin and a meal at the end of the day, will be better than wandering the country at the mercy of an unknown future.

"The markets for our cotton are gone. They will come back, but not soon enough. So now we are going to grow root crops and corn. Vegetables. Food to eat. I have been purchasing and storing seeds for the past two years. There will always be a market for food.

"To prevent problems with the invading army, if you decide to stay, I will give you your freedom now and the papers that guarantee that freedom."

For the third time, he cast his eyes around the room. He had never been a good man, nor a considerate man, and he accepted those facts. But he also accepted that desperation was causing him to make unpleasant decisions. He had a role to play. It would be best to play it well.

"I'll give you until tomorrow morning to make a decision."

He ended his plea with a warning.

"Whatever you do, don't leave this farm until you know for certain that the war is over and the government has declared you as free. If you leave before that time, the slave catchers may pick you up and you could be carried off. There would be no telling what would become of you if that happened. Here, at least, you are safe.

"Now, go back to work.

"John, you and your family wait here."

As the men and women walked back to the fields and the grandmas gathered up the children, four members of John's family huddled against the back wall of the shed, as far from the farmer as the space allowed.

"Stop cowering! Step up close so I don't have to shout."

The parents and their two oldest children shuffled closer.

"John, step up here."

John was just turned twenty years, as best anyone could figure. He was the oldest in the large family. An unusually strong, yet gentle young man. Not handsome, plain in most respects, he had never known a day of freedom.

Trembling with fear, the young man took a step forward, his terrified eyes cast to the floor. His parents looked on in equal dread.

"John. I have a special job for you. It is a job I would normally have my sons do but that cannot be anymore. If you will do this for me you will have a horse to ride and keep at the end of the job, enough cash money to see you through several weeks, and an open path to the western lands."

As a slave owner, Jedediah Akins had thought of simply assigning the special task to his slave but he was cunning enough to know that once John was down the road a few miles and away from his owner's influence, he could sell the horse, or just turn it loose, and run. No, he would need John's promise. He would have to play this carefully.

Too terrified to respond, John simply stared, unable to imagine what his owner had just said.

"You are the best horseman we have ever had on this plantation John. Maybe the best I have ever seen. It seems to come natural to you. Sometimes it almost appears like you and the horses can talk to each other. Understand each other.

"We have our last two horses hidden down in the hollow, as you well know. The only animals the army didn't find and steal. You know those animals better than anyone. The black stallion is promised to a breeder in Tennessee. Delivery was to take place as soon as the animal reached two years. That time has come. You have done a fine job of gentling and training the stallion, without breaking its spirit.

"The buyer has purchased horses from me before. I know he will pay well if the stallion is delivered safely. The farm will need that money to survive and pay the wages I have just promised.

"I want you to deliver that horse. I will give you names and directions. It is a long ride. You will be many days on the road. You will need clothes and money. I will provide all of that. You will take the bay gelding to ride. You will lead the black. You will take a good saddle and whatever gear you need for sleeping along the way.

"I will give you three letters.

"The first letter gives you your freedom. You will need that in case there is some delay in government action.

"The second letter will tell whoever asks that you are delivering the horse on my orders. That you are in my employ. The letter will also tell the breeder that he is to see that you are safely on your way to the west after he has the black and that the gelding belongs to you free and clear after your safe arrival at the Macintyre Farm.

"The third letter I will give you will tell anyone you ask for employment that you are a good worker and a good horseman. It may help you as you look for work.

"You can't read or write John. I am suggesting that you call into the Black church in town. Show the pastor the letters. Let him read them to you. Then you will know that what I have just said is the truth.

"When you need guidance along the way, you might be best to rely on church ministers. In some towns, the sheriff might be trustworthy but you can't be sure.

"You won't know who to trust, so trust no one too much. You will need to be careful at all times.

"You will have to buy food along the way. You have done that for the farm, so you know how to buy and pay. I have a sack of small coins I will give you. Small coins will raise less suspicion than larger coins when you are buying supplies. Again, a Black minister may be a help with that in strange towns.

"When you deliver the stallion, you will keep the bay gelding and your freedom. You may go wherever you wish after that. I would suggest you head west. Texas, perhaps. Or into Indian Territory. One of the tribes might make you welcome.

"There is little time. You must leave right away. If the army finds those two horses, we will lose them.

"Now, you talk with your family. Decide what you want to do. But think on this. You're a horseman John, not a farmer. My offer will take you to horse and cattle country if you manage to stay safe.

"I will be back in one hour. I will need your answer."

Chapter 4

"What have you decided John?"

"Me and my family have talked, Boss. It be a hard thing, this leav'n. Might never see dem no mo'. But I's surely want'n to see this Texas yo talk'n bout. Maybe work wit de horses 'n de cattle. I's go. Take good care a de horses as I can. I ready now."

"Good. Good. You get the saddle and gear ready. Get a halter and lead on the black. Take some bedding and new clothes from the storehouse. I'll have Maude put together a food pack for you from up at the big house.

"I'm trusting you, John. But I know you can do this job.

"You have to ride fast but carefully. I know maps are strange to you. But you have no problem with directions. You keep going north a bit but, mostly, west. That's the way most roads lead anyway, so it won't be too difficult. Keep an eye on the sun to point your way. Ask directions from time to time when you feel it is safe to do so. And, again, be careful. The war has done strange things to folks.

"You might be challenged. Try not to come crossways with anyone. Don't get into any fights with renegades or townsmen, or anyone else. You can't win. Whatever you do, don't strike a white man. You would be hung within the hour if you did that.

"I'll thank you now and wish you good riding. And John, you have no reason to believe me but I do wish you a good life. Take care of yourself and take care of those horses."

With a quick step and a twist on the sole of his boot, the farmer turned towards the big house. John's father called after him, something he would have been whipped for before this day.

"Boss. We's ready to talk about de farm'n."

Akins turned with a scowl on his face.

"Boss, de people, dey ask me ta speak fo dem. We's all goi'n stay 'n work de farm. Only thing is, we's not stay'n if'n Mr. Hobart be stay'n."

Hobart, the long-term slave overseer on Shady Acres Farm flashed a hateful look at the old man before shuffling his feet and glancing back at Akins.

They all stood in silence for a long sixty seconds. Finally, Akins turned to his foreman.

"You knew this day would come Hobart. It's just one of the many changes coming upon us. Pack your gear and come to the house. I'll have your pay and a bit of traveling money ready for you."

With a nod at the slave family, the farmer again turned towards the house.

Chapter 5

John's first stop after leaving the farm was at the little Black church in the village. The gathering of believers was pastored by a pensioned-out slave, no longer able to work. His master had felt it was less costly to give him his freedom than it would be to feed and house him. Pastor George acknowledged no second or family name. The name George was given to him long before, by his owner. He had little choice but to accept it. But to take the owner's family name as his own was more than his limited pride could bear.

George. Nothing more. George. It was good enough. And everyone in the village knew him as such. It may have brought just a bit of closeness between him and John, as well. John had adamantly refused to have anyone assign him a name other than John.

The slaves also knew the pastor was one of the few Blacks who could read and write, thanks to his owner's eldest daughter who, many years ago, had been determined to teach at least a few of the slaves, in spite of the South Carolina law against the practice. She was headstrong about the matter, defying both her parents and the law.

"Morn'n George. Gots some papers here. Needs you should read dem fo' me."

"Well, John. I'll be happy to do that if you will step down from that horse and tell me what it's all about."

"Bout tak'n dis here horse to de buyer in Tennessee. Don't rightly know where dat is but I got's ta get him dere."

Stepping to the ground, John reached in his pocket and lifted out the three pieces of paper. He peeled off the one he identified as meaning his freedom.

"Boss man, he say I get dis stallion to de new owner, I gets to go free and keep de geld'n. This here paper say so. If'n Boss tell de truth."

George unfolded the paper, took a long look at John, glanced over at the horses, and then back down at the letter. He read it once silently, adjusted his shoulders inside his ragged shirt, took another look at John and read aloud. John could remember the excitement growing in his much-abused spirit as the old black man read.

Now, two weeks of worrying travel, much of it while he watched behind him as often as he did ahead, had brought him to this small shack behind the church in a tiny village. He stretched the kinks out of his weary body, relieved himself in the uncleaned horse stall and pushed the door open. It wasn't quite full light yet.

Before he did anything else, John took the water bucket to the well pump and cared for the animal's needs. He then stroked both horses and talked with them, assuring each one that he was a good boy, and that life would be fine that day. He hoped it was all true.

As he was washing his hands and face in the cold, well water, he could smell bacon frying. A glance towards the house showed the back door to be open. A glimmer of yellowish light from a turned-low oil lamp shone through a double layer of cheese cloth stretched over the window opening on the outer door.

John wasn't sure how to approach his situation, so he went back to the horses. There, he knew what to do. As each minute brought more daylight to the yard, he could see that the grass in the small corral was now eaten down. The horses appeared to be content.

At a quiet, 'hey, you horses', the two animals stepped to the gate and hung their heads over, waiting for more of the friendly words and caresses that John spoiled them with every morning. He saddled the gelding, readying the animal for the day.

The slam of the outer door closing on its spring caused the horseman to turn around.

"Good morning John, I trust you got some sleep."

"Yassir, Boss. Did fine."

"Well, you can wash up at the basin outside the door. Mrs. Grimsley will have breakfast ready directly. Then we can get you on your way. If the sheriff managed to find Lefty, we'll have a talk with him. As soon as you eat and meet this fella, you're free to go your way.

"I don't think Elmer or Bronco will bother you again. I'm sure the sheriff put a proper scare into them last night."

John followed the old man to the back stoop. The elderly pastor wordlessly pointed at the wash basin, a pail and dipper and a bar of soap. John washed again, this time with soap. Although there was a greying towel hanging from a nail driven into the unpainted siding, he would let his hands dry in the rising warmth of the day. He didn't mention that he had already washed in the bucket.

A sleepy-eyed Mrs. Grimsley nodded wordlessly at John and pointed to a chair. John sat and waited. It wasn't long before there were three loaded plates on the table and Mrs. Grimsley joined the men. She folded her hands under her chin and closed her eyes. John, never exactly sure how to act around white folks, glanced at Grimsley himself. The pastor had his elbows bent on the table before him, his arms wrapped around his breakfast plate as if he feared its theft. He sat there with his head bent and his eyes closed. Within seconds he began praying. He prayed, first, for the new day God had given them and then he gave thanks for their health and wellbeing and the food provided so generously. He spent a few seconds remembering their children and grandchildren to the Lord, and then prayed for peace in the nation. He closed by asking for guidance and protection for John and the horses as they traveled on.

At the amen, John opened his own eyes and glanced at his hosts. They were both bent to serious eating. John followed their example, even to folding a slice of homemade bread over two strips of hot, crisp bacon. Within seconds, the homemade butter Mrs. Grimsley had encouraged him to slather on the bread was melting from the heat of the bacon and dripping onto his fingers. He licked it off in eager anticipation and then tied into the bacon sandwich. There was no talk during the meal.

John wondered how the wealthy Akins family ate, up in the big house on Shady Acres Farm, if these modest folks could share such luxuries so easily.

He had much to learn about life. About white folks especially.

Mrs. Grimsley gathered the used dishes and laid them on the counter beside the stove. She then poured three cups of coffee, placing one before each of the men. She stood beside the warmth of the stove while she cradled her cup in both hands. John said nothing but he guessed the woman would be back under her bed covers, given a choice.

At the crunching of hooves over the bit of rock-strewn grass on the side of the house, the pastor said, "That will be Lefty."

He stood and stepped to the door, opening it just enough to push the outer door an inch or so until he confirmed who the visitor was. When the door finally swung open and the cheese-cloth covered outer door pushed aside, a man stomped dust from his boots and stepped up onto the door stoop.

"Come in Lefty."

John was surprised to see a one armed and facially disfigured young man standing there. He noticed a slight limp as the man stepped into the kitchen. The visitor wore street clothing except for a worn and stained Confederate coat. John wondered if the stains were from Lefty's own blood. The scowl on the man's face told John the visitor was not there completely by choice.

Without the scowl and the wound damage, John could see that the new man would be considered handsome, sought out by the ladies. His one arm was covered by a pinned-back shirt sleeve. The way the material was filled out it was clear that Lefty, lacking an arm, was not lacking in strength.

Mrs. Grimsley poured another cup of coffee and set it in front of the last chair at the table. The pastor indicated the chair to Lefty who reluctantly, and suspiciously, sat down, never taking his eyes off John. The way Lefty attacked the coffee indicated to John that it may have been a while since he had enjoyed the caffeinated treasure.

The pastor noisily slurped his own cup dry before speaking again.

"Lefty, this is John. John has a job to do, delivering a horse to a stable in Tennessee. He's carrying papers from a plantation over by the coast, confirming this.

"Now Lefty, I am going to remind you that I've known you since before you knew yourself. I was there at your birthing. Not right in the room, you understand, but close by just the same. Your mother was young and frightened. She sought the comfort of the Lord in her distress. I was pleased to share what little encouragement I brought to her and to your father, who was beside himself with worry. It was the Lord, Himself, who was to provide their real comfort."

Impatiently, and somewhat angrily, Lefty broke into the pastor's monologue.

"I know the story. Why tell it again? Especially in front of the…?"

He was looking with an unfriendly eye at John as he spoke although he didn't finish all he started out to say, knowing the reverend wouldn't approve.

"I repeat the story Lefty, to remind you again that you come from good stock. Steady stock. Christian stock. I remind you, as well, that you were a credit to your loving parents until the past year or so. You were a good student and you showed great promise in whatever you turned your efforts towards.

"You sustained terrible wounds in battle. I understand that. God knows we've seen enough of wounds and death the past few years. But you've allowed your wounds to change who you are. And not in a good way."

Lefty was about to interrupt but the pastor held up his hand. As Lefty clamped his mouth shut, John learned a lesson about respect. Clearly, Lefty respected this elderly, modest pastor. All John had ever known was force and fear and the threat of the whip. Akins had never attempted to gain respect. He might have gotten more work out of his people if he had tried that.

"Lefty, you are well on the way of letting anger and bitterness rule your life. You need a change. A change of scenery, away from here, where you have fallen in with other complainers. I want you to accompany this man to Tennessee. I want you to be his guide and his protector. And as you go, I want you to look around you. See the beauty of the world. See the grandeur of God's great creation. And I want you to learn to give thanks that you are not in a grave, as so many thousands of other good Southern boys are.

"The war will soon be over. Yes, we will have lost but we are still alive. And we will find a way to live in the situation as it is presented to us. That way will not be the way of anger and bitterness.

"Now, go home and put together a few traveling clothes. Get rid of the grey jacket. Kiss your mother farewell and shake your father's hand. Promise them that you'll write often. Take John and the horses with you. John will tell you where he needs to deliver the stallion to. For now, all you need to know is to follow the shortest and fastest road to Tennessee. And Lefty, my advice would be for you to stay away from here or even go further west. Make a new life for yourself. Find new friends. Learn to be happy."

With barely concealed anger flashing from his eyes and with his lips sealed so tightly together that they were turning white around the edges, Lefty rose to his feet. As he turned towards the door, Mrs. Grimsley spoke.

"You're a good man Lefty. Don't ever let anyone tell you differently."

Lefty gave her a long look before turning back to the door. He said nothing at all to John but at a nod from the pastor, John rose from the chair and picked his hat from the floor.

"Thank you, Suh. And Missus. Thank yo for the meals 'n all. You'se good folk."

He followed Lefty into the yard and went to the horses. Lefty rose to the saddle and trotted the horse out of the yard. If John was to join him, it was clearly up to him. Lefty wasn't waiting.

Within an hour the duo was on the road out of town, heading west. Lefty's goodbyes had been made, and his saddlebags were stuffed with a change of clothing and a few camp supplies. A bedroll was secured behind the saddle. At the last moment, Lefty's father quietly approached and held out a small canvas sack.

"It's not a lot son but if you're careful how you spend it, you'll have grub along the way. We'll miss you more than words can tell son. But you will do well, with a fresh start. I have confidence in saying that. Let us know where you land. You never know what might happen. Ain't much holding us here. Could be we'll make a move ourselves if you should find a better place."

The two parents then stood silently as they watched the strange parade ride out of their yard and out of their immediate lives.

Chapter 6

As they rode westward, Lefty made no attempt to speak with John. The couple of times John rode up beside him, Lefty pushed his riding animal a bit more and John was soon left behind again. After a lifetime of slavery, being ignored by whites, except when receiving orders, John thought little about the matter. He contented himself with following, trusting that Lefty knew where he was going.

Neither man spoke for the first three hours. With Lefty leading and the duo looking like a typical owner/slave situation, they covered more miles than John had on any day since he left the plantation. Many people along the way glanced at the pair and especially at the proudly prancing black stallion but no one attempted to interfere. Clearly, it was going to be a help to have a white man riding along, even if there was no effort at communication between the two of them.

A glance at the position of the sun told John it

was nearing noon. He saw a small creek in the near distance. He trotted up to Lefty and said, "Need ta water dese animals, Boss. Best we stop here fo a bit."

Lefty grimaced at the idea of a black man offering advice. He knew John was correct but, still, his stubbornness came near to forcing him to object. Finally, accepting that the horses needed a rest and a chance at the water, he swung his animal towards the creek. He pulled off the trail at a grassy area and dismounted. Being one-handed, if he should happen to let loose of a single rein while he was riding, he would be in difficulty. He had tied the reins in a knot at the end. He now laid the leathers across the horse's neck and turned it loose, watching it closely, lest it start to wander off. The animal went quickly to the water and then started tearing into the succulent grass.

John held his gelding's reins while it drank. The length of the rope lead allowed the stallion to reach the water. Only when both horses went to grazing, did John drop some slack into the reins and lay them across the gelding's neck, and relieve the cinch. None of the horses showed any signs of wanting to leave the green grass and plentiful water.

Lefty hesitated about relieving the cinch pressure on his own animal, again being reluctant to be seen following John's lead, even in so small a matter. He finally turned the horse so he would be on the offside from John and eased some slack into the saddle harness. John paid no attention. He had never been free to question any white man and he wasn't about to start now.

*'dis freedom, it not be a easy thing fo old John
ta learn'*

Both men bent to the water themselves with
Lefty making a point of picking a spot well upstream from John. The black man was unaffected
by any of this. It had all been a part of his life for as
long as he could remember.

While they rested and allowed the horses to eat
and drink as they pleased, John walked a few paces
down the stream just to ease his muscles. He made
his way slowly back, studying Lefty's gelding.

"Good look'n horse there, Boss. How'd you keep
him from the thiev'n armies?"

Lefty, at first, had no intention of answering the
question or speaking to John at all, as far as that
went. But, at heart, he was a garrulous man, a talker. At least he had been before bitterness and anger
had taken over his mind. The exploding artillery
shell that tore his arm off, almost to the elbow, and
drove shrapnel into his thigh, along with ripping
off most of one ear and a large piece of his right
cheek left him with more than physical injuries.

After a half minute of silence, the words just
seemed to pop into existence and he found himself
telling the story.

"Stoled him my own self. Probably stoled from
some poor farmer in the first place. Army got me
all shot up and then cut upon by the butchers at
the medic tent. Then they turned me loose to walk
all the long miles home, me with one arm and the
stump of the other still leaking blood and pus and
hurting like all the fires of perdition were upon it.

"The idea of walking held no appeal. Wasn't sure I could do it, even if I wanted to. Which I didn't. Just bided my time, hanging around the mess tent. Then come a dark night with the clouds holding back the bright of the moon. Saw my chance. Sauntered over to the big corral with no one say'n, aye, no, nor maybe. Picked me a good one. Threw a saddle on him, slipped this good carbine rifle into the scabbard, grabbed up a short gun and holster and rode out like I owned the place. Rode him straight up, like somebody come, right to home. Kept that grey brute hid in the bushes since then."

John asked no more questions, simply studying Lefty as he told the short tale, nodding in understanding at the end. Lefty offered no more information. He never once made eye contact with John as they talked.

As evening started to roll around, the travelers were twenty-five miles from the little village they had started out from. When a small town showed in the near distance John took the chance on another suggestion.

"Dark soon, Boss. Yo feel'n like look'n at a church yard or maybe-so de livery barn?"

Lefty made no response but as they neared town, a church yard came in sight. Behind the church was a large, grassed area backed by some bush and then a full-on forest of mixed trees. A hand pump mounted over a dug well could be seen beside the building. The minister must live elsewhere. There was no sign of a manse.

A pair of outhouses were discreetly tucked into

the edge of the bush, hidden behind the church building. Lefty turned in, rode to the edge of the grassy field and dismounted. Wordlessly, he dropped the saddle from the grey. He exchanged a halter for the bridle and staked the animal out. It was all done awkwardly with just the one arm but he got it done. John followed his example and soon all three animals were pulling grass. John went searching for a bucket and found one in the woodshed. It took several trips to the pump but soon all three horses were watered and set for the night.

John pumped clean water to rinse the bucket before he re-filled it and brought it to their camping area. There would be no fire as neither man had coffee. They had enough cold fare to see them both through a couple of days, provided by Mrs. Grimsley and Lefty's mother. They would make do with cold well water in place of the coffee they both longed for.

Each man did as they pleased with no thought for the other. When Lefty laid out his bedroll, John moved a good twenty feet away before unrolling his blankets. There would be no hint of friendship or comradery.

Where John would have tried to search out the minister before staking out the camping area, Lefty showed no concern. When no one showed up to challenge them, John relaxed and enjoyed the evening and the quiet. He strolled around the church, studying its features. He looked long at a leaded, stained glass window, the first he had ever seen. He wondered what the various pictures represented but he wasn't about to challenge Lefty's reluctance to talk or his clear animosity at the entire event he found himself trapped within.

Just before full dark was upon them, three riders stopped on the road, taking a long study of the campers and the horses. John and Lefty glanced at the men but neither made a comment. Before long, the riders kicked their mounts into motion and were out of sight.

John was first to go to his blankets, after once again scouting the surrounding area and then checking the horses. Sleep took him almost immediately. He never knew when Lefty took to his bedroll but each of the three times he woke during the night, Lefty was there, holding to the twenty-foot spacing.

With a simple breakfast of leftovers cooked and wrapped up and sent along by Mrs. Grimsley and a cup of cold well water, the travelers were ready for the trail. As John was securing his saddle and rig, Lefty took a turn at the outhouse. John waited for his return, watching over the horses, before going to the bush, avoiding the little building with the poorly fitted door, himself.

When he heard voices at the campground, John stopped and listened, holding himself behind the brush that bordered the larger trees of the forest. There was loud argument developing. Lefty's voice was the loudest, warning of dire consequences if the others didn't ride off immediately.

"Ya, and what's a one arm freak and a scared to death Black fella gonna do? Y'all just stand aside and ya won't git yourselves hurt none. We'll just relieve ya of these here horses and be on our way. Ya can be thankful to be left alive. If'n I had my way, I'd just as soon shoot y'all. But that might raise a fuss."

John quietly walked from the brush. The way the men were sitting their horses, in a semi-circle, facing Lefty, he was able to walk right up behind them. Walking carefully so as to make no noise, John stepped up beside the talker's horse. That animal, and the one beside it, were close enough for John to touch both of them if he should so choose. Knowing he had only seconds before someone would sense his presence, John stiffened the fingers of his right hand and jammed them hard into the tender spot just before the horse's hind leg. John was a strong man. The stiffened fingers went deep into the animal's belly, setting the surprised animal into a whirl of bucking and gyrating. The rider that had been doing all the talking was caught totally by surprise. After a squeal from the startled animal and a couple of sideways jumps, the rider was flung from the saddle.

The man on the second horse sat unmoving, startled by what had happened. Before the rider could react, John reached up and grabbed his arm, pulling him from the saddle. Lying on his back in the grass, gasping for the breath that had been knocked from his lungs, he looked up at John. Never believing a Black slave would dare touch him, he was momentarily unsure what to do. John placed a foot on the man's chest and bent to relieve him of his handgun.

"Best yo jest keeps still now, Boss."

The third rider, noticing for the first time that Lefty was armed with a handgun, wanted no more of the confrontation. He whirled his horse and kicked him into a run towards the road, leaving his two friends behind.

When the talker regained his wits a bit, he pushed himself to his feet and turned towards Lefty, pulling his cap and ball handgun as he turned. Lefty pulled his own weapon. Blinded with rage, the would-be horse thief started lifting his weapon to typical aiming position, intent on taking Lefty down. He had no chance. Lefty squeezed the trigger, firing his weapon from waist height, when it became clear what the attacker's intentions were.

Know that a killing would raise all kinds of difficulties, Lefty dropped his aim. With a roar of exploding powder and a flash of flame, Lefty's shot brought a scream from the thief, along with blood and bits of hot flesh from the man's thigh. He crumbled to the ground, dropping the gun and clutching his leg. Lefty calmly walked over and picked up the gun, tucking it behind his own belt. He re-holstered his weapon and looked over at John.

"Y'all OK over there?

"All's fine here, Boss."

"Drop the saddles and head gear from those two horses. Get yourself mounted and let's get out of here. Gather up the loose animals. We'll push them off a ways."

With that, Lefty calmly pulled his weapon again. Reversing his hold, taking a grip on the barrel, he motioned for John to step away from the man he had pulled from the saddle. He then bent down and slammed the butt of the gun against the side of the cringing man's head.

"I expect that will hold him for a while."

Mounting his own horse, Lefty swung up beside John. Pointing, he said, "There's an opening through that brush. Leads onto a back road. Several trails from there. Push those other two animals ahead of you and let's ride. Follow me."

Lefty charged ahead, with John pushing the thieves' horses close behind. The black stallion followed along, leaving slack in his lead line as he ran.

Not much more than one hundred yards through the forest, the trail widened and split. Lefty took the westerly trail and kicked his animal into a run. Another quarter mile of fast riding led them into a large clearing. Lefty looked back at John and hollered, "Turn those two loose."

With John frightened by all that had happened, he stuck close behind Lefty. Their geldings, followed by the led stallion, thundered along the trail. The forest thinned somewhat when the trail led along the side of a low hill. Lefty pulled his horse onto another split in the road, heading south west. They ran full out for another mile before pulling to a trot and then to a walk.

A wordless half mile went past while the horses gathered their strength. Lefty finally looked back. What he had to say just might be the most difficult words he had ever uttered but he knew he had to say them. His father's teaching about gratitude and his mother's on manners allowed for no other option. And that was without bringing the Rev. Grimsley and his teachings into mind.

"Y'all done fine back there, John. Might've saved a killing, either theirs or ours."

A full half minute went past while Lefty fought against every instinct in his slave dominated life.

"Thanks."

John had never heard the word directed towards himself before. Hearing it was as strange to him as saying it was to Lefty. He had no clear idea what was to come next. But he did know that deferring to whites had always been his safest route through life.

"Glad y'all' alright there, Boss. Glad too that y'all didn't have to kill that man."

Both men were comfortable with no more being said.

Chapter 7

If there was any pursuit after the fight in the church yard, Lefty and John knew nothing about it. They rode carefully all the next couple of days with few words shared between them. John did finally work up the courage to ask one question.

"Worked well, us leav'n outa that church yard, you know'n bout them back trials, 'n all. You been there before, I'm figur'in."

"Once or twice. A few secluded spots back in there. Knew a girl... Well, that don't hardly matter none no more."

Lefty was going to have to be careful or the first thing he knew he would be talking freely to a Black slave. Proper was still proper, in his prejudiced mind, even if it was mostly pretense. Still, the strain of the hours surely did drag on with no talk between them. And Lefty admitted, at least to himself, that he enjoyed talking.

In the meanwhile, Lefty took his place as the

obvious leader of the little pack. As they entered new towns, John cared for and found water for the horses while Lefty spent a few coins on trail supplies. As they made their camps, the duties were shared. Overall, the ride was going well. They should manage to locate their destination soon if they could continue avoiding uniformed patrols. From either army.

Almost a week later, John saw something, a sign of some sort, nailed to a tree on the side of the road, He had no idea what it said or meant. He had seldom been curious on the farm. There was no need. Someone had always done his thinking for him, simply expecting that he would follow orders. But now he wondered about it. Perhaps that was an indication of interest in his impending freedom.

Lefty, knowing nothing of John's thoughts, inadvertently came to his rescue.

"You're no longer in North Carolina John. Sign says we're in Tennessee. How about that?"

"Yassir. How bout dat."

John was silent for a short while, looking all around as they rode on, before observing, "Don't hardly look no different. Don't know how folks would know one place from de other."

Another short time crept past before John said, "We'uns was in South Carolina and now you say we'uns in North Carolina."

Lefty didn't offer to explain about surveys, maps and such.

"Just following the road John. Tak'n us to this here horse ranch your letter talks about. Borders don't much matter if the road takes us where we need to go."

They rode along slowly for a while before another thought formed in John's mind.

"Be there slavery in this here Tennessee, lak back to Carolina?"

Lefty was starting to get just the briefest glimpse at the true barriers between himself and his riding companion. Being born and raised in a slave environment and not being particularly introspective, Lefty had given the matter little thought. Slavery was no more than a natural aspect of his life.

As he rode along in the next few minutes, for the first time in his life, he tried to put himself in the place of a slave; a man with no freedoms. He didn't like the feelings that started coming over him. If he wasn't careful, he might find himself sympathizing, or even respecting this black man who knew horses so well, and who had proven, in the few days they had been together, to be steady and dependable.

He had seen right from the start that John was a better horseman than he was himself. Where Lefty, a good enough rider by most lights, still showed some daylight from time to time, between the saddle and himself, John almost seemed to be glued to the leather, flowing with the tempo of the animal. Lefty could only guess how much that would ease the burden on the horse over a long day of riding. And the thought that the owner of the stallion held John in high enough esteem to trust him with the difficult challenge of safely delivering the animal, through dangerous times and conditions, put Lefty in the position of not knowing what to think. It was all very confusing.

"No more freedom here than back to home John. You still need to ride careful and stay close to me."

Two days into Tennessee found the travelers camped in a pretty little hollow in the hills. There were hardwood forests all around, watered by a hillside creek that tumbled toward the campground with considerable energy.

Both men chuckled at the antics of several squirrels that visited, hoping to scavenge a morsel or two. The forest was alive with birds of many sorts. Neither man knew their names.

Upstream from the campground was a ten-foot-high waterfall, ending in a deep, clear, cold pool, before tripping again over a rocky lip and into a channel that carried the life-giving water down the valley. Two smaller streams, searching out their crooked ways through the forested hillsides, also fed into the pool, forming an ideal fishing hole.

Neither man had brought fishing line or hooks. John, pulling his boots off and, with infinite patience, standing knee deep in the shallows along the edge, managed to scoop out three decent-sized trout, sliding his hands under the lazy fish and flipping them onto the grass. Lefty cleaned the fish and stoked up a fire. They ate better than they had for some days.

They went early to their blankets and slept soundly until Lefty heard the jingling of horse harness and the crunching of iron-rimmed wagon wheels on the road. Full dawn was a half hour away but it was light enough to see a bit of the forest and the trail from the main road.

Lefty rolled silently out of his blankets and crept to the edge of the campsite. He was in time to hear someone shout, "Captain, I see water just down below there. Hear what might be a bit of a falls too. We've been riding since midnight. I'm thinking these horses could use a watering. Maybe even a bit of a rest."

"Lead us down, Sarg. Leave the wagons here. Just unhitch, and take the teams down."

The faint light was barely strong enough to show the blue of the riders' uniforms.

Lefty scurried back to camp as quickly and silently as he could, in a crouching walk. He scrambled into camp and touched John on the shoulder.

"John. John. Federals. Git yourself up and let's get out of here."

John sprang to his feet, scrambled into his boots, jammed his beat-up hat onto his head, and grabbed an armful of bedding. He had no need to fear Federal troops but he purely didn't wish to lose the horses. Not after so much trouble and so many miles.

Considering he was working with one arm, it was amazing how quickly Lefty had his horse saddled and ready. John swung aboard the gelding and snubbed the stallion's lead rope to the saddle horn. The rolls behind their saddles were a jumble of bedding and spare clothing, carelessly tied down in no particular order. They could roll them properly and straighten out their gear later if they managed to escape the threat.

With no words, Lefty led into the forest. There was no possibility of being silent but Lefty hoped the jingle of the army's wagons and horse accouterments, and the talking of the troops, would cover their exit. The still-smoldering fire would be clear evidence that someone had been in the campsite but with any mercy at all, the troops would be headed somewhere in a hurry and would lack the time to investigate. For a moment, Lefty wished they had put out the fire. But there was no chance to hide the tromped down grass or the grazed-over area so the campsite would be obvious, fire or no fire. Their hope, now, was in running, not hiding.

The men forced their horses through the brush and watched for more open forest. After a half mile of struggle, stepping over fallen trees and ducking under low hanging branches, in the semi-light of dawn, they came to a small trail that appeared to be headed back towards the main road. Lefty turned onto it with no words. John followed, right on the heels of Lefty's grey gelding. The buildup of years of dead leaves served to partially silence their hoof falls, although they had put enough distance between the army patrol and themselves to dampen any noise.

Where they had camped wasn't far off the main road. Following the narrow foot trail, they were soon back to that same road. Lefty pulled his horse to a nervous stop, glancing carefully both ways, hoping to see an open road to the west.

There were no troops, just one black man walking slowly towards them, leading a mule. He looked harmless enough so Lefty kicked the gelding back into motion and turned west, taking the road at a smart lope.

John found the whole, never before experienced, incident exhilarating.

Five days after entering Tennessee, they rode into a small village straddling the main road. A sign as they entered read, "Hapner City, Tennessee". Lefty figured the 'city' part was a bit of a stretch but he didn't bother thinking further about it. At first glance, Hapner City was a pleasant enough little town. Like all the settlements they had passed along the road, it was showing the weariness of war. There was barely a scattering of people on the boardwalks. The various retail outlets, businesses that, in peace time, might have displayed life's abundance in their display windows, or even piled their wares on the boardwalk, were now only dimly lit, lending a forlorn appearance to the eye of the travelers. Lefty was momentarily saddened, thinking of the damage done to the nation beyond the battlefields themselves.

The men were tired of make-do meals. Although they had never spoken of it, Lefty figured they were both hankering for a cup of coffee and a plate of woman cooked food. Or at least food neither he nor John had managed to ruin.

After taking turns over the fire, the two men had decided it was a tossup who was the worst cook.

They rode past an edge-of-town livery and a six-room hotel. Several small businesses were crowded along the lone street, including one large general store and a small bank. There was a sheriff's office with one barred window showing near the rear of the building. A few larger, attractive homes could be seen along a road that paralleled the main trail and a scramble of worn-out shacks, scattered throughout the surrounding bush.

The town lay lazy in the late spring heat. A few townsfolks studied the men and horses as they rode along. Here and there, a merchant was sweeping a walkway or leaning on the doorpost, his anxious eyes watching for a paying customer. A few hens pecked at the sparse grass growing along the walkway. Two dogs snarled and barked at each other before deciding it was too hot to fight. Each trotted off in its own direction.

Finally, Lefty spotted a small café pushed back from the road. The old building and the broken-down steps leading to the small wooden porch entry showed no particular sign of prosperity. But Lefty caught the mouth-watering odors, carried into the open in a small cloud of grease smoke, pushed along by the light, southeast wind. Without consulting John, Lefty turned his horse to the rail on the shady side of the small building. John followed him in. Dismounting, the two men's actions were nearly identical, leaning back to stretch shoulder muscles and then twisting from side to side to straighten their backs after hours in the saddle.

Towards the rear of the building was a half full water trough, with a hand pump mounted over it. The horses were led to the trough and all three dipped their heads to the cooling water. John went to the pump. Lefty allowed the animals to have their fill before tying them to the rail as John continued to re-fill the trough. Lefty then removed his hat and scrubbed his face, hair and hands with fresh, cold water directly from the spigot, as John pumped.

Lefty worked the pump as John had a wash, something he would never have considered doing a few weeks before.

John held back as Lefty headed to the front door of the eating house. Never in his wildest dreams had he imagined entering an eating house in town, no matter how modest.

Lefty stepped inside to see an apron-wrapped black man standing at the big iron cook stove and four customers, all white, lined along the benches siding a large communal table. A similar table sat empty nearby. Lefty spoke to the cook, making no effort to keep his question from the men at the table.

"Traveling with a Black fella. Any objection to feeding him?"

The question wasn't belligerent but wasn't designed to be particularly friendly either. Without even turning from his stove, the cook answered, "No one be turned away from 'ol Bose's eat'n house Boss. You march 'im right in here. I be cook'n nuff fer all."

At Lefty's invite, John nervously lifted the battered hat from his head and kicked a bit of dust from his boots. Lefty pointed to the empty table across the room and the two men took their seats.

The cook hollered out, "Beef, taters 'n greens. Take it er leave it. Dat be de choice today. Same cit-iation as every day. Only make de one thing fer each day. Had fish yest'day. Might be hav'n de poke chops tomorry, if'n ol' Grady done cetch thet hog. Hog, he got out'n da gate,'n took to the brush. He be runn'n pretty fas, las I sees of 'em. Mind, that was last evn'n. Could be cotched 'n killed 'n cut up by this here time. Won't know till in the mo'n'n.

Lefty answered, "Beef sounds good to me. Don't much care about tomorrow. Just travl'n through. Look'n for the Macintyre Horse Ranch. Figure it might be close by here. Judging by the miles we've ridden, is what I mean. Any one of you fellas recollect where that might be?"

One of the men at the other table turned to look at Lefty and John. He studied the two men for some time, trying to discern a threat, Lefty figured, but finally said, "Macintyre place is just a short piece further along to the west. You stay to this road. Bout seven, eight miles out you come to a big 'ol gate, off on the left side. Road leads through the Macintyre grass land. White painted fence all along the trail into the farm. Jesse Macintyre, he likes things nice. White painted fences bout everywhere you go on his place. Peel'n some now, gett'n no attention, what with the war and all.

"Built that place up after his Pa, and his Pa before him, passed on to their rewards. Good family. Good horses too. That is until the army helped themselves to most all of 'em."

When the cook waddled out of the kitchen with two overloaded plates, piled high with beef and taters, and steaming with rich brown gravy, the conversation stopped.

John was overwhelmed with the offered feast. He stared big-eyed at the plate and then up at the cook. The cook showed no facial expression but, after glancing to see if Lefty was watching, he flashed a slow wink at John. Lefty was already laying the edge of his fork into his beef, hoping it was tender enough to break apart with just his one hand. He missed the interaction between the two Blacks. But he did manage to say, around a mouthful, "Is that coffee I smell?"

"I be bring'n de coffee in jes' a minute, Boss."

Lefty dropped the asked for coins on the table after the huge meal was consumed, along with three cups of coffee. When Lefty turned to leave, John reached into his pocket and pulled out another small coin, placing it beside his own coffee mug. He caught the cook's eye and returned the man's wink with a grin and a nod. With no words shared between them, the two Black men acknowledged their understanding.

Lefty and John were not long covering the few miles to the Macintyre Horse Ranch. But before they got there the trail passed along another slow running stream. John studied it with longing and purpose.

"Best we be stopping here fo jest a bit, Boss. Thet water be good fo the drinking and fo de wash'n up, both."

Without waiting for Lefty's agreement, he turned off the trail and pointed the horses into some covering brush, along the side of the stream. He pulled the animals to a stop and swung out of the saddle. In a matter of a minute or so, his saddle was on the ground and the horses taken to water. Lefty led his gelding to water but left the saddle in place. It had not been long since the stop at the small eating house, so the animals were soon satisfied.

John staked out his gelding and led the stallion into the stream. He left the animal standing, while he went behind the bush and stripped off his own clothes. Barefoot and naked except for a ragged pair of cut-down long johns, he waded into the stream with a well-worn shirt he had dug out of his blanket roll, balled up in his hand. While all the while talking softly to the stallion, he dipped the old shirt into the stream and gave the animal a thorough wash down. The stallion showed his appreciation by shaking water all over John, causing the first laugh Lefty had ever heard from his riding companion.

John staked the shiny black stallion on the sun-warmed grass and led his gelding into the water. It received the same refreshing treatment the stallion had been given. With that done John said, "Mights jest as well I give de grey a wash'n down too. We's want to show dis Macintyre fella de best o' de horses. Show dey got de good car'n fer along de way. Goin ta have myself a overall wash after dat. Can't wash de stink outa de pants nor de shirt. Dey take too long fer ta dry up. Jest have ta be what it be."

Lefty dropped his saddle into the grass and led the gelding to the creek and turned him over to John. The horses plainly enjoyed the cleaning, although John knew they would roll in the dust at their first opportunity.

When John was as clean and dried off as he could make himself, he donned the old clothing again and saddled both geldings. Without a word, Lefty had gone a bit further into the brush, seeking privacy, and took this first good wash since leaving home.

Chapter 8

Neither man found it necessary to point out the road with its big entry posts and the sign that John couldn't read. Lefty read it to himself but he could find no good purpose in reading it aloud for John. With the big posts and the white painted fences, matching what they had been told, this could be nothing other than the entry to the Macintyre Horse Ranch.

The ranch road was little more than a two-track wagon trail but it wound around a couple of small hills and through some hardwood forest before crossing a creek on a wooden bridge. All the horses trembled a bit at the echo from their hoof falls on the wood but they kept going. When the ranch buildings came in sight, both men automatically pulled their rides to a halt. They sat silently, taking in the big house and the many structures, all fanning out from a white painted stable that fed into a series of corrals.

John was the first to speak.

"My, dis be maybe de biggest fa'm I ever did see."

Lefty offered nothing to support or disagree. He simply kicked the grey gelding into motion and moved towards the fancy ranch gate. The gate was closed and held in place by a blacksmith-made, metal loop that pivoted from the corner post and dropped over the top of the gate post.

Mounted horse high on the corner post was a large brass bell, with a short, braided, leather thong hanging down from the clapper.

John was puzzled and Lefty hesitated. To lift the loop and open the gate would be a simple act. But would it be the right or welcomed action? The gate was closed and the bell was there. They would wait a bit.

But when two minutes had gone past with no one taking notice of the new arrivals, Lefty leaned from the saddle, put his hand to the leather thong and gave the bell three solid clangs. His grey gelding came close to dumping him on the ground. He stayed mounted only by dropping the thong and taking a fierce grip on the saddle horn.

John, having an idea what was about to happen, stroked his riding animal gently on the neck and spoke soothing words. The gelding stood fast but the black stallion jumped, lurching to the end of the lead rope, nearly upsetting the gelding and John, both, before settling down.

While the ringing from the bell was still resonating through the yard, a black man poked his head out of the stable doorway, taking a study of the arrivals. Seeming to show no hurry, the man sauntered towards the gate. It took all of a frustrating minute for him to walk the distance. He was studying the guests all the while.

Arriving at the gate, he looked first at the horses, spending most of that time on the black stallion. When he had satisfied his curiosity about the animals, he looked at Lefty and then, for a longer time, he studied John. Only then did he speak.

"That be a good look'n stallion ya got there. What fer er ya here? Ya got business on the Macintyre?"

Lefty, for the first time, deferred to John. With a glance back at his riding partner, he nodded. John took the hint.

"We be deliverin' dis here stallion from Mr. Akins, over to de Shady Acres Farm, back down to Carolina. Mr. Macintyre be expect'n him, bout dis time."

Again, the Black ranch worker was slow to respond. Before he had thought it through, a voice spoke from behind him.

Both John and Lefty had watched the well put together white man walking across the ranch yard.

"Open the gate, Benj. These men have come a long way."

With a creak of unoiled metal hinges, Benj pulled the gate wide enough for the riders to enter the yard. Both waited for an invitation to dismount.

"Jessie Macintyre. Welcome to the Macintyre Horse Ranch. Or at least, what's left of it. Step down, take your ease.

"That's a stallion to be proud of. Akins always

knew horses. Knows horses better than he does men. But, nonetheless, I'm some happy to see that black.

"Come up to the cookhouse. We'll find a cup of coffee and something to eat. I'm sure you're ready for a rest after your long trip. Benj will care for the animals. I'll want to hear your story."

As the men stepped to the ground, Macintyre moved to each one, shaking hands and asking their names. He then followed the short lead rope up to the black stallion's head. He held the rope lightly in his hand while he talked to the animal and studied every line. When he saw that the horse was steady and not inclined to back off, he dropped the lead and did a more thorough inspection, walking around the animal twice. He turned to John, one horseman recognizing another horseman, and smiled.

"Fine animal. Fine animal."

Chapter 9

After the silent walk across the farmyard, the horses disappeared into the cavernous barn. Without the use of rope or rein, the animals followed Benj, encouraged by a black and white collie dog. Lefty didn't seem to notice the dog but John watched him intently. Not wishing to speak openly, he said to himself, '*dat be a valuable dog when der be horse work to be done*'.

Jessie Macintyre sauntered, as if time was of little essence, towards the cook house. Lefty and John followed along. Kicking the dust from their boots, they entered. An old and wizened black man poked his head around the partition at the back of the room.

"Got anything left to go with some coffee Sammy? Just something to tide over until dinner time. These men have come some distance."

Lefty saw no point in explaining about the huge lunch back in the village.

Jessie Macintyre turned a chair around at one of the square tables and straddled it. Lefty sat at his right while John chose the chair opposite.

"So first, tell me what's happened on the Akins farm. You know, the war and all. Then tell me about your trip. It's quite a thing you two undertook, coming all those miles, with every risk imaginable bound to pop up and cause you grief. I had about given up on the stallion. Then, too, if Akins somehow managed to send it along, I'd have expected one of his sons to have the task.

"You'll understand that my dealing with Akins has always been done by mail. Oh, I was down there just the once. Didn't buy my first animal from him until I'd seen the layout and the conditions of the animals' raising. Wanted to eyeball the sire, too. But with the war getting in the way, there's been no more traveling and the mail service has been unreliable.

"I don't remember seeing either of you on my visit. Mind, that's some years ago now."

Lefty said, "I'm only along to help John through those risks you mentioned. I have no connection with the Akins' farm, although I've heard of it. Never been there my own self. John was probably there when you visited but he might have been kept out of sight too.

"I can tell you that we had just a couple of smaller issues getting here. Nothing that seriously threatened either the animals or our own lives. Still, I'm happy to have it behind me. John can tell you the rest."

Jessie swung his gaze from Lefty to John and waited.

"Y'assir Boss. Been lots a troubles, down to de Shady Acres Fa'm. Army men, dey come and dey take mos all de ho'ses. I's been work'n 'n train'n de ho'ses, maybe fo', five year now.

"Army be rid'n down de lane. Boss Akins, he say quick 'hide de stallion an de geld'n'. I's tak dem to de brush, on de run. After de army left, I be put together a corral far inta de woods. I keep dese two animals down ta de woods mos of de las year. Sleep'n down der wid them too, mostly. Army, dey come back fer de cattle 'n den de hogs, but dey missed see'n de corral in de forest. So, Boss Akins, he say ta keep de hos's down to de bush. Keep work'n wit de train'n of de stallion. I train him to lead an ta take de saddle. I's jest take a few rides an he settle down. Good horse, dat one."

Lefty offered, "I might add that the black sniffed every mare we passed along the way, rolling his upper lip and baring his teeth when he scented a welcome. Doing just what you'd expect of a good breeder."

Jessie again swung his head from Lefty and back to John.

"You still haven't told me how it is that you got the dangerous and difficult job of delivering the horse, John."

"Oh, Boss, not much left a de Shady Acres Fa'm no mo. Both de sons, dey be kilt in da war. Both work'n teams, dey be took. No animal left ta pull de plow. Boss man, he hop'n de Blacks be stay'n ta plant de farm to potatoes 'n sech. Says he goin pay de wages 'n free de folks."

"Well, I'm sorry to hear about the boys. Terrible what the war has done across the land. We had all our horses taken too, except for a handful of older mares that wouldn't be much good under saddle or in harness, either one. But the war will soon be over and we have to make plans. Actually, I've been making plans right along but the time isn't right yet to move ahead. The stallion will hold an important part in those plans.

"What are your intentions, John? Is Akins expecting you to ride back? The way the war is going, I expect you'll be declared free before long."

John reached inside his shirt and pulled out the folded and creased, rain and sweat damaged envelope. He laid it on the table and opened the flap. Pulling out the papers, he said, "Plans be mostly made a'ready. Dis here paper say I's free when de stallion, he be at dis place. Also say de gelding be mine."

He slid the papers across the table, where Macintyre picked them up. He studied John's face as he opened the first letter. His lips moved as he read but no sounds came forth. He pulled out two more papers and read them, glancing up at John several times. Only when he returned the papers to the table and leaned back in his chair, did John speak again.

"Be what I's been told by Boss Akins and de preacher over to da village be true?"

"I take it you can't read John."

"No Boss. Been de law back to Carolina. Cain't no Black fella be showed to read no' write no' do de sums. Boss Akins, he show me de sums. I's been go to da store in de town fo de farm things, time to time. But not show de read'n, nor de write'n."

"Well John, what you have been told is correct by this letter. And this form is your letter of freedom. It's called a letter of manumission. That's simply a big word that means you're free. Congratulations young man! I'm very happy for you."

With that said, Jessie Macintyre reached across the table and shook the black man's hand firmly and positively. Lefty, clearly still uncomfortable with the changing situation, held out his left hand. It was all he had to offer. John smiled and gripped it awkwardly with his right hand.

Jessie Macintyre called, "Sammy. Come out here please." With quick steps that belied the age of the man, Sammy arrived at the table.

"Sammy, shake hands with the newly freed John. His papers were in this envelope he brought with him."

Wordlessly, Sammy stepped around the table and grabbed John's offered hand with a grip that matched the energy of his quick steps. Giving a tug, he motioned for John to rise to his feet. As soon as John was standing, the old cook threw his arms around him and gripped him tightly. John had no idea how to respond. No one but his mother had ever hugged him before. Finally, Sammy loosened his grip and looked up into the taller man's face. With a smile that could light up the room, he wordlessly nodded, patted John on the chest and made his way back to the kitchen.

Lefty turned his head back to Jessie.

"I take it the cook is a freed man?"

"All my workers are free. I've never owned a slave. Neither my father nor his father would have anything to do with slavery. We've had a few white wranglers over the years but the work wasn't exciting enough for most of them. So, we hired Black workers. But they were either free when they arrived here or we granted them freedom before they went to work on the farm. It cost us some money buying workers and then freeing them but when we were a big operation, we needed the help. Dad looked for men who could work the animals with gentleness and care before he looked at the color of their skin."

Jessie pushed the letter back to John with a smile.

"You'll want to take good care of this letter John, although, as I said, I expect freedom will come anyway, soon enough."

They sat in silence for a minute while Sammy refilled their heavy crockery coffee mugs. Jessie then picked up the letter of instruction from Akins.

"This other letter, John, says that you now own the gelding. You'll need to care for these ownership papers too. It could be that someone will challenge you for ownership, even after freedom. And then it asks me to help you on your way. Says you plan to try for Texas. Is that still your plan?"

John didn't answer the question right away. He had wondered and changed his mind a dozen times on the long road from the Shady Acres Farm to the Jessie Macintyre Farm. Instead, he reached into another pocket and extracted a second, smaller envelope. He passed it across the table.

"What's this, John?"

"That be the papers fo da black stallion, Boss."

Jessie took a quick glance and set the papers aside, with a question for Lefty.

"I don't fully understand how you got involved in this matter Lefty, but I want to thank you for helping John. I'm not sure either John or our new herd sire would have arrived safely without you. I know that sometimes a white man can smooth an otherwise bumpy path. I expect you have done that a good many times on the trail. Thank you."

Lefty had relaxed and mellowed considerably since being summoned by the Rev. Grimsley. He offered a lopsided grin at the horse rancher.

"I didn't start out on this venture of my own idea or volition. After this wounding, that you can easily see, I knew my folks were concerned about my future, but it was the town preacher who gave me the kind of care and attention that made the difference."

He stopped and hesitated for a moment, fearing to put his next thought into words.

"Well, I guess I would have to say the Rev. Grimsley showed me caring and love when I needed it most. He seemed to understand in ways that my folks didn't. He lost a son years ago in some kind of accident. Maybe that helped him see through my anger and confusion. Anyway, he spent a lot of time with me while I was home and recovering from these wounds. I came to respect him more than I ever had as I was growing up.

"When John showed up at the Reverend's door with two knocked senseless fellas, town rabble who had tried to steal the horses and threatened to capture and sell John to the slave trader, the Rev. Grimsley came to John's aid. When he read those letters and knew that John was on a legitimate assignment, he called me and insisted that getting out of town and away from my troubles was the best thing for me. That, and helping John stay safe. I didn't agree but I came along anyway. Now, I don't know what my next step should be."

Chapter 10

Jessie Macintyre stood from the table.

"You men hang around here this afternoon, take your ease. Have Benj show you around. You'll find any number of unused bunks over in the bunkhouse. We've been on skeleton crew since the army took our horses, so there's lots of space. Take whatever bunk suits you. Fire up the stove and heat water for a bath or washing clothes if you wish. You'll hear the dinner triangle when Sammy has food ready. We can talk about your futures another time."

With that, he was gone.

Having had a cold-water bath just hours before, neither man wished to repeat the process, even if the water was heated. But washing their clothing was another matter. After a quick walk through the cavernous barn with Benj and a look at the remaining mares, they were shown the bunkhouse. Both men threw their kits on unused cots and unrolled their blankets and spare clothing.

Lefty was becoming more at ease working beside John but it was still stretching his lifelong beliefs near to their breaking point. There was a limit to how far this familiarity could be taken. But he wasn't at all sure where that limit lay. He decided to let John heat water and wash his clothing first, while he wandered around the big yard. He would pump and heat fresh water when his turn came.

On a horse ranch that employed twenty workers before the war, only six, two whites and four blacks, sat down to the evening meal Sammy had prepared. They gathered at a single big table, leaving the rest of the dining room unused. First name only introductions were made. There were no offered handshakes. Jessie Macintyre did not join them.

Lefty found himself halfway between startled awareness of his past and some realization of what the future was shaping up to look like. If asked, he would be forced to admit that he had never once considered that slavery might one day come to an end. Even during the war, that thought had not come to him any more than the possibility of losing the war had entered his mind. The idea was somehow beyond his limited imagination.

Now, here in a dining room with a Black cook and four Black workers, plus John, sitting at the same table as he was himself, his mind was a jumble of thoughts. Or perhaps they couldn't rightly be called thoughts. Shouldn't a thought start somewhere and carry the thinker to some kind of a conclusion? Well, whatever was rattling around in his mind had a beginning in his upbringing. But he certainly had no idea where it was taking him. And there was no sign of any understandable conclusion.

Lefty's beliefs were further strained, later that evening, when it was time to blow out the kerosene lantern and roll into his blanket. The two white-skinned workers showed no reluctance at the arrangement, having lived with it for some time. But it was almost more than Lefty could reconcile. Even on the trail up from South Carolina, he and John had maintained a respectful distance between their bedrolls.

He considered taking his blankets to the loft. There would be hay enough to make himself comfortable. But a rational part of his brain told him that Jessie Macintyre would take a dim view of his actions. And, after all, he had already passed what was probably going to be his most difficult test. Not that he would ever talk about it. Things like that were not talked about in polite company. But using the same outhouse as the Blacks almost had Lefty saddling his gelding and heading home.

When he awoke in the morning no worse off than any other morning, he moved deeper into his personal compromise process which had started in the kitchen at the Rev. Grimsley's small home. It had grown with each mile and each day of the trip west.

As he lay awake, his eyes still closed, he contemplated the situation the country found itself in. The war was going badly for his side. He hadn't known that when he was in the midst of battle.

The officers were not known for passing that discouraging information to the troops. Looking back, he found himself wondering if even the officers had up to date information.

Now, with the news on everyone's lips, he knew the end couldn't be far off. All things were going to change. He somehow, instinctively, knew that there were hard times ahead. He didn't know the number of dead and wounded but he knew it was heartachingly large. The carnage of war that he had seen and somehow lived through, was indescribable. The destruction of homes, farms and city properties was almost beyond understanding.

There were thousands upon thousands of widows spread across the south. He expected it was the same across the north. Women who would be left with little opportunity to earn a living for themselves and their children. With so much industry and agriculture destroyed and major offshore markets dried up, many of the returning soldiers were doomed to unemployment.

All of these thoughts led Lefty to consider John's original plan, suggested to him by Akins, before John left the Shady Lane Farm.

Texas. All hope lay in Texas. The sun always shone in Texas. Everyone was getting rich in Texas. He had heard it said so often, over so many years, it had almost taken on the aura of folklore, a story passed down from others, a tale to be believed and longed for. Whether those tales of freedom and wealth were true or not, he had no clear idea.

Texas. The word kind of rolled off the tongue.

Texas. Texas and the West. All things could be new and fresh in the West.

Yes, indeed. They must go to Texas. After all, he told himself, folks from Carolina and Tennessee had been seeking refuge and hope in Texas for forty years or more, ever since "The Father of Texas," Stephen F. Austin had opened the way.

That Texas was war torn and suffering too, he had no knowledge of.

But why had he thought 'they'? Where did that come from? Surely he was only thinking of his own wellbeing. Had his undisciplined mind somehow included John?

Lefty rolled out of bed and dressed. Outside, at the back of the bunkhouse, there was a washstand. It included a bench with four basins, a bar of soap for each basin and two roller towels. Lefty looked with considerable doubt at the towels. Did any of these towels ever get changed or washed?

Above the wash bench, built into a wooden stand, was a large, metal tank, holding, perhaps, twenty gallons of water. The men worked together after each washing-up to pump and haul pails of fresh water, passing them to a man standing on the bench, who would dump them into the galvanized tank. The sun would warm the water during the day, taking the bite out of the cold-water shock the next morning.

Jessie Macintyre showed up at the barn shortly after breakfast. He gave a few unnecessary, repetitive instructions to Benj and the other workers. Lefty, listening in, thought immediately that they might be the same instructions that had been given since the army helped itself to the horse herd.

Clearly, there was little to do anywhere on the many acres of the Macintyre Horse Ranch.

With the crew set to their mundane tasks, Jessie turned to Lefty and John.

"Men, I'll be back in one-half hour, after I take care of a small situation up at the house. Benj will have my riding horse saddled. If you could ready your own animals, I'll show you around the spread.

"When we return from our ride John, I'd like if you would introduce the black stallion to Benj. Work together on him, helping the stallion to understand he can trust a new face."

With that, he turned toward the house.

The tour of the land and facilities took most of the morning. At lunch, Jessie sat at a table in the far corner of the spacious room, after inviting the two guests to join him. As was traditional, they ate in silence. When the meal was done and the crew had returned to their duties, Jessie pushed his plate far enough back to lay his elbows on the table. He cast his eyes from John to Lefty and back again.

Sammy quietly walked from the kitchen and picked up the plates the men had used. He would never have done that for the crew but for the boss and his guests, well, it just seemed like the right thing.

"Men. I know you both have thoughts in your minds of what to do next. Although you expressed some doubt yesterday Lefty, you said your original thought was to guide John here and then return home. If you should follow through on that plan, I want you to know how much I appreciate a job well done. Getting that stallion here was no small matter to Akins or myself.

"But I would also caution you to hold on to your plans until this war grinds to a halt. The violence is winding down but it's not over yet. And I'm afraid a different type of violence could erupt on our streets."

Lefty kept his newer thought, the thoughts of Texas, to himself.

"John, you expressed interest in going to Texas. You also mentioned the possibility of tying in with an Indian band in Oklahoma. Either one could be a good choice. It will depend on what you're trying to accomplish. You're free now, you can do what you wish. Setting your own goals and working towards them will be new to you. But you now have that right.

"If I can be forgiven a piece of advice, I would advise that you set your goals high. Push yourself into new challenges. Don't settle for being only a farm worker, although there is nothing wrong with being a farm worker. But being chosen by Akins and getting that stallion here safely, even with help, tells me that you have abilities you may not have recognized yet."

The three men allowed a few moments of silence to slide between them before Jessie spoke again.

"But now I have a thought for the both of you. These are dangerous times for all of us. Here in the eastern part of the state, we have a large Southern force still somewhat in control, although that can change from week to week. The odd Union patrol wends its way through the land but, so far, it hasn't amounted to much. To the west, from here to the big river, is heavily controlled by the Blue Coats. And everyone involved seems to want more horses.

"Even the road back to South Carolina could easily prove dangerous for you Lefty. When this thing ends, there will be soldiers by the thousands walking home. And that's saying nothing at all about the Northern troops who have been riding just about anywhere they wish for the past couple of months. Then there's the deserters and the freelancers, men who ride for themselves, not caring who or what they hurt. That grey of yours could be a grave temptation to anyone you meet along the way.

"I'm going to suggest that you both stay right here. It's not a perfect sanctuary but you'll be safer here than on the road. You could work with Benj, John. Work with the horses. And Lefty, we'll find something for you to do. I haven't given it much thought yet, what with you planning on going home and all.

"For now, your wages would be a safe place to sleep and three-square meals. When the situation finds a new balance, we'll take another look at it all. If the farm could somehow restock its mares, there will be a lot of work to do. We did manage to hold onto one team. Haying season isn't too far away. If you can drive a team one handed Lefty, you could be a big help to the farm. We put up a lot of hay."

After a thorough discussion, the three men decided to leave matters as they were for a while. There was much to learn about the politics facing them. John and Lefty would have to await the arrival of news through the usual channels. But Jessie had contacts in Hepner City who seemed to hear things that others weren't aware of. He would depend on this bit of information to help him make plans. He would share that information and his plans with the crew, at the appropriate time.

Lefty and John found themselves agreeing on the dangers of travel. They would never see Texas or South Carolina if they were captured or killed along the way.

Chapter 11

The war finally ground to a halt, one troubling front at a time. The fractured army in grey was left in tatters through distance and lack of communication. It almost seemed like no single officer really had the big picture. But the one truth no one could honestly deny was that the old South was no more. The boys gave it a valiant effort but it wasn't enough. Many of the officers, tired of the hopeless bloodshed and the loss of the cream of Southern manhood, were secretly hoping and praying for an end. Others, established in their own rightness, and the rightness of their cause, were determined to fight on.

But, end it finally did. The news was slow getting out. But, eventually, official word arrived at the Macintyre Horse Ranch, by way of a friend from town who rode out. Jessie Macintyre, although following the generations before in his dislike of slavery, was Southern. The loss hurt him deeply, even though he had long seen it as inevitable.

His solution for dealing with the turmoil of thoughts struggling for supremacy in his mind was to saddle a horse and ride. Once he was out of sight of the ranch buildings, he lay the reins across the horse's neck, sat back in the saddle, folded his arms in front of him, closed his eyes and went where the horse took him.

After three hours of aimless riding, pondering, imagining what could have been, suffering again as he tried to sort out the terrible losses he and his countrymen had endured, he rode back to the barn and turned the horse over to Benj. John and Benj worked together to clean and brush the animal, although with the slow ride it had not even worked up a sweat.

Jessie made his reluctant way back to the big house. He kicked his boots off, left them lying on the veranda floor, and stepped into the big kitchen. After his ride, he felt strong enough to share the news with Trudy, his wife and Abby, his daughter.

Trudy saw him coming and knew, from the way he walked, that he had news. As he reached for the doorknob on the outside, Trudy pressed down on the big brass latch on the inside. The door opened under her hand. Wordlessly, the two stood looking at each other. In the background, across the kitchen, her sagging shoulder and twisted spine making standing difficult and awkward and painful, stood Abby, Jessie's twenty-five-year-old daughter.

Trudy didn't ask, waiting for Jessie to speak at the right time. They looked at each other and then Jessie glanced over at Abby. He held out his hand toward her.

"Come here Abby, we'll all take a seat."

As they waited for Abby to make her slow way across the room, Trudy ran out of patience.

"It's over, isn't it?"

"Yes. Pastor Reynolds just rode out from town with the news. Came on the wire a while ago. I wasn't sure how to tell you. I've been riding."

Jessie took his daughter's arm as she struggled into her chair. The three finally sat around the small, decorative, wood-cut trimmed table with matching chairs.

A full minute of silence followed the brief sharing of news. After thinking of the loss to the horse ranch and to the South in general, Trudy said, "There is some good news. Howard will soon be home."

Jessie nodded in agreement but followed that with, "Yes we can pray to that ending. But we haven't heard from him in months. So many southern sons have been lost. Although I pray for our son all day long, as I'm working around, I'm also praying that we will be strong, no matter what happens."

Abby, a handsome young lady with light brown waves throughout her long hair and magical brown eyes, said, "We have all been praying, Papa. And we could pray again now."

"Indeed, we could. Would you lead us? And there is no hurry. Nothing is calling me back to the yard. We can take our time in prayer."

So, this hurting, wondering, devout family prayed for their son, their ranch, and their country.

Chapter 12

When he heard the news, Lefty was grateful for the advice he had followed. This wouldn't be a good time to be on the road. The Macintyre Horse Ranch was looking a bit better each day.

John didn't have enough understanding of the politics involved to make an independent decision. He was also not mature enough in his new freedom to fully understand the variance in human nature. If anything, in spite of deeply held suspicions, he was often too trusting. He found safety in followed Jessie's advice. Sammy and Benj both privately assured him on his decision.

John and Benj had the stallion settled down and familiar with his new home. He appeared to have accepted Benj as his new handler with no problems. The first time Benj threw a saddle onto the black's back and stepped into the stirrup, he sat prepared for the worst. Looking over at John who had watched the entire matter, he asked a silent question. John answered with a big smile.

"Dat ol' boy forgot how to be mean. I's be work'n wit him since he be borned. Never let him buck nor be mean. He give'n you no trouble."

The big stallion had serviced his first mare just a few days after arriving at the farm. If enthusiasm was any indication, the black should have a long career with rebuilding a Macintyre herd.

Benj noted the date of breeding in a hard-covered book that was kept in the tack room. With the breeding and raising of quality horses being the only business of the Macintyre Horse Ranch, it was essential that dates and records of the dam and sire be kept. This had long been Benj's job, along with the care of the animals. When the birth took place the date, description and sex of the foal would be noted below that of the breeding record.

Shortly after the news of the war was received, Jessie sought out Lefty down at the big barn. He led him off to the side for privacy before speaking to him. Satisfied that no one else could hear, he said, "Lefty, I have something needs doing that you might be admirably fitted for. My daughter, Abby, has a heart for flowers and trees and beauty. Wherever you see beauty on the farm, the credit goes to her. She has all the ideas, but the planting and weeding are difficult for her. She has trouble bending and is often in pain. If you felt that you could be patient with assisting her, that would be a big help. She would give you directions. You would only have to follow her lead. What do you think about that?"

Lefty studied Jessie for just a moment before saying, "My mother is a great gardener. But all I ever got to do was dig and hoe and weed. Didn't learn much that way. There's probably no one you could find who knows less about gardens than me, Jessie, but if it would help make up for some of the good meals Sammy has put in front of me, I'll do what I can."

"Come, I'll introduce you. Abby won't want you to do much more than what your mother did, so if you can handle some tools with one hand, you should do alright."

"Well, it's really one and a half arms when it comes to long handled tools. I'll do what I can. Show me the way."

The two men walked slowly up to the house. It seemed to Lefty that everything around the farm was done slowly. He suspected that if the country ever settled back down and they got a decent herd of mares back, the pace of operations would change considerably.

Standing beside a workbench placed outside the rear door of the big, white, painted house stood the very attractive Abby Macintyre. She appeared to be sorting small paper packets into three piles. She hadn't heard the men coming. At her father's call, she turned just her head. Her twisted and aching back and shoulder didn't follow the move. She looked at her father and then shrunk back when she saw a strange young man accompanying him. Neither Abby, since her injury forced her to quit riding, nor her mother, ever bothered much with things down at the working end of the farm. There was no familiarity with the two newest crew. This was the first Abby and Lefty had seen of each other.

Jessie stopped a few feet short of the workbench.

"Lefty, this is my daughter Abby. Lefty will give you a hand getting those seeds into the ground Abby. He claims his mother was a gardener but all he ever did was dig and hoe and weed. Since that's what you need doing, he sounds like just the man for the job."

That last was said with a smile, as Jessie was turning to go back to the barn.

The two young people stood watching the horse rancher walk away, feeling awkward together. Finally, although not particularly comfortable around women, since his injury, and somewhat in awe of Abby's beauty, Lefty took the few steps that would close in on the workbench the young lady was standing beside.

"Don't know how much help I'll be but you point and I'll jump right to it. I'm what you might call a nonpaying guest on the farm. Need to do something to earn some of my keep. I came along as guide to a man who was delivering a stallion from way down in South Carolina. A black man. You might say I was encouraged to sign on as guide. Had some little bit of trouble along the way but John, the horse and I all arrived safe and sound. Now we're kind of stuck until the peace is worked out. So, I'm pleased to help you."

Abby hadn't talked with a young man for a long time. She hadn't even been to town for more than supplies since the accident. She found she paid too heavy a price for sitting through the church service, so she had given that up also. Her life was spent either indoors, in the big house, or fussing over her flowers and her flock of chickens. She had started a small growing shed, a greenhouse of sorts, but the physical effort of mixing soil, placing it in the planter boxes and carrying water had proven to be too much for her.

Abby immediately figured out what her father had in mind when he chose Lefty to help with the planting. Her father was always supportive but not particularly subtle.

She took a quick study of her appointed helper. His right arm gone, leaving just a stump that reached a few inches below his elbow, enclosed in a folded-back shirt. A quite noticeable limp that she had spotted when he stepped to the workbench. Most of his right ear missing. A poorly repaired gouge on his right cheek, the surgeon's hurried stitching running diagonally from near the base of his nose, to end close to the damaged ear. Clearly, this man had paid a price for his part in whatever battle he had been in. His soft accent pegged him as being from Carolina. His initial mannerisms supported that assumption.

One wounded person helping another. Plainly, her father hoped she would get over some of her self-consciousness if she saw another damaged person getting along in life.

Chapter 13

Although the little wooden bridge on the two-track trail leading into the Macintyre Horse Ranch was some distance from the big metal entry gate, the thunder of many horses cantering across, two abreast, in line, could be heard all the way to the big barn. Jessie and two of the workers stepped to the open doorway to see what was happening. Within a few seconds, a squad of blue-clad riders was pulling up at the gate. The captain in charge studied the brass bell and the loop that held the gate closed, choosing between politely ringing the bell or simply lifting the loop and charging in. The sight of Jessie walking quickly from the barn made the choice unnecessary.

"Good morning Captain. What can I do for you?"

"You can open this gate."

"Well now, Captain, I don't mind doing that. Folks are always welcome on the Macintyre. But it's common for visitors to state their purpose upon their arrival."

"I am under no requirement to state my purpose. Perhaps you haven't heard. The war is over. You will now cooperate with me and my men or pay the price."

"Well, Captain, as surprising as it may seem, we do occasionally receive the news. Of course, I know the war is over. And I'm not inclined in any way to oppose you. I simply wish to know your purpose. And victor or not, this is still my ranch and still private property."

The Captain seemed to remember whatever was left of his war-damaged manners. He could remember his father telling him 'it costs you nothing to be polite and you'll gain your purpose faster, and with less trouble. Remember, the other fellow has a point of view also.'

"I have been tasked with assuring that all slaves in this sector are indeed set free, as declared by Federal law. I'll need to examine your premises and talk with your people."

Jessie smiled at the surprised Captain as he lifted the loop, allowing the gate to swing wide.

"Well, then sir, come right on in. I don't have any 'people', as you phrased it. I do have a few employees. We had a considerably larger crew before the war, Black and white both, but that was before your army stole our horses. Unfortunately, I have but a few men in my employ anymore. You will find five Blacks. Four are on the Macintyre payroll. The fifth man is a temporary guest. Three are working with the horses in the barn. I will call them out for you. I would ask that you do not disturb the animals.

"One man is preparing dinner in the cookhouse, and one is sleeping, after completing a night's work with a sick animal. All are free. The Macintyre Horse Ranch has never owned or worked slaves. Three generations of Macintyres now and never a slave. But you're welcome to talk with the men. I would only ask that not all of you try to crowd your way into the barn or cookhouse. That would serve no purpose. If you'll wait while I walk up, I'll guide you around the place."

A half hour later, the still suspicious Captain Mulcair could find no purpose in staying longer.

"I'll leave it for now, Mr. Macintyre. But I'll be back. If you're holding out on me, I'll, sooner or later, find out."

"Duly noted Sir. Come any time it suits your purpose. Simply come for a visit if you wish. We hope to be a civilized people. And to show you our simple hospitality, Sammy has put on a big supply of coffee. He might have something to take with it as well. Your men are invited to tie their animals and slake their thirst."

The Captain tried, unsuccessfully, to stare down the horseman, looking for deception. He finally gave in and turned to his men.

"All right men. You have been invited to rest and have a coffee. Tie your animals. One of you stay with the horses. The rest make your way to the cookhouse. You have one quarter hour."

As the Captain led his handful of troops out of

the yard after the rest time, Jessie asked John to walk with him as he went to close the gate.

"John, you can see what the country is like now and imagine what it's going to be like in the near future. All officers are not like that Captain. We could very well find ourselves faced with a truly belligerent man the next time. We need to take care. And you, especially, need to take care if you decide to move on west.

"There is going to be huge resentment in many southerners over the loss of the war. And then, more than just a few farmers are going to have a difficult time getting crops into the ground and worked, without their slaves. It's true they could do as Akins did over east, on the Shady Acres, and hire their workers back but most won't think of that. Even if they think of it, their pride is likely to stand in the way. Eventually, they will give in to the inevitable, but that time is not yet.

"Akins is not a good man, nor a man I would want for a friend, but he raises good horses and he has a wisdom of sorts. Or perhaps it is more of a cunning. That wisdom is not built on his love for mankind. It's far more selfish than that. But he just might be successful with the farm where others are failing due to their stubbornness. Or what they would think of as their pride.

"I'm concerned there could be all kinds of violence for a long time to come. And Blacks will bear the brunt of that violence.

"What I'm trying to say, I guess, John, is that although you are free to do as you wish, I'd advise again that you stay right here. I think your chances of getting to Texas safely are not very good. It is a powerful long way from here. Then, there is the big river to somehow get across. You will need money for food and other expenses.

"You stay here for a year and work with Benj and that beautiful stallion. I'll pay you a wage and your keep. You save your money. In a year, perhaps traveling will be safe enough for you to move forward."

"Yas, Boss. Benj and Lefty, dey both say de same. I's be stay'n 'n work'n. Do de work yo ask of me. And I be thank'n yo Boss."

The men were silent as the gate was swung closed and the loop put into place. Jessie leaned his folded arms on the top of the gate, looking out over the beautiful country to the south and east. The Macintyre Horse Ranch was situated approximately two hundred feet higher than the surrounded country. The view from the gate was magnificent. Rolling hills, hardwood forests that he knew held several cleared-out spots where other farmers were working out a living on the well-watered land. Leaves flashing that peculiar green freshness of spring. A truly beautiful land. But a troubled land. A war-torn land.

That the two conflicting truths should be forced to co-exist was an abomination in his eyes. Sadly, he had no choice but to accept the facts. Wordlessly, he turned back towards the barn with John following.

John still had considerable suspicion and reluctance about talking with white men in authority. It was true that he and Lefty had found a way to be together but Lefty was not an owner or any other kind of man in authority. He thought briefly of the good Pastor Grimsley who had helped him along his way. And the sheriff who believed his story and gave back the letters. But he had met others who meant him harm. Nevertheless, Jessie Macintyre had shown himself friendly, at the very least. John could see no reason not to trust the man.

When they reached the barn, Jessie showed his approval of John's decision with a light slap on the shoulder and a small smile.

"The problem with this freedom thing John, is that we have to make our own decisions and pray they're correct. When we're free we live by those decisions, good or not so good, with no one to blame. But we're also free to think and not to simply follow others. You've a good head on your shoulders John. You use that head to think your way forward. I believe you're going to come to enjoy every minute of your freedom."

Without giving John any time to respond, he turned towards the house.

John had, unintentionally, flinched at the ranchman's touch. The only other touches he had ever experienced from white men were anything but friendly. Or gentle. But he had heard the words from this good man.

Never before had he heard words like those. Encouragement? John hardly understood the meaning of the word. Good head? Think? Make his own decisions?

Until that time, John's understanding of freedom had been surface and shallow. He knew he was free to come or go without asking anyone's permission. But he had given almost no thought to the consequences arising from his decisions. He knew enough to understand that the world held traps for the unprepared or for those that chose the wrong road. But he had never tried to think through how to avoid those traps.

Nor had he considered the possibilities of thinking his way forward. Thinking carefully before he acted. What did he really want? Would he find it in some unknown land known as Texas? What, after all, did he really know of Texas? Had he, perhaps, already found what he wanted, on the Macintyre? Or should he be looking for something else altogether?

He had, from time to time, thought he should learn to read and write. Still, he failed to carry that thought forward.

There was a lot to consider and learn. Perhaps a year with the Macintyre horses would give him the time he needed to do that considering, that learning.

Chapter 14

Lefty put his belt gun away the day after reaching the Macintyre. It was rolled up on his bunk, covered by the pillow. His carbine was safely stowed in its scabbard, attached to the saddle, stored in the tack room. No one on the Macintyre wore a gun in sight. He was surprised to find out that Skeeter and Daniel, the two white workers, and Jessie, himself, carried weapons belted under their long vests. No Black wore a weapon, although they had all been trained in the use of long guns.

When Jessie came the second time to tell Lefty that Abby could use an hour or two of help, he brought the subject up.

Jessie hesitated before speaking but finally answered the question.

"We've had very little trouble over the years, Lefty, but there have been a few times I was glad those men had their handguns. Both Skeeter and Daniel have demonstrated their skill with weapons as well as considerable discretion in their use. We don't want any gun handy folks around here that can't think before they shoot. At the same time, with the disruption of our society that's bound to follow the war's loss, I'm wishful of being prepared. I'm talking defense only here, Lefty."

Lefty nodded his agreement without interrupting his employer's line of talk.

"We've never been attacked or challenged right here in the yard but the Macintyre is a large farm. There are many gullies and wooded stream beds. Although the land is fenced, it's not difficult to tear down a fence if a person is determined to steal a horse or two. It has happened.

"With the herd now so small, we've kept the animals close to the home place and take hay off the other pastures. We don't need the hay but taking it off keeps the risk of grass fires down to a minimum and gives us a store of feed against future dry years or a series of hard winters."

Lefty thought on this for just a moment before asking, "Do you wish me to carry my handgun? I could dig it out of my gear. I have a carbine in the tack room too."

Jessie couldn't help looking at Lefty's shortened right arm, all that remained after the wounding.

"How do you manage a carbine, Lefty?"

"Well, first you have to understand that I was born left-handed. I've carried this name most of my life. So, shooting left is no new thing for me. Then, I have just enough of a stump to take the weight of the long gun. I did a lot of shooting in the war. Of course, that was before I lost the arm. But still, the familiarity with long guns remains. As to the handgun, that's the same as it always was, shooting left. Come to a troublesome situation, I could hold my own."

Jessie lifted his eyes to Lefty's face.

"You go ahead and wear the short gun. It might add another layer of comfort. Leave the carbine where it is.

"With the anger that I'm sure is coming upon us, I fear for the Blacks and, perhaps, for my family, more than the horses now. I am truly expecting violence to reign around the land for some time. Whether it will stay in the towns or along the roadways or find its way to the Macintyre and other farms, I can't guess. I'd feel better if all of us were armed. But arming the Blacks would be asking for trouble. You go ahead and wear the pistol. Keep an eye out for trouble. Especially when you're working with Abby.

"And that reminds me of why I came down here."

With a grin he said, "You have been summoned. I've never before heard of a one-armed shovel man but you must have done a satisfactory job. Abby has more work for you."

Jessie wandered down to the barn while Lefty made his way to the bunkhouse. He emerged just minutes later with his Smith & Wesson #2 Army, belted to hang, in its holster, on his left side.

He didn't own a long vest like Skeeter and Daniel wore or any other piece of clothing that would cover the weapon. He wore the Smith & Wesson for all to see, just as he had done during the war and since he had been invalided home.

As he slung the gun belt around his hips he thought about Jessie's words and where they might lead. 'Anger. Anger and violence across his beloved homeland'. Could it really come to that?

With thousands of Blacks freed and wandering across the land, taking up jobs the returning soldiers wanted, attempting to push their way into the general white society, demanding more and more freedom, demanding an opportunity for education, showing their own anger at their lifetimes of slavery, claiming their equality. And the whites, reluctant to change, pushing back.

Yes, indeed the south could easily become violent.

For perhaps the first time, Lefty could see that the old order was not going to be pushed aside easily. Not easily at all. He thought of John, the first Black he had ever talked with long enough to get to know, even a little bit. Inwardly, he was still struggling with the revelation, the one overriding thought from the long ride to the Macintyre: John was a man he could learn to like and even admire when his faithfulness to his assigned task and his adroitness with horses were considered.

There was no possibility of him openly speaking about any of that. He was nowhere near ready to go that far.

His own internal struggle with anger and self-pity had been picked up almost immediately by the Rev Grimsley when he first rode home from the battlefield. His parents were slower to see the changes in his life. While his mother was tending towards pity and sorrow over his injuries, his father had finally seen the situation more clearly.

"An arm doesn't make the man, son, and the losing of an arm doesn't take away from his manliness. You've spoken angrily about how your scarred face will stop any woman from wanting you. You have much to learn. Any woman who judges a man on such superficial things isn't a woman you want. And if you, in turn, was to judge a woman on such things, she would be right to walk away.

"None of us can change what is. You took on some serious injuries. You will carry the scars all your life through. That's nothing more than the facts. But there's a good life just waiting for you. It's up to you to go find it. And anger or self-pity will not help in that search."

Lefty had become sullen and unresponsive following that short lecture from his father, knowing somewhere, in the depth of his soul, the rightness of the words, but still not welcoming them. It wasn't until he started understanding the depth of despair and the life robbing hopelessness that slavery had left in John, that he dared to make even a cursory comparison. Losing an arm didn't compare to a lifetime of slavery. Didn't compare at all.

He couldn't talk of that openly either.

Thinking to pick up at least his portion of the pace around the farm, Lefty walked smartly up to the big house. Abby was just emerging from her growing shed. Lefty had been wondering about the small building with the mismatched windows worked into the roof.

"Good morning Abby. What's with the shed? I've never seen windows in a roof before."

"Good morning Lefty. That was going to be my growing shed. Some would call it a greenhouse. But I soon found out the work was too heavy for me. I gave it up after just a couple of months, last summer."

Lefty couldn't find an adequate response, so he asked, "What are we doing today?"

He soon found himself on his knees in the flower bed along the front of the big house. He prepared the soil and pulled the few weeds that had found growing space. Abby passed him some flower bulbs.

"It's really pretty late in the year to be planting these but we'll see how they do. They'll just die by next spring if they don't go in the ground now."

Lefty turned his head upwards so he could make eye contact.

"You just watch to make sure I don't get these in upside down. I did that once some years ago, before the war. I was pretty young. Probably wasn't paying much attention to my task. Ma came and saw. Made me pull them all out again and then went up one side of me and down the other for not watching what I was doing. It was a lasting lesson on where my skilled areas lie. And where they don't lie."

Abby laughed at the vision and assured Lefty he was doing just fine.

Was it his imagination or was Abby a bit more at ease on their second day of working together? He waited for a bit of time to pass before working up his courage to ask, "Mind telling me what happened to your back? I'm sensing that it's a fairly new thing."

"It's no secret around the farm. Any of the men could tell you the story. I took a bad tumble off my horse. No call for it really. The horse didn't do anything unusual. I was daydreaming, I guess. Wool gathering. Enjoying the motion of the cantering horse and looking at the clouds. Of course, I always knew better. I've been riding all my life. But the clouds rolling across the blue sky caught my attention. I've always thought of clouds as sailing ships, sailing to the far corners of the world. I read that one time in a children's book. I guess I kind of took it to heart. Clouds. Ships going to places I've never been or have any hope of ever seeing. I guess I was sailing along with the clouds when, all of a sudden, I really was sailing. Only I didn't land on a sandy beach with waiving palm trees. I landed in a heap against the trunk of a tree.

"Silly, right? I mean when you consider that I've never seen the ocean and never really expect to. And I don't even remember when I first started riding. Seems like I might have been born on a horse. Anyway, I lay there until the crew found me. It simply hurt too much to move. The horse returned to the barn alone. It took a couple of hours for the men to find me and then go for a wagon to carry me home.

"Anyway, things happen. You lost an arm and I ruined my shoulder and twisted my spine. We have to make the best of life."

Lefty paused in his work to think through what was said. First, it was Jessie, not an hour ago. Then all his own thoughts crashing through his mind. And now Abby. Were they ganging up on him? He shrugged off the silly thought.

He knew his own attitude after the wounding didn't measure up. He had fought deep anger and despair. He still did, occasionally. He came close to feeling sorry for himself from time to time. Remembering the horror of the battlefield and the many, friends and comrades, who weren't coming home, pulled him back from that emotional trap.

Surprisingly, he found that the couple of hours working with Abby lifted his thoughts and his spirits. Perhaps it was because she hadn't flinched in horror when she first cast her eyes on him and his scarred face.

Not wishing to discuss his own situation, he returned to digging and pulling weeds. When he had more soil prepared, he asked, "You got any more of those bulbs?"

Chapter 15

Three weeks after his first visit to the Macintyre, the Captain returned. This time, perhaps acknowledging the lack of resistance on the horse ranch, he was accompanied by a much smaller group of soldiers. At the clang of the big brass bell, Benj trotted down to the gate. Benj hadn't moved above a slow shuffle since the army confiscated the horse herd. The pace of movement on the ranch was beginning to pick up.

"Morn'n Captain. You's jest in time for de noon dinner, should you an dem fellas wit you be hungry. I's be open de gate. De Boss, he be up to de big house. I git him jest as soon as I kin close dis gate back up."

The soldiers rode to the big corral and dismounted, waiting for Jessie to arrive. Within a few minutes, the owner of the Macintyre walked down to the corral with an outstretched hand.

"Welcome, Captain. What brings you around again so soon?

The two men shook before Captain Mulcair said, "Orders, Mr. Macintyre. Orders. We've been pretty well everywhere in this sector and now we're doing a follow-up."

With a bit of a sloppy grin, the military man continued. "So, tell me Mr. Macintyre, how many un-freed slaves am I going to find here today?"

Jessie returned the grin with, "Pretty much exactly the same number you found on your last visit Captain."

"Well, I'll just take a saunter around anyway so I can be honest in my reporting."

"That's fine. You go anywhere you wish. In the meantime, if your men were to come with me to the cookhouse, we'll see what Sammy has that he can spare, after feeding our own crew. You'll find most of our men up there."

The Captain turned to the man beside him.

"Corporal, I'd like if you would detail one man to stay with the horses and one man to come with me. Then you and the others make your way the cookhouse. Spell off the man with the horses."

A bit later, Jessie Macintyre and Captain Mulcair sat at a table alone, drinking coffee and eating a liberal slice of dried apple pie Sammy had rescued before the hungry crew got to it. After discussing the general happenings around the county, the Captain said, "There's another reason I chose today to return, Jessie. The army has delivered a large herd of horses to our keeping. The poor brutes were gathered up from several locations and brought down to Adelaide. Some of them were extras, superfluous to our current needs, now that the battles have ceased and a large part of the army sent home. Some are impounded from the Confederates and a few were captured from two or three gangs of free riders. All in all, there's around two hundred fifty animals the military has no need of and can't feed or care for. Some are in simply dreadful condition and some, in fact, may not live out the week. The circumstances these poor creatures survived through during the last weeks of the war is indescribable. But if a buyer were to look beneath the scars and shedding hair, I believe there's some good stock there.

"The whole bunch is going on the auction block in two days. Anyone with the ready cash can buy them. The army wants the word spread quickly. A large, fenced field was commandeered just outside town but now there's little forage left. The animals have to go. They're going to perish if we don't find new owners. I thought you might like to take a look. If you can raise some cash that is.

"I'm told this has always been a breeding farm. There are some likely looking mares in the bunch and you might find a few geldings worth saving and bringing along for either ranch work or pleasure riding. I thought you might wish to come down to Adelaide and take a look, at least. It's only about a ten-mile ride to the west. Of course, you already know where it is, no need of me telling you."

After a few more questions about the horses, the Captain and Jessie shook hands and parted. The men had long since returned to their duties.

Jessie made his way to the big barn.

"Benj. I'd like it if you would gather up Skeeter and Daniel. Might bring John along too. Saddle me a horse and get one for yourself. We're going to take a quick ride over to Adelaide. Have a look at some horses."

With that, he walked up to the house and lifted his carbine off the deer horn rack above the kitchen door. He checked it for loads and then dropped a few more shells into his pocket.

Trudy walked in as he was checking the weapon. With a quizzical look, she asked, "What's going on?"

"I just got word that the army has a bunch of horses they can't feed or look after. They're desperate to see them gone from their possession. They plan an auction in two days but I don't see any hope of that working for them. There's little money left in the country for buying anything, let alone misused and worn-out horses. But we might find a use for them. Might even be the key to getting us back on our feet."

"Can we spare the money for their purchase?"

"Depends on what the army will settle for on the deal. I'll make them an offer. If they accept it, I'll give them a bank check. By the time they get to cashing the check I'll have enough gold taken in to cover it."

"Yes. But you need to be careful. Breeding and raising salable riding animals isn't an overnight venture. We need enough cash on hand to make expenses along the way. And speaking of expenses, is that transfer for the stallion complete?"

"I talked to the banker just a few days ago. I'm not

sure how the banks do it but, somehow, Akins had the bank certificate delivered to him. So, he's paid and our account is reduced by the same amount. Plus, of course, the fees the bank charges."

Jessie placed his hands on his wife's waist and pulled her to him, giving her a hug.

"You needn't worry, my love. I'll take no foolish chances."

He turned, picked up the carbine again and left the house.

Within one-half hour, the five men rode out of the Macintyre gate. Lefty, who had followed them down the lane, closed the iron gate, then leaned on the top of it, watching them ride off.

An hour later, they were sitting their animals, strung along a sagging and partly dismantled pole fence, looking at the horses. Each man seemed to be focused on a different animal or grouping of animals. Jessie, himself, was studying the yard. The grass was eaten almost to the roots, the horses were in small groups, head to tail, swatting flies off one another, heads hanging as if in defeat. There was no sign of a creek or other source of water. He seemed to recall a bit of a pond towards the back of the property. With the size of the herd needing water, there would probably be little left but mud and rank dregs of scummy water.

A man in a blue coat, riding a big grey gelding, and all decked out in Cavalry brass, including a sword, trotted his well-fed animal over to join them. Behind the man were a half dozen cavalry riders. Their horses, too, appeared to be properly cared for.

"One of you Macintyre?"

"That would be me."

"Captain Mulcair suggested that you might be in. I take it you could have some interest in attending the auction. Do you care to ride into the yard? Take a closer look?"

Jessie was a long time answering, as he continued to scan the group with a knowing, horseman's eye. Finally, he sat back in his saddle, pushed his hat a little higher on his forehead, studied the officer for few seconds before giving up on sorting out the man's rank, and said, "Sir. I'm interested but only if that means an immediate purchase. I'm talking about right now. This afternoon. Some of these horses will be dead in two days and most of them won't be worth trying to pull back from the brink. They have no feed and I don't see any source of water.

"As to holding an auction, that's not going to gain you much, if anything at all. There's no money left in the country and little need for sick and abused horses, when most folks are having trouble feeding their families."

There was a full minute of silence between the men before the officer spoke.

"But I take it you have some funds available."

"Sir. The Macintyre is three generations old. It was a well-known and sizable horse operation before our animals were impounded from us. We have bred, trained, and sold quality riding horses, as well as light teams, for nearly a century. My father was a wise man. He never failed to put away against a rainy day, as he called it. He is no longer with us but I, and the farm, are benefiting from his wisdom.

"Yes, if you and I can come to an agreement on a price for the entire herd, I will give you a check which the bank will cover. I will need two days to make a deposit. But in the meantime, you will know where the horses are if you wish to have that bit of security against my making good on payment."

Without talking further or asking permission, Jessie spoke to his crew.

"Fellas, let down that gate bar and take a ride among those animals. Have a close look and come back with a count and with your advice. I will want to know how many will have to be culled out. We will wait here."

With the order given, Jessie looked back at the cavalry officer.

"Are you in the position to make a decision, Sir, or will I be working with a chain of command somewhere?"

The man showed the first hint of a smile.

"Are you ex-military, Mr. Macintyre?"

"No, Sir, I'm not? Does that make a difference?"

"No difference at all. I'm just smiling to myself at your understanding of military protocol. In this case though, you can set your fears aside. The command understands that this matter can't be delayed. The decision will be mine alone."

Jessie nodded and smiled himself.

"We didn't really introduce ourselves. I'm Jessie Macintyre. Civilian with no rank except family man and horse breeder."

The cavalry man held out his hand. "I'm Ted Crowley. Major. At least until I can arrange a discharge. I'm not career. I'm also a family man who has been away far too long."

The Macintyre crew were a full half hour seeing to their duties with the horses. Before they rode back to the gate, they met to compare counts. They settled on two hundred fifty-seven animals, eight of which might not live out the week and forty-five more that would require special attention. Furthest away from the gate they had entered through, in a small cluster of bushes, they found one heavy team and two medium teams. The heavy animals appeared to be in reasonable health. They left it to Benj to report their finding to Jessie.

The Major seemed a bit perplexed when Jessie received the report from a black man, while the other two whites stood back. Although he studied on Jessie's reaction, he decided that saying nothing was the best approach.

Again, they sat in silence for a quarter hour while Jessie wrote columns of numbers in a small notebook he took from his pocket. The Major's horse was fidgeting and the Major, himself, was becoming restless. The men accompanying him were clearly wishing the duty to be drawn to a close. He finally turned to the Sergeant.

"Sergeant, move the men to that grove of shade trees across the way. Have them dismount and take their ease. I'll call if anything is needed."

The men had heard, so there was no need for

orders to be passed down.

Jessie studied the numbers on the page again, pushed his hat further back, took a deep breath and let it out slowly, and turned to the Major. He tore a page from the book and passed it to the military man.

"This is an offer good for one-half hour. After that, we ride for home."

Ted Crowley studied on the page for an uncomfortably long time. It didn't take that long to read a few numbers but he fully understood that Jessie was serious about the one-time offer. It was low but if he was the one purchasing it probably wouldn't be any higher. Still, he felt he had to bargain, just a bit.

"That's hitting the army pretty hard, Jessie. Let's bring it up, at least some."

"This country was stripped bare of horses Ted, including mine, and nary a one of them paid for or returned with the surrender. The Macintyre herd was bigger than the one in this pasture and far better mounts, as well. I don't expect to ever see them again and any hope of payment went out the window long ago.

"That's my offer. These animals need to get on grass and water. There's no time for delay if you want them to live through this ordeal. We're willing to take on that chore but only if we can start now. If we ride home, we won't be back."

The major held out his hand.

"Does a handshake still mean something Jessie?"

Jessie completed the handshake as he said,

"Between men of goodwill, it does, Ted. Between the Macintyre Horse Ranch and the US Army, I'll be wanting a formal sales contract in the next couple of days."

The Major nodded and smiled.

"Looks to me like you might have learned more than just a few things from your old pappy. Get them out of there Jessie and luck to you."

Jessie turned to Benj. "Gather those beasts and push them this way Benj. Bring them along slowly. We don't want them running. Skeeter, you hang back in there. Scour every corner of that property. Shake out every bush and hiding place. We'll move out but we'll be moving slowly. You can catch up. Get at it, men."

The major crossed the road and dismounted, watching to see how the operation unfolded.

With John placed on the road, outside the gate to direct the animals to the east and with Jessie holding place on the road to prevent the animals from running, Daniel and Benj were left to gather and push the horses towards the gate. Once the first few found the gate, the rest followed with almost no pushing.

The herd was slow-walking towards the Macintyre home place when Skeeter trotted up behind, pushing the last of the purchased animals.

Twenty minutes down the road they stopped beside a running stream. The sides were sheltered by an almost solid line of light brush but Jessie figured that wouldn't stop the desperately thirsty animals from finding their relief. He was correct on that.

When the herd was finally watered, most of the covering brush had been trampled flat. Jessie knew it wouldn't be long growing back.

It took more than two hours to reach the Macintyre. The animals showed their lack of strength as they followed along with no attempt to run or break out of the group. When they crossed the wooden bridge, Jessie pushed his horse into a fast trot. He needed to get the gate open. He didn't want any bunching up at that late point in the drive.

Lefty heard the bell as Jessie rang it solidly. Running from the barn, he caught Jessie's signaling arm wave.

"Open the gate to the big pasture,"

Lefty turned and ran to obey. He then had just time enough to swing onto a horse bareback and stake out a guiding position in the yard.

Before long, the horses were spreading out, their noses pressed deep into the fresh, late spring grass of the Macintyre Horse Ranch. No one had to show them where the water troughs were. Even after the stop at the stream on the way in, it took two men, working the iron handle in turns, to pump enough water to keep ahead of the thirsty animals.

Jessie called over to Lefty, "How's Sammy doing for dinner? We're a bit late but we're ready if he is."

"Just came from there a few minutes ago. Dinner is laid out and the old man's worried about y'all."

The crew had gathered outside the pasture gate. Jessie rode up to them there.

"Well done, men. I half expected a couple of those brutes might lay down and die before we got them here. Well done. Now, Lefty tells me dinner is ready. See to your horses and then make your way to the grub pile. We'll let the horses rest this evening. First thing tomorrow morning, I want Benj and John to sort out that bunch. Any that need special attention you push into the barn. We'll stall them there until they either recover or show us they're not going to. Do whatever you think needs doing with them. Save as many as you can.

"Skeeter and Daniel, I want you to lead one animal at a time into the blacksmith shed. Check their feet. Pull any shoes they may still be wearing. Trim the hooves. Look them over carefully for injuries or poorly healed cuts. Watch for scald, ringworm, mange. Well, shucks, you know as well as I do what to look for. Keep a record of any branded animals. We'll try to track down as many owners as we can. When you're done with an animal, put the mares in the small pasture and the geldings into the horse trap. I want the heavy animals in the barn after you finish with them.

"I'll be up at the house if I'm needed."

Chapter 16

Over the next few weeks, and with many hours of grooming and care, the horses lost the last of their winter coats. With the long hair gone, the men were able to better judge the overall condition of the animals.

With the treatment of the Macintyre crew, the horses deemed to be the most at risk were all looking and acting better, except for one grey gelding. His skin lesions refused to heal, he was often found lying in his stall, unable to get up, and he didn't take to his feed well enough to put his lost weight back on. He refused every tempting bit of special nourishment John and Benj could come up with.

With sadness, Jessie had John remove the animal from the barn and put a halter and lead rope on him. Jessie mounted his big gelding with his carbine stowed in the scabbard. John passed him the lead. Skeeter, watching from a short distance away offered, "You want me to take care of that, Boss?"

"Thanks Skeeter. It's my job to do."

With that, he slowly led the animal across the big pasture and into the timber two miles southwest of the ranch buildings. He was too far away and too sheltered by forest for the crew to hear the shot but they all understood. Jessie returned an hour later, wordlessly passed the halter and lead to John, and dismounted. John stepped over and silently reached for the gelding's reins. Jessie was about to object, seldom allowing anyone but Benj to care for his animal.

Let me, Boss. Jest dis once."

Jessie nodded his thanks and walked to the house. He never had gotten over the losing of a horse.

The activity of the horse ranch had picked up to near where it was before the war. The black stallion had been put to work on a few of the recently purchased mares. John and Benj were riding and gentling a group of geldings with John doing most of the riding. The horses had all been under saddle before but had taken up some bad habits. John would try to work those habits out of them. It would take the patience of Job to accomplish the task. Or in this case, the patience of John.

Benj was more knowledgeable with matters of horse health, while John, clearly, was the best rider.

Lefty was busy trying to track down the few brands the animals carried when he wasn't busy grooming the horses John and Benj currently had in the barn.

Jessie watched the three men work for over an hour on a slightly cloudy, drizzly morning. He was long familiar with Benj's work but John was the new hand. Benj had sung John's praises to Jessie in a private conversation but to see the man put the animals through their paces, gently, but tolerating no nonsense, ignoring the rain running off the brim of his tattered hat, firmed it all up for the boss. As John stepped off one animal, turning it loose and swinging his saddle onto another, Jessie spoke, his arms resting on the top rail of the corral.

"John. I've prided myself in my horsemanship and the Macintyre has had many a competent rider and trainer over the years. But I do believe you outshine the lot of us. Are you sure you can't actually talk to those animals? You have them obeying you and I don't always see your signals to them. I know you have your eyes fixed on Texas but I want you to know you have a long-term position here if you should change your mind.

"In the meantime, consider yourself on full wages. You and Lefty, both. Good work, young man."

In times past, laying in his rude bunk in the small family shack back on the Shady Lane Farm, John had imagined what freedom must be like. Or, at least, he tried to imagine it. But without a starting point, the dreams seemed to sputter and die, vanishing like the campfire smoke that so easily found its way into his and Lefty's eyes, on the trip to Tennessee, before rising and disappearing into the sky, never to be seen again.

In his most vivid and hopeful dreams, John could have never imagined having a white man say such things to him. And, really, this was the second time Jessie offered words of encouragement. John had no idea what to say in return, so he made no reply to the Boss of the Macintyre Horse Ranch. He simply nodded with a bit of a smile.

Each step he took into the white man's world was putting a growing distance between John's slave thinking and his current situation. He was finding the change difficult and not altogether comfortable. As ugly as the slave life had been, it had been his life, all he knew, and he had found a fit within it. It was not quite a comfortable fit; it was more a lack of conflict. Since slavery left him without choices, he accepted the life as it was. Now, to throw off the mental and emotional shackles of slavery threatened to leave him without a foundation. To leave him vulnerable.

Freedom was demanding a whole new way of thinking, forcing him into making his own decisions and standing with the results of those decisions. John wasn't altogether sure he was going to be able to manage, or adapt, to that new way. Certainly, it would take some time. Perhaps much time.

The acceptance and encouragements of Benj and the others were, perhaps, a temporary support to lean on.

Along with the surprising acceptance and appreciation of his work by his white employer, he admitted to himself that there was still a wide valley between the races. Or perhaps it was more between the cultures than the races. He was unable to sort it all out, so he quit trying and concentrated on the horses.

Later that day, Jessie was fussing over one of the pair of heavy animals, wondering if he should keep the team for the farm or find a market for them, when he heard a blood-curdling scream emanating from the house. He ran to the doorway of the barn in time to see his wife pour out of the kitchen door, run across the small porch and literally leap down the four stairs. She continued her screaming, running as she hadn't run in years, and waving her arms.

Every man on the farm had rushed to the yard expecting to see disaster unfolding.

Jessie had his eyes firmly on Trudy and Abby, who was coming across the yard as quickly as her twisted spine would allow. As Trudy got closer, Jessie moved to intercept her. With her arms still flailing over her head, she ducked past her husband, running towards the gate. As she passed, Jessie could just barely make out her out-of-breath words: "Howard. Howard. He's home. It's Howard."

Jessie snapped his head toward the big gate in time to see a thin, bedraggled, ill-looking man turning back from dropping the gate's security loop into place. It took a moment for his eyes to convince him that his wife was correct. The scarecrow at the gate looked very little like their son but the slowly waving hat and the weary grin, even hidden behind the black, unruly beard, confirmed the identity. Jessie, who hadn't tried to run in years, joined his wife in that exercise. Abby was still doing her awkward and painful best to catch up with her parents.

Trudy arrived at the gate just steps before Jessie. She threw herself into the arms of the bedraggled man, nearly bowling him over but backing him against the metal gate, instead. Her hugging arms threatened to crush him. The weary walker returned the hug and then opened one arm to receive his father's embrace. The three of them stood there, wordlessly, long enough for Abby to hobble the distance. With Howard and Trudy opening their arms, they included her and again the hugging continued.

Finally, Jessie, tears streaming down both cheeks, moved a half step away. He ran his rough hand over his son's whiskered, hollowed-out cheek and down his arm, feeling for the bulk of muscle that used to be there, knowing he wouldn't find it. He couldn't tear his eyes off the filth and blood-encrusted remnants of the grey uniform or the pitiful and badly used man inside it.

His son. This was his son who had endured. Endured just what, Jessie couldn't guess. Perhaps he didn't want to know.

The Macintyre family, with Jessie walking alone while the two women held Howard's arms, walked towards the big house. As they came close to the cookhouse, Howard shook off his mother and sister and stepped towards the assembled and watching crew. They were all there, side by side, looking on in wonder and happiness that this young man was home.

Howard stepped up to Sammy, the eldest of the black workers, the man who, when younger, before he'd been semi-pensioned off to the cookhouse, had spent many happy hours teaching the young Howard the skills of riding. Howard looked at the Black cook with a smile of loving remembrance.

Sammy's grin was threatening to split his face asunder.

"I's more den happy to see you ta home, son. Been pray'n mighty hard fo you."

Howard responded with a tight squeeze, one hand on each of the cook's shoulders.

"It's good to be here Sammy. And it's good to see you looking well."

"Y'all look'n tired, son, but mighty fine, all the same. Mighty fine."

"Tired? Yes, I should say so. I've done some walking Sammy. Getting home."

Taking just a short step to the side, Howard threw his arms around Benj, before doing the same to Skeeter and Daniel.

"I'm happy to see every one of you and to see y'all are still here on the ranch."

Jessie had walked up beside his son. When Howard looked at John, Jessie said, "This is John and standing beside him is Lefty. They've recently joined us."

Howard shook hands with the two men, taking his longest look at Lefty. With no shame at his staring, Howard looked up into the taller man's eyes.

"We all have a story, Lefty. I'd like to hear yours. But not yet, a while."

Lefty simply nodded silently.

At the house, Howard took a seat at the big kitchen table and stared around the room as if seeing it for the first time. His mother placed a cup of coffee before him while Abby went to the pantry and dug out a plate of sweet rolls she had baked the day before.

Howard took a sip of the coffee, set the cup back on the table, bowed his head just a bit, and closed his eyes. As tears ran down his cheeks, no one said anything.

With new tears threatening to overflow his eyes, Jessie laid his work-hardened hand on his son's forearm. For those few moments no one talked.

The family was complete again. It wasn't the same. Probably would never be the same. Maybe it couldn't be the same. But it was complete.

Abby was learning to cope with her injury. Both Jessie and Trudy had faced up to their advancing years and bodies that had been wracked by hard work and accidents, over those years. Howard would recover. Given time. Yes, the family was not the same but they were all there. They could, and would, give thanks for that. And if nothing in his war experience had changed Howard's thinking, he would be there to take over the horses when his time came.

Chapter 17

Howard contributed very little to the farm work for his first couple of weeks home. But gradually, with hours and hours of sleep, good and plentiful food, and the love of everyone on the farm, he began to regain his strength. Although he spent considerable time riding and talking with Lefty, he found it difficult, bordering on impossible, to share his war experiences with the family.

At mid-morning, a few weeks after arriving home, Howard walked down to the barn to find Lefty. When he located him, he grinned at the one-armed man and said, "You have been assigned the task of escorting my sister and me to town. We'll need the buckboard and a light team. It's time to fetch the month's supply of grub and fixings for both the house and Sammy's cookhouse. If you'll bring in the team, I'll help you harness them."

With Lefty one-handing the reins and Howard sitting on the other side of Abby, the three young people headed off to town. The shopping was entrusted to no one but Abby while Lefty was along to lend his one-armed assistance as the general store clerk loaded the wagon. Howard was mostly along for the ride.

Abby made two attempts to prod the men into describing their military experiences before she finally figured out that wasn't going to happen. The rest of the trip to town was taken in silence with only the rattle of the empty wagon for company.

Abby laid the long shopping list on the general store counter for the clerk, before slowly making her way to a table bearing bolts of cloth and other sewing needs.

"Young Lady, may I speak with you for a moment please?"

Abby turned, searching out the source of the voice. Howard and Lefty heard, as well. They were heading towards the door, intent on escaping the drudgery of shopping, while they took in the sights and activities of the town from the bench in front of the store.

Abby turned and studied the man who had spoken. She saw a well-groomed, military man wearing the blue coat of the Union army. Abby had no idea what the insignia on his sleeve meant.

Howard and Lefty, suspecting trouble or an improper approach to Abby, both turned away from the door and stepped towards the speaker. Their holstered handguns were hanging in plain sight.

The speaker spoke first to the approaching men.

"Are you men accompanying this lady?"

"I'm her brother."

"Fine. I am Capt. Tobias Blakely. Medical officer. I would very much like to talk with you and the young lady if you would walk with me to the end of the aisle where it is a bit more private. I promise you I present no threat or anything unbecoming."

With grave suspicion, they followed the doctor. Having found a bit of space where they could speak without being overheard, Capt. Blakely, talking quietly, said, "Miss, I couldn't help noticing your twisted spine and dislocated shoulder. I wasn't staring. It's just a part of my job and training. Beyond normal medical training, I have done considerable study on the skeletal system. Some medical schools are beginning to believe that study has been too long ignored. I admit the science is rudimentary and at the very beginning of the discipline but it is interesting and informative in any case. I wonder, Miss, if you would feel free to tell me about this deformity? It doesn't look like a birth defect, so I am assuming it is an injury."

Howard wasn't happy to have a man who was his shooting enemy just weeks before, taking what he considered to be liberties with his sister. And to have that man approaching his sister, a woman unknown to him, in public, went against all he held to be proper.

"There was a time, sir, when I would have challenged you for speaking to my sister without a proper introduction. But I'm as weary of fighting as I am of Blue Bellies cluttering up our land. State your purpose and be gone with you."

The two men tried to outstare each other for several seconds before the medical man let his held breath escape and his shoulders slump to a relaxed position.

"You might not believe me young man, but I really do understand. I understand protocol and I understand the weariness of war. One could not possibly spend time in a medical tent, such as I have, without becoming weary of the entire matter. Can we both just let it go for this one time? My interest in your sister is purely professional."

Turning back to Abby, he said, "Miss, I'm wondering what medical assistance you have received and why you would live in such obvious discomfort with what looks like no more than a dislocated shoulder. Will you tell me what happened and what your doctor has told you?"

Abby pulled her eyes away from the doctor long enough to look first at Howard and then at Lefty. She then spoke directly, as an equal, to this doctor who was wearing the uniform of their victorious enemy. It was an inwardly proud moment for her, even if no one else could see what her actions meant.

"In a moment of carelessness, I took a tumble off my running horse. I jammed my shoulder and back against a tree trunk. This is the result."

"And your medical help?"

"The army hauled our only doctor away a couple of years ago. He hasn't come back."

"So, you have not consulted a doctor. May I make a quick examination of the situation? I promise no inappropriate actions."

Abby again looked from one man to the other before making her own decision.

"I'll agree to almost anything that might help if you'll call me Abby or Miss Macintyre. I don't like the sounds of 'young lady'. Or 'Miss', either, for that matter. Somehow, it makes me feel uncomfortable."

"Fine Abby. Then if you would please turn your back to me and just relax. I am going to see if I can feel where the bones have come out of alignment."

Capt. Tobias Blakely, Union Army medical man, stood in the general store in the little village of Hepner, Tennessee, his fingers searching for the probable dislocation of a shoulder on an unfamiliar woman who was a part of the defeated enemy. It was almost surreal when he briefly thought about it all before he brought his mind back to the task before him. He prodded gently and then, sure he felt the tip of the offending bone, he pressed harder. That brought a gasp of pain from Abby. Still pressing fairly hard, he said, "That's the troublesome spot isn't it?"

Abby was near to tears but, for a few moments, her hopes of some kind of help had risen. She wasn't ready to quit just yet.

"Well, it hurts all over but where you have your finger is the most painful."

Stepping back and touching her shoulder to turn Abby back towards himself, he said, "Well, Abby, you have been through a lot of misery over something that could have been easily treated right at the start. How long ago did this happen?"

"A bit more than a year."

Tobias Blakely nodded, thinking.

"It is always easier if treatment is timely. When treatment is delayed the muscles tend to adjust to the new position of the bone. Then the surrounding bones and muscles will adapt in sympathy with the injury, making the whole matter appear much worse than it really is. Putting the bone back into place is not difficult but can be quite painful. Then, of course, the muscles and the straightened spine have to find their new homes. That can take some time and, occasionally, the bone will slip back out of position. The good news is that putting it back into position a second time will be nowhere near as troublesome as it is the first time.

"Over against that reality is a lifetime of pain and discomfort like you are going through now. Wouldn't you rather have a moment of pain if relief can be had?"

This time Abby neither looked at her brother, not consulted him.

"Doctor. If you can put this back in place, I'll stand up to whatever it takes. Just tell me what I can do to help."

"All right, here's what I need you to do. Turn just a bit to your right and bend your elbow. Take a good hold on that counter beside you with your other hand. I'm going to be pulling you this way. I'll pull you off your feet if you don't have a good grip. Perhaps one of you men could walk behind the counter and hold Abby's wrist, ready to counteract my pulling. Understand please, I will not be giving your arm a sudden jolt. Expect a simple, steady pull.

"I need your brother, Abby, to help you hold your bent arm in place. I will be overpowering what you can do yourself.

"So, brother, if you would hold Abby's other shoulder and take a grip on her right wrist and simply hold it in position. Don't pull back. Just see that it stays bent the way it is now and allow it to move as I pull but not straighten out."

When all was in place, Capt. Dr. Tobias Blakely slowly, but firmly, as gently as possible, pulled on the bent arm while his other hand massaged the bone at the point of dislocation. He had no intention of making any fast or jerky moves. Slow pressure and some manipulation, some back and forth movement. That was the plan. Abby gasped and bit her lips, holding back any outcry. The pain increased as the pressure increased. Finally, with a slightly quicker but more firm pull the bone slid and then snapped back into the socket it had vacated those many months before.

This time, Abby couldn't hold back her scream. The pain was excruciating. A startled outcry escaped her trembling lips. Her entire body shook in sympathy with her throbbing shoulder. Tears ran freely. Her breath came in gasps.

The store clerk and two lady customers turned their startled eyes towards the make-do medical clinic at the end of the dry goods and clothing aisle.

Lefty turned to them and promised, "No problem folks. Just the doctor helping out. No problem."

The customers said nothing but neither did they take their eyes off the back corner of the store.

Capt. Tobias Blakely gently massaged the wounded area, feeling again for the bones. With some satisfaction, he said, "Try gently moving the shoulder Abby. Although there may well be a bit of discomfort from having moved the bone, it should be tolerable. Stop if the full pain returns."

Abby, expecting the worst, slowly rolled her shoulder and then lifted her arm and let it drop again. She had been walking with a forward bend in her spine for more than a year, hoping to find a less painful way of walking and moving. Slowly, she straightened up, even bending backwards just a bit. She stood tall, slowly moving her shoulders and spine from side to side. It took a couple of minutes but, finally, she turned to the doctor. Her pain-driven tears had been replaced with happy tears.

"I don't know if it's fully fixed Doctor but whatever happened, it's sure a far leap from where it was. How can I thank you? Does the army allow you to receive payment for private service?"

With a smile, the doctor answered, "There's no payment required or wanted, Abby. That smile on your face is payment enough. I hope to see a smile such as that on my wife's face if I ever get rid of this uniform so I can return home. I'm very happy for you."

Smiling at the patient, he said, "I'm not sure we haven't worn out our welcome in the general store. If I had a clinic, I'd suggest you come in sometime soon so we can take another look and see how it's healing. But I can't even promise I'll be here. The army can send me wherever they wish, anytime they wish. If I see you again, that would be my pleasure and honor. If not, I bid you God's blessings."

He turned to Howard and Lefty with an offered handshake. "Thank you too men. For your help and your understanding. If you wished to help Abby even more, one of you would ride in the back of that wagon on the way home. It wouldn't do to crowd that shoulder."

Both men shook the doctor's hand with another thank you. Howard gave the simple directions to the farm with an invitation for the medical man to ride out if he got the chance.

Chapter 18

Abby's shoulder mended about the way the doctor had told her it would. It wasn't yet perfect, or fully healed, but she considered the improvement to be wonderful, just the same. Much of her previous life had been reclaimed and restored. She was riding again and the growing shed, with Lefty's frequent help, was back in use.

Her spine, which had followed her out-of-kilter body in sympathy, was only slowly straightening up. She found herself stretching and back-leaning often during the day, to relieve the healing tension.

Capt. Tobias Blakely visited the farm just once. Although he was made welcome and had the freedom to examine Abby in privacy, there was a bit of tension when Howard felt the man had spoken out of turn. The doctor had been shown around the farm, walking through the big barn with its stalls full of horses and with the white workers shoulder to shoulder with the Blacks.

He had been treated to a long lunch, sitting around a table with Jessie, Lefty and Howard. He appeared to be surprised when the owner and his son lined up with the rest of the crew to serve themselves from the tubs and pans of food prepared by the Black cook. That the working crew, including all the Blacks, was expected to get their food first was something he simply didn't understand.

Having recently arrived in the south, and with only a cursory knowledge of the country he found himself in, he had become convinced, or had been convinced by others, about what he would find was normal in the culture.

Being uninformed about the situation on the Macintyre Horse Ranch, he made an assumption and a comment that followed that assumption. Abby had joined the men for pie and coffee by that time.

"Am I correct in assuming, Jessie, that these Blacks working with you are your freed slaves or are they hired on new?"

"There has never been a slave on the Macintyre, Tobias. The men you see are on full wages, the same as the whites. John, our prize horse trainer, who you met, is new to us. The others are long term employees."

"But I thought…"

Howard, still hurting from the war, was short in his response. He made no attempt to keep his voice or emotions under control.

"On the contrary Doc. Perhaps you didn't think at all, like most of your Blue Bellies didn't think."

The tension around the table brought the entire cookhouse to silence. As the silence dragged on, with everyone frightened to take the next step, to utter the next word, the crew quietly laid down their forks, took another quick gulp of coffee, dropped their dishes into the crash bucket and left the cookhouse.

The doctor understood instinctively that it was he who would have to break the silence. But how to do that without aggravating the situation?

Making another poor decision, he looked from Howard to Lefty and back again before saying, "But I thought that was why you went to war. Without the slavery issue, why have a war?"

Howard was equally unwise in his words.

"I didn't suffer in your damnable prison camp, nor fight you over hill and hollow, over slaves that we've never had. Lefty didn't lose an arm and half his face over some imaginary slaves his family never owned either. There were slaves enough. No one is denying that. But the fact is that the large majority of southerners have never owned a slave. Of course, there's slaves enough in the north too but you never want to talk about that."

"Then why were you fighting?"

"Mostly to keep you Blue Bellies out of our land. And to keep your taxes off our exports. As thankful as I am that you were able to help Abby, you have to understand that none of you are wanted here nor will you ever be welcome."

The doctor nodded his head in acceptance of Howard's position. He understood that nothing else would bring this discussion to any kind of a peaceful conclusion.

"Abby, Jessie, men, my fullest apology. I did not intend to bring offense. I can see that my medical education outshines my knowledge of my own nation. I have much to learn. I promise, I will endeavor to learn as I go along. Now, I thank you for your hospitality and for this fine lunch.

"Abby, you are doing well. That shoulder just might pop out again if you strain it the wrong way. You might try to put it back in with the help of a couple of these men or you might have a doctor in town before long. In any case, I wish you well and I want you all to know that it has been a pleasure to meet you and your family and see this lovely farm.

"Now, if you will excuse me."

Jessie pushed his chair back and stood, as a signal that the lunch and the visit were completed. He gave the doctor a firm and sincere handshake.

"Tobias, we will always remember that a stranger, a man of compassion and medical knowledge dared to speak to Abby and offer assistance. Our thanks will be unending. I wish you well and I wish you that discharge soon and a safe trip home."

Abby thanked the doctor earnestly. Lefty offered his left hand. Howard walked to the kitchen, spoke this thanks to Sammy for the lunch, and slipped out the back door. Dr. Tobias Blakely noted his actions but said nothing.

Chapter 19

The pattern of work on the Macintyre had been set with the purchase of the army herd. The animals they had to work with were lacking the quality and breeding of the original Macintyre stock but the crew was managing to get some reasonably acceptable riding and work animals settled down and re-trained, ready for sale. The most difficult task, left almost exclusively to John, was the breaking of war-induced habits. With the breaking of these unwelcome habits would come the introduction of obedience to a new set of directions, felt by the animals through rein and knee action, plus a few kind words and loving touches.

Only a skilled and observant horseman would have recognized the army animals in the sleek, well-groomed, carefully fattened-up and fleshed-out bunch the Macintyre offered for sale. Advertisements run in newspapers from Memphis to Knoxville, and many smaller places in between, had a small but steady stream of buyers visiting the horse ranch or sending letters of inquiry. The heavy team was sold, along with one of the lighter teams.

Slowly, the cash fortunes of the Macintyre were taking on a breath of new life.

Lefty managed to place just two branded animals back with their original owners, receiving volumes of thanks but no payment in return from the poor-as-church-mice farmers. Jessie felt the goodwill generated through that action was worth more than the cost of two horses.

Jessie was cautious with his spending. In a broke and broken country, it would be unwise to flash any sign of new wealth. Anger and hopelessness were rampant across the land. There would be nothing to gain by attracting attention to the horse ranch.

And so, month followed month on the horse ranch, until the new green, breaking out in the surrounding forest was a sure sign that another spring was upon the land. Most of the invading army had been posted elsewhere or discharged. There was periodic violence against freed Blacks. Out of work men, with no skills to offer other than the simple farm work they had done in slavery, often led their starving and desperate families from village to village, on foot, begging for some work, any work that would put food in their mouths. Theft almost always led to violence, and, often enough, even death. But desperate people do desperate things and a man has to feed the hungry mouths he's responsible for. It was a much different freedom for most Blacks than what they had dreamed of.

Jessie kept his own Black workers as close to the safety of the farm as possible, cautioning them to never visit the village alone.

Full spring finally arrived with its warming air, greening grass and new hope. But the new hope didn't touch everyone equally. Families abandoned devasted farms, having no workers to plant and care for the crops or the money to pay them. Hundreds of footloose southern soldiers wandered the land looking for any kind of opportunity, since the family farms they had hoped to return to were destroyed. Or sold out from under them for delinquent taxes.

The farms would produce again. Some day. But not by the hands of the sons of dead or destitute fathers. Or conversely, by the dead sons of the remaining farm owners. And none of it would happen soon enough to meet anyone's needs.

Widows by the hundreds were reduced to begging, or worse, to feed themselves and their children.

From this tide of unrest and weariness came a single thought for many people. Texas. The West. Few bothered to look at the real facts on the ground in the West. The name and the idea were enough. There was hope in Texas. The very word conjured up enchantment. As far as that went, there was hope anywhere in the West. The West was magic. The West had a draw to it that was as difficult to ignore as gravity.

The West was big. No one really knew how big. But big. Big enough for everyone to have their share and perhaps a bit more.

The stories of almost instant wealth from the mines had found listening ears in the shattered Eastern states. Tales of the millions of acres of empty grasslands, just waiting for the arrival of the cattle that would feed a nation, were like a giant magnet. Free land. Who could imagine such a thing? One quarter section, one hundred sixty acres, for a man alone. Two quarters, three hundred twenty acres for a man and wife. In Texas, a man could have three hundred twenty acres of good farmland for himself. More if he had a wife with him. Further west, he could have all the grassland he could claim and hold against others.

And so, the stories were told. Stories of success and happiness. And people listened. The result was a great tide of humanity rolling across the Big River and onward. Onward and westward.

'Turn your back on the old troubles and follow the sun west, moving across the land.' That was the cry heard everywhere men gathered.

People by their thousands were going west. Texas, California, Colorado, Nevada. Few could have found any of those places on a map but that didn't matter. The names alone, and the hopes they offered, were the draw. No one had accurate maps anyway. Nor did they have any way of reckoning with the vast distances, or the days, weeks, months the journey would require. They ignored the fact that there were rivers that would need crossing. The dangers from outlaws or Indians, either one, were set aside, to be dealt with when the time came. Most were blissfully unaware of the many other problems that might beset them. They were going west and would cross their rivers when they reached them.

Like a rolling tide, they patched up their old wagons, greased the hubs and put their mismatched teams into harness. Loading what tools and household goods they could cram into the tight space under canvas, provision with foodstuffs as well as their limited funds would allow, and gathering with other like-minded movers, they were ready to roll west. To Texas. What a name. Easy to say. It almost rolled off the tongue. Easy to remember. Just five simple letters. Enticing to imagine. Such promise. Who could resist the draw?

Big Hammond Gates proudly rode his seventeen-hand crossbred stallion into the Macintyre yard. Hammond did everything with panache and pride. He had the rare ability to truly let yesterday be yesterday. To Big Hammond Gates, every day was totally new. Yesterday's troubles belonged to yesterday. Each sunrise brought new opportunity, new hope. Even with his farm grown to weeds, the taxes unpaid and the house reduced to blackened timbers and char, he still rode and spoke with pride, with hope.

"Morning Hammond. Good to see you. What brings you to the Macintyre this spring morning?"

"Morn'n Jessie. Ain't seen you in a while. Heard your boy got home safe. Awful glad to hear that. I should have come over to shake his hand." He paused and took a deep breath before saying, "but you know how it is."

The moment passed as quickly as it came. Still, it was one of the rare insights into the big man's single vulnerability.

"I know and yet I don't really know Hammond. I wondered a thousand times how I would respond if I lost a son. I've seen you just the once since you received the news about Jerry. How are you and Rosa doing?"

"Aw, you know, day by day. Ain't anyone really happy, nor full of joy, as old Pastor used to say. Left a hole in our lives, Jerry did."

He looked off to the southeast, towards the mid-morning's spring sun and the few fluffy white clouds that occasionally drifted in front of the sun, casting a shadow across the land. He seemed to put the brief conversation and memory behind him too, in that simple glance upwards.

"But ain't it a bright morn'n? It's good to be alive and free to enjoy God's fresh air.

"We're going west, Jessie. Texas. Or perhaps somewhere beyond. Going to fill that hole in our lives with new horizons. Came over to ask you to come along. Empty land in the West. The country will need knowing folks. Ain't no one knows horses better than Jessie Macintyre. Turn this whole thing over to Howard and get your wagon down to the crossroads. We're pulling out, five families of us. Leaving in just one week. Love to have you there with us."

Jessie smiled up at his old friend.

"Step down from that animal. We'll find a coffee and have a chat."

As the two men pulled chairs up to Jessie's usual corner table and set their filled coffee mugs down, Sammy appeared with a plate of hot buns, directly from the oven in one hand and a small tub of home-churned butter and a couple of knives in the other hand. Wordlessly, he laid the mid-morning fare before the Boss and retreated to his kitchen.

Hammond watched the Black cook as he walked away, before turning to Jessie with a bright smile.

"Wouldn't hurt none if you was to bring Sammy along with you. Always room for a good cook, on the trail or on the ranches or farms we're going to set up."

Jessie didn't bother responding to the suggestion before asking, "You thought this all through carefully, Hammond? It might be easier to bring the land you already own back into production rather that driving a team and wagon a thousand miles towards the unknown."

Hammond nodded. He had already considered Jessie's point of view.

"Probably cost more to bring this land back than it would to start over with free land. There's no stable market for anything we might grow, anyway. Then there's the memories and the deep hate that's taken over this land since the war. Like you, I never owned slaves but now that they're free, the Blacks are everywhere, poor beggars. Their situation seems hopeless. It's a huge problem and I see no ready answers. There's no easy solutions and no willingness across the land to take on the difficult ones.

"At my age, I don't know as I have the heart to face up to it. Rather start fresh in a new country."

Jessie slowly buttered a hot bun while he thought of a response. There was no consideration at all, in his mind, to going west. He simply had no interest. What if he offered some financial help to get Hammond back on his feet? As soon as the thought entered his mind, he cast it out. The danger of offending his good friend was a risk he was not prepared to take. Anyway, all the money in Tennessee wouldn't replace Hammond's lost son.

Jessie took a bite of the bun and chewed while he looked across the table at his old friend.

Although the outward actions of the big man had changed very little, Jessie thought he could see an underlying weariness. Or perhaps it was sadness. Hammond had to be nearing the fifty-year mark. He had married late and his eldest child, his only son, Jerry, was around Howard's age, perhaps twenty-five. Fifty was old for a man to begin again, in Texas or in Tennessee, either one. Still, he would say nothing to discourage this lifelong friend.

"The girls all going with you?"

"Yep. Two married ones will have their own wagons. Melody will ride along with her mother and me. We'll probably let her sleep under canvas while the wife and I roll out our bed beneath the wagon. Won't be as comfortable as the feather quilt at home but the reality is that the bed, the feather quilt and the roof they used to shelter under are all burned to the ground. Nothing left but memories and sadness. Kind of helps understand the anger taking over the country. Stupid, burning folks' homes. What was that supposed to accomplish? Stealing their livestock?

"But no one ever accused any army of being smart."

He seemed to hesitate as if he was reliving the whole nightmare of the past few years, before saying, "No, my friend we need to see the sun come up over new land."

"Believe it or not Hammond, I understand. But that doesn't mean I'll be joining you. It's kind of you to think of us but we're getting a bit of a new start here with a small herd to work with. We'll have a batch of new foals coming along in a few months. No, we'll be holding here. But there's a couple of men I want you to meet, if you'll walk down to the corral with me."

The two men made their way through the big barn, with Hammond admiring the horses as he walked along. He stopped at the oversized stall holding the black stallion. He looked for a long time and then turned to Jessie.

"Now, that there is a fine-looking animal. I don't recognize it though. Don't recall you having an animal like that."

As they moved on towards the corral, Jessie told Hammond about purchasing the horse from South Carolina and how the two men somehow managed to deliver it through the war-torn country, and right to the Macintyre.

"I rode down to the breeder's farm before the war. Liked what I saw with his herd sire and a black mare, with a foal at foot. The pair's next two foals were already spoken for but I got the promise of the third. That took some time, of course. The mare and stallion were lost to the army but not before this black wonder was brought into the world. Hid him in the bush. Raised and trained by this man I want you to meet."

John was working with an army gelding, sitting tall and proud as he put the animal through its training paces.

"John, pull up over here and meet a friend of mine."

John nudged the horse to the side of the big corral with only his leg pressure. The reins were lying across the animal's neck. John sat with his arms folded in front of him. With a quiet "whoa" the horse stopped a few feet away from Jessie and Hammond.

"Stand." The horse stood like a statue.

"John, I'd like you to meet my friend Hammond Gates. Hammond is leading a group west in a few days. Heading for Texas. I thought if you still planned to go, you might see if Hammond would take you along with him. It's not anywhere near safe to ride alone. What are your plans now John? We'd miss you if you go but I'd understand too."

John seemed stunned for just a moment by the opportunity and the possibilities. When he had gathered his wits again, he asked, "Dat be right, Mr. Hammond? You be tak'n Ol' John to Texas wit you if'n I's ta ask?"

"Well, John, Jessie kind of threw this at me without warning but if you wished to come, we'll make a place for you. We can't outfit you but we'll feed you if you'll work with the animals along the way. We'll be driving some extra stock, horses and a few cattle, enough to get a leg up on a good grade of beef animal. One milk cow. You would have to be ready to leave in one week."

"I's be ready Boss, and I sure do thank you. Don' know much about de cows but I's be glad to keep de horses head'n right. Maybe learn about de cows along de way."

Jessie then called Lefty from the work he was doing and made the introduction, explaining the opportunity. Lefty begged off on making an immediate decision but promised to get a message to Hammond within a day or two.

By the next morning, after giving the matter serious thought, and discussing it with Jessie to assure himself of a job if he stayed on the Macintyre, Lefty announced his decision.

Arriving alone, as a stranger in Texas, having to somehow find his one-armed way in the new land, with very little wealth to his name, didn't hold as much charm as it had one year before. He admired the Macintyre family and their dedication to raising quality horseflesh.

Over the months together, he and Howard had become fast friends and, of course, the time spent with Abby held a certain attraction as well. He would stay on the Macintyre.

Jessie harnessed a light team. He and Trudy

drove the buggy over to have a last visit with Hammond and Rosa. They carried Lefty's decision, and thanks, with them.

After some discussion between Lefty, Howard and Jessie, with a bewildered John listening in, a list of items John would need for the trek west was produced. It was decided that everything would be available at the general store in Hapner City.

Lefty, Howard and John would ride in the next morning to see to the purchases.

John dug out his savings cache which he kept snugged down in a coffee can Sammy had given him. As a matter of trust and to add a level of security, he had shared his secret location with Bose. Bose spent almost all his time in the barn. If anyone went searching around, he would surely notice. With the farm paydays only coming around once each month, the treasure can sat undisturbed, safely gathering dust and cobwebs for weeks at a time, tucked behind a gap where the barn wall structure met the floor of the loft.

By mid-morning the next day, after caring for the early chores on the farm. The three men pulled up and tied off at the hitch rail in front of the general store. Howard entered the store while Lefty took a few minutes to reassure John about his plans to stay on the Macintyre.

"Are you be sure you'se not want'n ta come on ta Texas wit de rest o' us Lefty?"

Lefty chuckled a bit and turned his eyes away, wondering how much to tell John. He didn't want to make presumptions about his growing friendship with Abby. But, on the other hand, she had specifically said she would miss him if he left and she preferred that he not go. What was he to read into that? Although he had no solid answer to that question, he did have the answer to his own question. Or whatever was left of his own question after the many hours with the lovely lady.

He most certainly was enjoying his side of the arrangement with Abby and would very much like it to continue. And to grow. Definitely grow beyond gardening and riding the beautiful acres of the Macintyre farm.

In musing about his decision, he remembered Abby insisting that it be Lefty who escorted her on her many shopping trips to town. And as she found her self-confidence in riding again, always careful of reinjuring her shoulder, she asked Lefty to ride along. "Just in case".

He admitted that he might be misreading the matter. Could a woman as beautiful and potentially well off as Abby love a one-armed man with a badly scarred face and no wealth at all? Could she make a life with someone like him?

If only he could sort it all out while the opportunity to move on to Texas was before him. Admitting to himself that whatever answer came, it would not be coming in the following few days, he confirmed his decision.

He needed to give the friendship between Abby and himself time to mature. To percolate. To grow to fruition, one way or another. He could always move on to Texas, anytime he wished, if things didn't go the way he hoped they would go. He would quit trying to sort it all out, knowing it sure wasn't going to end in his favor if he went off to Texas, leaving Abby behind. He would stay with the Macintyre. That was final!

"Well John. You know I've seen considerable change in myself in the past year. Old Pastor Grimsley was right. Again. Seems to have a sight of wisdom most folks lack, that old man does. I've benefited from a new location and new friends, including you. And you know I would not have said that one year ago. I like my job…"

John interrupted, which would have gotten him whipped in another era.

"I's thinking that Miss Abby might be fit'n inta de picture somewhere."

Lefty slapped John on the shoulder and turned to the store, laughing. John followed close on his footsteps.

"Hey, Blacky. Whatcha think y'all are doin? This here's a store for white folks. No Black fella goin' to be buying in there if they want my business."

John and Lefty turned to see a hulking bulk of a young man with his hands on his hips and a foolish smirk on his face. Beside him stood two other young men.

John was more than capable of fending for himself. But even with his freedom, he knew that fighting with a white man simply could not end well for him.

Lefty stepped to the front. He carried his pistol on his hip but hoped to not have to use it.

"Back off there, fella. And close your filthy mouth. Go on your way and leave us alone."

The big man turned his head just enough to speak to his friend beside him.

"See here, Spike? Here's a Blacky lover standing in for a scared to death and useless Blacky. Only thing I hate worse than a Blacky is a Blacky lover.

"You best take your pet black man with you crip and get gone."

Lefty looked the three of them over and wondered what his best approach should be. In his younger years, what his father had referred to as his misspent youth, it wasn't at all unknown for Lefty to enter into a fight. There were occasions when he seemed almost eager for a fight. Sometimes, just for the fun of it. He had found, by the time he was around eighteen years of age, that he kind of enjoyed fighting. At least, he enjoyed winning. The fights were rough and tumble affairs, with few rules, but no one was ever really hurt. He won more than he lost and the few times he lost were best forgotten.

His time in the army had done nothing at all to calm his aggressive spirit. Even the wounding hadn't totally taken the fight out of him.

Still, facing the town bully, he decided to try once more for peace, understanding fully that there would be no peace. He knew that because just one year earlier he could well have been the bully confronting him and John. He understood the man's thinking.

"Mister, we're not looking for trouble. You go your way and we'll go ours. Leave each other alone."

"Yeh, or what, Crip? What's a one arm cripple and a sorry slave going to do about anything?"

Howard finally heard the raised voices outside and walked back to the door. Speaking from the doorway behind Lefty, he said, "Gomer, you useless waste of flesh and bones. You were too stupid to keep up in grade school and now you're just plain dumb. Get on your way. You'll never come up to the worth of either of these men, you and your two friends, all together."

"You want to fight me Walter? I'd love to take a whoop'n to you. Just you set that gun aside and step down here."

Howard started to step around John and Lefty but Lefty held his arm out and said, "No. This one is on me. This goon's big mouth has caused enough grief for this morning."

Lefty stepped close to Gomer and said, "All right, if you insist on roughing it up, we'll make this fair. I'll stand still and you take your first swing. That way at least you will have tried. Unless you're scared and want to run for yer Mama."

The taunt was too much for the bully. With a sealed-lip grimace, he snapped his right arm back, his hand making a fist, and flashed it forward. A blind man could have read his intentions from the start of the swing. Gomer was a big man and undoubtedly strong. There was no doubt the punch would do serious damage if it landed. But it didn't land.

Lefty deftly bent his knees, dropping below the big fist, and tipped his head sideways. The punch sailed past his ear and over his shoulder, pulling Gomer forward and off balance when there was nothing to stop the fist's forward motion. Lefty straightened up and responded with a short, sharp rap on the bully's nose and lips, starting his fist driving from his standing position, and following it in with a twist of the shoulder, laying all his weight and the strength of his legs and shoulders behind the blow. Blood spurted in all directions and then poured down the bully's face and onto his shirt. He sealed his eyes shut in pain.

Before Gomer could react, Lefty stepped in with a series of hard, well-timed slashes to the big man's face, with more sharp, short jabs, leaving cuts and bruises in three places and completely putting Gomer, his arms flailing uselessly, out of the fight. He followed up with one last blow to Gomer's belly, bending the big man over and down to the sidewalk. His two friends looked on with astonishment.

Lefty looked at Spike and Clay.

"You fellas want in here or do you just want to drag this fool off the sidewalk and out of our sight?"

Without any words, the two men took Gomer by his arms and dragged him to the side of the store. Howard and John were staring intently at Lefty. It took a moment before Howard gathered up words to speak.

"I'd say you wrapped that deal up good and proper, Lefty. Can't imagine what you might do if'n you were to have two good hands. You'll have to watch that Gomer though. He's too dumb to learn.

He'll come at you again. He'd come at John too if he were to stay here."

Lefty nodded and said, "The really sad thing is that I'd likely be standing beside the big goon just one year ago. Been some changes in that year."

With a wordless headshake, Howard turned back into the store. John stood silently, carefully studying his protector. Lefty walked into the store alone. John followed a few moments later. Several people, men and women alike, who had been looking on, hesitated for a bit and then turned back to their own business.

Chapter 20

Several days later, at the appointed hour, Jessie, Abby, Lefty and Howard all rode with John as he left to meet up with the western travelers.

There was much excitement around the five wagons gathered in a rough line. They had made camp there the evening before, using the grassy, roadside clearing as a demarcation place for the westward trek. The horses were harnessed and hitched, ready for a day's work. An early breakfast was over, the dishes washed and put away. A few of the movers were alternating between sipping on their last cup of coffee and either checking over harnessed teams or saddling horses.

Rosa had milked the cow earlier and was just storing the milk that was left after breakfast in a two-gallon crockery jug. She had poured a few cups of milk into the watering dish in the chicken cage attached to the side of the wagon. She hoped the extra protein would hold the weight on the birds during the weeks of travel.

Two of the young men were gathering the small herd of cattle and the several additional horses, making a difficult and raucous job of it.

When John and the men from the Macintyre pulled close to the noisy, excited circle, activity stopped.

"Morn'n all," hollered Big Hammond Gates, much louder than the distance between them, or the occasion called for. "Welcome. All of ya. Wish y'all were joining us. Got yer trav'ln' boots on John?"

John, somewhat intimidated by the crowd of strangers and the loudness of the welcoming voice, could only stammer a quiet, "Yass'r, Boss. I's rar'n to leave outta here."

Hammond looked on as Howard and Lefty pushed three horses, a spare for John, plus one light team, towards the gathered bunch. John chose to carry his bedroll and small gather of fixings behind the saddle, rather than burden his spare animal with such a small pack.

"What's with the team John? You figur'n on finding a wagon?"

Jessie prevented John from having to answer the question when he said, "Think of it as a gift from the Macintyre Ranch, my friend. That's a good team. A bit rangy at the first but John got them settled down and thinking right. We'll never know what the army used them for but I expect they've heard the roar of more than one cannon. And smelled the powder's sulfurous stink. Made them skittish. But they're good now. Never know when you might need a spare. Long ways to Texas. Could lose a horse or two. You take them and God Bless."

For once, Hammond was stuck for words. He simply walked over to where Jessie sat his horse and stuck out his hand.

"All I can say is thanks. Never saw nor met a better man than Jessie Macintyre, nor a better friend. Sure wish you was coming with us."

The two old friends studied each other's eyes for another short while, then the moment was broken. With a simple nod from each to the other, Hammond turned back to the group. His voice, full of enthusiasm, could be heard back in the small village.

"Get aboard there, ladies. Get those kids in the wagons. Step into your saddles, men. We're going to Texas."

With a wave of his hat, Hammond drove his horse to the front of the group, ready to lead. He had no more time or inclination for goodbyes or introductions of his family and a couple of neighbors to John. That could all come as they moved along.

Ignoring the fact that there was only the one road, he needlessly pointed in a more or less westerly direction.

"Step it up there everyone, Texas is that a way."

There was that word again. That magic word that sounded like freedom and hope and prosperity all tied up in five simple letters. Texas.

Silently, Jessie watched his old friend move out,

never looking back. Wordlessly he prayed, *"God, make it all these folks need and believe in."* His own goodbye was as silent as the prayer.

Howard, Abby and Lefty sat their animals a few feet behind Jessie, saying nothing as they watched the westward movement of the wagons. They had all said their goodbyes to John, back on the farm.

Howard's mind went back, briefly, to Jerry, his friend from younger years. *I can't imagine what this family is feeling, moving out with their son only a sad memory, not even knowing where he lies. All else left behind.*

Jessie made no indication that he was done watching until the road wound around a large rock outcrop, nearly a mile away, taking his friends out of sight. Remaining silent, he turned his riding animal and took the lead, back to the Macintyre.

Chapter 21

It didn't take many miles of the westward trek to start sorting the group out, deciding who might be competent at the different responsibilities. John hung back and watched in strained silence for an hour while two of the younger men, Hammond Gate's sons-in-law Lewis and Charles, tried, somewhat ineptly, to straighten out the horse gather and get them moving, along with the plodding cattle.

These men were farmers and skilled enough at that occupation. Their horses had been well broke, light saddle stock or work teams. Their cattle had been milk cows or yard animals, held for beef purposes. On the open road, with the cattle and several new, less disciplined horses moving together, the young men were out of their element, although willing enough.

Hammond's intent was to have the remuda and cattle a half mile distance to the front of the wagons. But due to the several times that one horse or another decided to either turn for home or stop and graze on the edges of the well-traveled road, the wagons caught up and had to stop.

The loose animals scattered at the sight of an approaching freight wagon, pulled by a heavy team, driven by a man seated high above his freight load. The cattle simply stood still, blocking the entire trail, while three of the loose horses ran, undisciplined towards the team. The angry freighter pulled his team to a halt, stood in his place and yelled ear-splitting profanities at Lewis and Charles, before turning his attention to Hammond.

"Man can't handle his bunch any better than you, mister, shouldn't aught to be on the road. You get this mess cleaned up or I'll climb down and do it for you. You won't enjoy that."

The short speech was laced with more words Hammond, foolishly, hoped the women didn't understand.

Hammond had finally reached the end of his patience.

"John, Jessie tells me you're a horseman, can you pull that mess together?"

His voice boomed, even over the teamster's raucous shouts.

At Hammond's instruction to his two sons-in-law, they backed off, attempting to hide their displeasure and their embarrassment. Reluctantly John nodded his head towards Hammond and silently kicked the gelding he had ridden all the way from South Carolina towards one unruly animal. With a few quiet words and the quick movements of his gelding, he soon had all but one horse lined out on the trail. A quick swing back along the road, circling around the homeward bound gelding, put John in the position to turn the horse back to the drive. When the bunch-quitter slowed to a reluctant walk, a nip on his flank from John's gelding had him moving again.

Although John had never heard the term, 'cutting horse' and would not yet have any idea what the term meant, his gelding was showing every instinct in that direction.

With the horses gathered and lined out in the chosen direction and the mess cleared from the trail so the freighter could proceed, the two younger men moved back in. John looked at the men, hesitated, and then said, "I's kin care fo de hos'es if y'all kin bring along de cows. Maybe best we don' mix 'em."

The suggestion was not welcomed by Lewis. He said nothing but his hard look, aimed directly at John was enough to say there was going to be trouble sooner or later.

With the horses under control and moving along, the teamster gave a slight tip of his hat to John before shouting at Hammond again, pointing his thumb at John.

"Best you keep that man, else you're going to have a long, hard time of it."

Hammond said nothing in reply but his embarrassment was beyond measure. It wasn't a good start. He would have to work and think, to make it better.

Never intending for the cattle or wagons to travel at more than a steady walk, Hammond was finally satisfied with their progress. The women were driving the wagons, while Hammond rode alongside his wife and daughter. The two young men took turns, one driving the cattle while the other spelled off his wife on the reins. The family wagons both held children needing care.

The first real sign of trouble raised its head at the noon lunching.

The wagons pulled to a stop beside a small stream and the teams were unhitched. Each animal was led to water and then staked on the grass at the side of the road. With their teams cared for, the two young men strolled back up to the fire that Hammond had lit, using a handful of kindling stowed in the back of the wagon against the possibility of rain.

John ushered his small remuda to the stream with a clear separation between them and the wagon teams. He sat his saddle while the horses satisfied their needs. He then held them on the grassy banks, although none showed any signs of venturing away from the green banquet nature had spread before them. With the remuda settled down, he stepped to the ground, and with a simple hold on the mane of his spare riding animal, led it to where the Shady Lane Farm gelding, named Hound Dog, stood, with his head bent to the grass. In a matter of seconds, he switched his saddle, ready for the afternoon's ride.

The cattle found the stream with no leading from their herders.

Hammond got the fire going well and then turned the lunch preparation over to the ladies. In a loud voice, he called the group together.

"Time for y'all to say hello to John. Step up here John and meet these folks. We're going to be together for some long while. Best you know a few names. Over here by the fire is my wife Rosa. If you chose to call her Mrs. Gates, that would work too. Standing beside her are our two daughters, Minnie and Gertie. That's their kids romping down there by the stream. Minnie's husband, Charles, is there by the wagon, and Gertie's husband Lewis is over by the tailgate of their wagon.

"This young lady standing beside us is our youngest. Melody by name.

"Those others are old neighbors and friends who have decided that Texas holds more promise than their burned our farms in Tennessee do."

Pointing, he said, "That's Dusty and Hattie."

Swinging his arm a bit to the left, he pointed again, "Jess and Clara."

Hammond turned his eyes back to look directly at John.

"Now John, I'm not expecting you to remember all that right off. But we'll get familiar soon enough."

Hammond hesitated, knowing that the feelings towards Blacks were not universally welcoming. He felt he had to say something to set the group straight on why John had joined them.

"Folks, I'd have you to understand that John was a man well trusted by a farm owner down in South Carolina. He was tasked with the delivery of a very valuable stallion to the Macintyre ranch that you're all familiar with. He got that job done in spite of war and suspicion and violence all along the way. Since then, he has shown Jessie Macintyre that he's an exceptionally talented horseman, quieting and training many animals for Macintyre over the past year. I expect he'll be a help to us with the horses.

"I made a promise to both John and to Jessie that we'd welcome John along with us and feed him in exchange for his care of the horses. I'd appreciate if you'd all join me in welcoming him."

There were a few nodding heads and a couple of mumbled 'welcome John', comments heard. Several heads were turned to the ground in embarrassed silence, knowing in their hearts that they would rather John not be there. But only one voice spoke out.

"I won't fight you on this Hammond but just keep him away from me and mine."

It was Hammond's son-in-law, Lewis, who had spoken.

The silence in the group was total and uncomfortable. Finally, knowing he had to say something, Hammond looked at the young man, replying, "Lewis, I know your thoughts and feelings. John will stay out of your way and I expect you to be at least decent, if not entirely cordial, and not cause any disturbance. Can we agree on that?"

All he got was a quiet stare, backed by a slight nod.

The first few days of travel were put behind them with minimal fuss over their Black guest. John stayed mostly to himself, unrolling his bedroll well away from the group, taking his plate of food to the side and eating by himself and speaking only when he was spoken to. He wasn't asked to join in the night guard rotation.

He did what needed to be done, caring for the horses, switching his saddle among the bunch on the theory that a horse needed a bit of work from time to time. Hammond picked up on the same theory, turning his own team out every half day, while the harness was draped on the Macintyre team. The more lightly loaded wagons hung in with their own animals in harness.

Only once did Lewis make a verbal objection. That was when John roped a young gelding, thinking to give the animal an afternoon of disciplined riding. It was the poorly trained bay that had turned before the freight wagon, heading back east and home. John had watched the gelding carefully ever since, alert for trouble.

"That's my horse. You keep your Black hands off. I won't tell you again."

The voice, raised in volume by anger and threat, brought the camp's lunch activities to a halt. John flicked the rope off the gelding and coiled it, hanging it over his saddle horn.

"Yass'ir, I's be sure to leave dat animal ta his'self."

With no more said than that, John moved his saddle to another horse, mounted and pushed the remuda onto the afternoon's trail. Behind him, he heard a woman's voice.

"I really don't think that was altogether necessary Lewis. From what I've seen, John's a good horseman.

That rangy brute you put so much stock in might benefit from an afternoon of restrained riding."

"You mind the kids. I'll mind the horses. And I'll do it without some good for nothing slave's help. Or any more advice from my wife."

The already quiet camp sank into a deep, embarrassed silence. Gertie's shame at being talked to like that by her husband only magnified Hammond's anger and frustration. It took all the self-control the usually easy-going man could dig up to hold his tongue. It wasn't his way to interfere in his children's marriages, but from time to time, Lewis had pushed him to a dangerous edge.

Gertie, angry and embarrassed beyond telling, lifted the two children into the rear of the wagon, climbed aboard herself, and slapping the reins on the rumps of the team, pulled her wagon out of line, passing her parent's wagon, nearly knocking Lewis over in the process, and taking the lead onto the trail. Her face was a-flame in shame. The pursed lips and tightened jaw warned everyone in the camp to keep their silence.

For the first time on the trip, she pushed the team into a slow trot, soon leaving the rest of the group, still picking up after the lunch stop, in her dust.

Lewis silently sat his horse, looking at the ground, understanding that his harsh words were excessive and out of line. Charles threw the saddle onto his afternoon horse and pushed the cattle into activity. Finally, loaded after the lunch stop, the other wagons rolled past.

After hesitating, while the other travelers slowly moved away from him, Lewis swung onto the trail, following behind. His misplaced anger and self-righteousness, somewhat tempered by his embarrassment, were still driving his thoughts and actions. With no further or deeper insight, he confirmed within himself what he had known from birth, that he was superior to any black man.

John had the remuda moving, falling in behind Gertie's wagon, before anything else could be said or done. It took in excess of a half mile to catch up and then move past Gertie's wagon and take up his normal position at the head of the troop. The remaining wagons and the cattle were a long hour overtaking Gertie who had finally slowed to a walk.

Hoping to brighten John's day, even a little bit, Dusty, an older and somewhat wiser man than the volatile Lewis, kicked his animal into a comfortable lope, catching up to John. The two men rode side by side for a few minutes with Dusty rehearsing his thoughts, afraid that a wrong word could make matters worse.

He finally looked directly at John and said, "Lewis ain't half as bad as he makes himself out to be John. He served in uniform but not for long and not in combat. He spent some time in a supply troop and never saw a Blue uniform until the surrender. But leading up to the war he was meeting up with a few young men who thought they knew it all and wouldn't listen to anyone.

"His father was a slave holder. All Lewis ever heard growing up in that home was that the Blacks were inferior, not to be trusted or seen as anywhere near equal. I expect he'll learn, given time. If he lives that long. In the meanwhile, he's bound to grate on a few folks and find favor with some others. I want to thank you for holding your peace. I expect you've seen worse than Lewis in your years.

"You're a good man John and a good horseman. Changes are going to be almighty slow in coming to this country. I'm hoping you can find your way to wait while that happens. And I truly hope that you can find your true freedom, and a good life in Texas, just like the rest of us want to."

Before John had a chance to respond, Dusty pulled his riding animal off to the side to await the wagons.

It was nearing the time for the midafternoon watering before Lewis rode up to his family wagon. Whatever words were spoken at that wagon were not heard by the others.

The first sizable town the travelers came to was Columbia. Hammond had visited once, well before the war. He searched his memory to pull up the images of a pleasant, genteel town, with homes and businesses showing the prosperity of the times, with a population of about four thousand souls. Well-groomed and dressed men and women had strolled the sidewalks. Although there were slaves and poor whites aplenty, it was the wealth of the landowners and the ruling class that had impressed the much younger Hammond.

Hammond well knew that other cities and towns had seen far more fighting than Columbia had, but still, to see parts of that pleasant town reduced to war rubble, with little sign of those handsome ladies with the beautiful gowns, brought out great regret in Hammond. Regret for the devastation brought on the property and the people, by leaders who couldn't find a way through the quagmire of politics.

When he thought of his son, buried somewhere far from home, he would never know where, he couldn't help asking himself, 'for what'? And then the follow-up question couldn't be avoided, 'what now? How long will it take to put it all back together. Or will it ever be put back together? Perhaps it never was truly together'.

Everything he saw and heard and thought, confirmed his decision to go to Texas. He didn't have the heart to stay and be a part of the repairing and rebuilding process. He believed, based on the evidence of the little history he knew, that people like him would be shoved aside, while the wealthy would grow wealthier yet, and the powerful would grab far more than what was right or just, leaving little for those who suffered most during the years of blood spilling. Thousands of young men like his Jerry had suffered and died in a lost cause. Now it would be the lawyers' turn. The bankers' turn. The men with soft hands would push their way forward to sort out and lay those soft, grasping hands on the spoils of war.

No, he'd had enough. He was going to Texas. He was taking his family and a couple of friends with him. He knew Texas had suffered its own divisions and would certainly have its own share of grasping men. It seemed that human nature leaned towards taking the easy path. But what Texas offered was space. Distance. More space and distance than a handful of greedy politicians could take or use.

Land. Opportunity. Freedom to be his own man and to care for what was his. That's really all he asked of the future.

Hammond found it interesting that John, a freed slave, surely ignorant of the deeper matters in the nation's history, or that of Texas, was still bent on looking for his final freedom in that state, as well. Where had the thought come from? What, really, did John expect to find on a new frontier? He didn't have the answers but, silently, he wished the Black horseman every success.

Thinking more about his own situation, he was comforted by the knowledge that he had enough coin secreted in the wagon to cover their travel costs, with a sufficient sum left over to get a start in their new home country. There was also a back-up stash on deposit in the small Hapner City bank. He had left the funds on deposit as a safeguard against loss on the trail. All your eggs in one basket and that sort of thing. There was enough in the Hapner bank to expand their new holding and sustain them while they waited for their first crops to mature.

Although he rehearsed the same reasoned-out speech silently, in his mind, day after day, really, there was no going back. The farm had been sold. Their beautiful home was in ashes. The son who was to take over the farm was dead and gone. There was nothing to go back to.

Chapter 22

Travel through Tennessee was eased by having established roads to follow. Depending on the weather, some roads were little more than muddy trails. Others were rough, rock encrusted, bone-jarring paths that tested the strength of both the wagons and those who rode them. But no matter, they were roads. At the very least, they didn't have to break trail, or search out water and graze for the animals, the way those travelling to the far western, uncharted lands would be forced to do.

Although he had no clear knowledge of what lay ahead, Hammond expected they wouldn't see actual frontier conditions until they crossed over the big river and, perhaps, not even then. There was much unknown lying before them. There must be roads in Arkansas. Of course, there would be roads. But how many or in what condition, he had no idea. But that situation could be dealt with when the many days of slow travel they faced just getting through Tennessee were over and behind them.

The tediousness of travel was somewhat lightened by the change of scenery as they moved through small villages, wound past farms and fields and forests, and crossed numerous creeks and streams. The river courses were all bridged or marked with established fords, although many of the bridges looked to be hastily constructed affairs.

The men were able to knock down a deer from time to time to supplement their fresh meat supply. The convenient replenishment of their foodstuffs the villages offered would mostly end across the river. Or so Hammond believed. But until then they would keep themselves well supplied.

John stayed far out of the way, herding his horses and doing what had to be done to remain with the group. He was wise enough in the ways of slavery, and the remaining hatreds, to see that he could easily fall into peril, away from Hammond and the rest.

But, almost unfelt within himself, very slowly, he was growing. Growing with the idea of freedom. Real freedom. Learning what it was and what it could mean to a man determined to make the most of it.

He started understanding that freedom was more than simply not being a slave. Freedom was the right and ability to do work along with white men and have that work acknowledged and appreciated. He had known and experienced that on the Macintyre and he was coming to know it here with these westward-bound travelers. In a small way, at least, with some of the folks. Lewis may never change but some of the others had or were beginning to.

With the horses in a rope corral and the evening meal behind them, John felt the need for a bath and clean clothing. After several long, hot, dusty days on the road, he was finding the grimy collar of his shirt chafing his neck and his long-worn socks feeling clammy between his toes. He gathered up his few belongings and, with the setting sun warning that there were fewer than sixty minutes of dimming daylight left, he walked well upstream from the group. There, hidden behind a streamside growth of forest and shrubbery, and stripped to his cut-off long johns, he scrubbed his clothes, draping them on the branches to dry, in what was left of the sun. The day had been hot. He hoped there was still enough energy left in the sun to drive out at least some of the cold wash water.

With the clothing washed, he laid out the clean pants and shirt he would put on after his bath. Checking again to assure himself that he was alone, he carefully stepped into the surprisingly cold, swiftly running stream.

Wishing to be no longer than necessary, John ducked his head under the water and vigorously massaged his long, curly hair, then his neck and face. Lifting his head, he blew out the held breath and began scrubbing the rest of his body.

He was interrupted by a blood-curdling scream.

Having no idea where the woman's voice was coming from, he turned his head from side to side searching for the source of the shriek. The first sign of activity came just seconds later when Lewis burst through the bush wielding a carbine, following Melody's pointing finger. Lewis was waving the weapon from side to side, looking for whatever had caused the terror in his young sister-in-law. He stopped and lifted the gun to firing position when he spotted the black man sitting in the stream. John froze in fear.

Before Lewis could complete his aim or pull the trigger, the gun was grabbed from behind and pushed down. Hammond's commanding voice said, "Put the weapon down you fool. There'll be no shooting here."

The others arrived, joined by the teen-aged Melody, who lagged somewhat behind, still holding her face between her hands and looking like she was either going to scream again or begin crying.

Lewis had all the evidence his closed mind required. He turned on his father-in-law with a look of triumph, even while he and Hammond were both gripping the weapon.

"I told you plain. Told you all but you wouldn't listen. Told you this man would be causing trouble. There ain't a one of them as can be trusted. Now he's gone and snuck up on your very own daughter. Look at her. She's terrified. And all because..."

"That's enough Lewis. Now stop and shut up."

Hammond's voice was not gentle as he yanked the carbine from Lewis's hands. Although there was a murmur of voices from the gathering, John heard no clearly spoken words except Hammonds, which could probably be heard on the far side of the mountain.

Hammond turned toward Melody and gently asked, "What's going on here Mel? What are you doing here and why the scream?"

The distraught young girl managed to pull one hand away from her face and point in John's general direction.

"I, I, I was just out for a bit of a stroll after sitting on the wagon seat all day. I thought it would be pleasant by the stream. Then, then, I see..." She could say no more.

"Settle down girl and tell us what you saw. Right now, what I see is a man sitting in water almost up to his chin, taking a bath, which more of us might benefit from, by the way. And I see clothing washed and laid out to dry on the bushes. Was John sitting there when you came upon him?"

Lewis was all set to re-state his opinion but Hammond stopped him with an upraised hand, stating, "No more from you. I told you to stay quiet and I meant it."

"Now girl, answer the question. "Where was John when you first saw him? Was he sitting right where he is now?"

Melody could only nod her head.

"So, in fact John did nothing we shouldn't all be doing. Having a bath and minding his own business. And you happened along. Is that correct?"

"I, I guess so."

"Alright listen up, all of you. You too John. Let's have a simple rule among us. When you're going for a bath, you let folks know. That way we should be able to eliminate another incident like this. Now get back to your wagons. And you, John, best you get out of that water. Your lips are turning blue with cold."

Hammond turned back to the camp, with one work-scarred hand resting on Melody's shoulder. He stopped just the once to indicate to Lewis that the fiery young man should walk ahead.

Lewis caught up and held out his hand.

"Give me the carbine."

"Naw. I expect it might be better in my wagon for a while."

Chapter 23

Entering Memphis brought everyone sitting upright in the saddle or on a wagon seat, anxious to see what a truly large city looked like. Hammond, who had eagerly absorbed whatever news he could pick up, over the years since Jerry had put on the gray, knew that Memphis had been won over by the Union forces, virtually without a fight.

Oh, there had been a fight alright. And it was close by Memphis. But it was a waterborne affair that cost the South most of their interior navy. Within literally hours, the Southern navy was beneath the waters of the mighty Mississippi. The City of Memphis was under the command of the Union shortly after. The old city had sustained almost no war damage.

Now, driving horses, cattle and wagons through the long-standing shipping center, the Hammond Gates' group was mesmerized by the buildings, the people and the businesses of the enterprising residents. None of the travelers had ever seen a big city before.

Knowing the ladies intended to outfit here in preparation for the supposed wilderness across the wide river, Hammond was sorry he hadn't held the loose animals outside the city. They could turn out to be a nuisance if a suitable camping spot couldn't be found close to the river.

Wishing to get the shopping done as quickly as possible, he detailed Dusty to ride along with John and the younger men who were caring for the cattle, to find a suitable place to camp and hold the stock, until they could secure a crossing.

The wagons were pulled into a row outside a large general merchandise store and the ladies stepped to the ground, stretching the day's stiffness out of their bodies.

Hamilton advised, "There appears to be a lot more than just the one store. If you find this one to be unsatisfactory, you can always search out another. Jess and Lewis will stay here with y'all. Charles has gone off to mind the cattle. John will stay with the horses. I'll go along and find out what the situation is for making a crossing. Dusty will come back and guide you to the campgrounds by and by."

With that, he turned his riding animal back onto the road and headed towards the river.

The entire group was pulled into a rough circle later that afternoon. Two cooking fires had been lit and supper was well under way when Hammond found them. The campground was ideal, lots of grass and just close enough to the big river to catch a glimpse of moving water.

Always seeming to be in a good mood, Dusty greeted Hammond with, "Well, do we have to swim the whole bunch across, or did you find a boat?"

Hammond rode to where John was holding the horses and dismounted. Lifting his saddle and cradling it under his arm, with the bridle draped from the horn, Hammond made his way the short distance to his own wagon before he answered. People began gathering around.

"Found what the owner called a 'barge', although he allowed as it wasn't really a barge. It just seemed to him to be a better name for his boat. Nothing fancy, just a big flat bottomed, open, stern wheel paddle boat. It's not much to look at but he says it floats and the price is right. The fellow can take us over in the morning. Early. I'm hoping y'all got the buying done. I'd hate to lose another day."

Chapter 24

River traffic was far heavier than any of the travelers had imagined. Of course, none of them had ever seen the Mississippi before or a paddle wheeler, as far as that went. They had no way of knowing what all the boats were doing or where they were going.

Someone brought up the question. Hammond, never taking his eyes off the Arkansas shoreline, put a stop to the query.

"Don't much matter where any of them are going. Texas is where we're going and that's still off to the west. This river don't go to Texas."

Steam whistles seemed to be sounding out warnings from every quarter. The captain of the barge took it all in stride but the first-time boat riders alternated between excitement and fear. The cattle that had plodded, uncaring, through the long miles, stood with heads hanging, thankful for the rest. The horses, however, threatened to be a problem, led by Lewis's half-tamed gelding. The men spotted themselves around the horses, tightly holding a long rope from man to man, forming a temporary corral. John, inside the rope circle, moved among the brutes, talking gently to them, assuring them with gentle caresses along necks and flanks that all was well in their world.

The women climbed off their wagons after the wheel chocks were in place and stood at their horse's heads, prepared to try to calm them if the unfamiliar movements of the boat had them acting up.

John found himself wondering why a boat offering transport to migrating families didn't have a corral built onto the deck. He didn't bother voicing his opinion. Since the bathing incident, he had remained withdrawn and almost silent.

After what the crew promised was a typical crossing, the barge floated up to the off ramp on the Arkansas side of the river. A half dozen shore workers awaited its arrival. The barge was soon tied securely to the big bollards dug firmly into the riverbank. It was none too soon as far as the anxious travelers were concerned.

The remuda, pushed by John, who was now mounted again, was the first to leave the barge. Lewis's gelding threatened to make a serious nuisance of himself. Without even looking at Lewis, or seeking his permission, John dropped a rope over the nervous animal's head and snubbed him tightly against his own saddle.

The horses were followed by the cattle. Most of the men hung back, holding the wagon team's bridles, as the ladies awaited their turns at disembarking.

With the big paddle wheel dominating the stern of the barge, everything had to be loaded and off-loaded from the one end. The wagon masters had to lead their teams in a tight curl of one hundred eighty degrees, across the deck, pointing them back to where they had come on. The movements had the men alternating between concern that they wouldn't complete the turn on the narrow deck, and have to back up to try again, and the fear that the tight radius would have the effect of jamming an iron-rimmed wheel under the wagon frame.

Their concerns were greatly enhanced by the nervousness of the horses, who clearly didn't like the feel of the moving deck beneath their feet.

When the last of the load finally set foot on dry land there was a great heave of satisfaction from everyone.

Hammond led them away from the shore and onto the flat land along, and above, the riverbank. Eager to take one more look at the big river and their homeland on the other side, he stopped and stepped to the ground.

Dusty and Jess and their wives stood arm and arm in front of their wagons, holding their mounts with their free hands. The three younger women stood on their wagon seats, staring back, across the white canvas tops. The young men sat horseback, silently thinking their own thoughts.

Hammond and Rosa stood a little off to the side, silently saying goodbye to what was. Hammond was eager to move into whatever was to come. Rosa was not quite sure about her feelings. But there truly was nothing to go back to, so she had voiced no objections to Hammond's plans.

John turned his gelding and watched the group. He dared not leave the remuda, lest they break out and scatter into the unfamiliar distance.

There was little chance that any of the travelers would be back this way again. The West was the future and what they left behind was well forgotten.

If the rails ever reached the area they eventually settled in, there might be a possibility of a return visit. But no one would willingly retrace the long wagon trip without a very good reason.

Hammond's only comment was, "I find myself wishing there was one of those picture taking fellas nearby. This would be something for you young ones to show your grandchildren."

With that comment and a quick explanation of where they were as they took a last look at the rough map Hammond had been following since leaving home, they were ready to head west by south and on to Texas. They had no clear idea what to expect in Arkansas but Hammond was sure the group was up to facing anything that might come their way.

"The boatman tells me this place held a decent town until the Union forces came over the river and burned it to the ground. Used to be called Hopefield. Looking at those blackened and charred timbers and the rock chimneys standing like statues to some lost, long ago dream, I'd say whatever hope the Confederate forces had in holding the town were put behind them with the burning."

Rosa gripped Hammond's arm as he held the reins. Looking around at the ruins that were at one time a Confederate stronghold, she asked, "Do you suppose our Jerry...?"

Hammond patted his still-grieving wife's arm with his hand and then drew his arm around her shoulders. Melody had chosen to ride for the rest of the morning. With just the two of them on the wagon, Rosa gave in to her continuing despair. Quietly, she leaned against Hammond's side while he held her and she wept.

Chapter 25

Hammond had been unable to secure a reliable map of the territory, although he held tight to the hand-drawn sketch of the area with a few roads marked in. He had been hoping for a military map. As soon as the boat captain told him about the burning of Hopefield, he knew he should have found a map in Memphis but it was too late for that.

They chose the best of the two roads a local resident said would take them where they wanted to go. There would be many adjoining trails along the way and many choices to make. They would have to seek advice where it was offered, or take their best guess, hoping against trapping themselves in some watery cul-de-sac.

They were certainly not the only westward-bound group of travelers. But, as they started away from the river, they seemed to have the road to themselves. Whether that would last or not, Hammond had no idea.

After crossing the river, the travelers seemed to relax and step up their pace. The parting from their familiar homes and villages was now done and behind them, separated by the wide expanse of the State of Tennessee and the rolling and roiling Mississippi River.

The river seemed to mark an unchangeable decision. There was no talk about it but Hammond felt that the demeanor of the movers signaled a decision made; a final decision if one hadn't been made before that time. From here forward, there were no decisions weighing them down, no room for second guessing. It was onward, westward, to Texas.

The trail was wide and well-traveled. How long it would remain that way was an open question. John led out with the remuda. He had the gathered horses under control except for the jug-headed animal that Lewis insisted John not ride. Day after weary day, the animal gave him problems. As they passed riders, freighters and caravans headed east, towards the big river, it was inevitably the one animal that would dart out of line, either mixing with the oncoming riders or causing a team to balk and turn aside.

The anger and profanity pouring from the offended teamsters were aimed at John with, seemingly, no one recognizing that it was only the one animal causing the problems. After fighting the brute for three days since the river crossing, on top of the many days gone by in Tennessee, John threw a rope around its neck and pulled him up short, forcing the gelding to walk close to his side. The foolish animal refused to settle down. It fought the rope and came close to upsetting John's animal a couple of times.

Finally, in desperation, he pulled a halter over the brute's ears and muzzle and tied a short rope to the metal ring worked into the bottom of the leather bindings. Turning back to where Lewis was riding beside his family wagon, John tied the recalcitrant animal to the rear of the wagon. Hammond was close enough to see what was happening.

"Troubles, John?"

"Dat horse, he be goi'n cause problems all de way ta Texas. Best he be kep from run'n free."

Hammond laughed out loud and said, "That horse should be shot. Ain't worth the grass it takes to keep him alive. Good for you John. Tied fast to the wagon is a good place for him."

Lewis took exception to the pointed remarks.

"That's a good horse. Just needs a little riding is all. In fact, I'll switch my saddle right now."

John trotted his own horse back to the remuda, leaving Lewis to do whatever he wished. He had learned years before that it was best to leave white men's questions for white men to solve. It took him only a minute to get the remuda back into a compact bunch.

It was just a few miles after Lewis switched his saddle. And it wasn't really much of a stream. It was similar to the many they had already waded through along the trail and one of the many they would undoubtedly see in future days. The trail led onto a rocky bottomed ford, clearly staked out by those who had gone before, and wide enough to easily support the loose animals as well as the wagons that were following behind.

The upstream flow of water piled up a bit as the raised bottom of the ford and the steep creek-side banks forced it into a faster running flood, putting pressure on the animals' legs. Looking ahead, from high on his own gelding's saddle, John saw the stream in the distance and assessed it as not being a problem. The horses and cattle would take it all in stride. It wasn't anything new. They had walked through flowing water many times in the past few weeks.

On the downstream side of the ford, the water dropped off to a depth of four or five feet in the center. The edges swirled around, and over a liberal sprinkling of rounded boulders. The rapid flow over the crossing created a bit of a waterfall on the downward side, with white water foaming up where the falling water re-entered the stream.

Lewis, sitting proudly on his jug-headed bay, had pushed his way to the front of the group, leading by a hundred yards. John could have warned him that the animal had balked at every crossing but he let it go. Lewis would have to learn his own lessons.

At the edge of the flooding water, the gelding, at first, hesitated, then plunged in at the touch of Lewis's heels on its flanks. As the horse neared the center of the flowing water, an inch thick, broken-off branch from upstream cascaded over the crossing and glanced off the gelding's right foreleg. Twisting and turning, it then tangled it-self in the gelding's left leg, before dropping over the edge. The horse, in unreasoning panic, picked both front feet off the solid floor of the ford, twisted a bit to the left and dropped down again, too near to the edge. With another slight shuffle, as Lewis tried in vain to bring the animal under control, one hoof fell off the rock bottom and into the void under the falls. Both horse and rider re-acted in startled alarm. As the animal scrambled for footing, leaning precariously to the left, both of the horse's front feet were suddenly well clear of the rocky bottom. Lewis's foolish response was to pull back on the reins while hollering, 'whoa, whoa'. But it was far too late to prevent what was to come in a matter of seconds.

With a twist, and rising on its hind legs again, the animal turned downstream. When it settled back down, neither front foot enjoyed anything under them but air and then water. Water over four feet deep. The horse went forward and down, with a whinny of terror, that reached back to the following riders. Every eye turned to Lewis and his quickly sinking horse.

The horse's front legs sunk into the rushing wa-ter, throwing its rider out of the saddle and over its head. Lewis was tossed towards the edge of the stream, doing a complete flip as he fell. He landed on his back in the shallows along the edge. Unable to control his downward momentum, his head, as it flopped backwards, smacked against a boulder. His body hung on the boulder for only a second or two before the flow caught his legs, drawing him back into deeper water, and downstream in a tumble that left him lying face down in the water.

Breaking loose from the rocks, Lewis was at the complete mercy of the stream. The unconscious young man made no effort to right himself.

The swirling water was quickly washing away the smear of blood that was left on the boulder.

The horse had completed its flip by the time Lewis hit the boulder. It thrashed the water for just a moment but finally got to its feet. At that point, the water was perhaps three feet deep.

As the air was rent with shouts from the men and screams from the women, John was just approaching the crossing with the remuda. At his first sight, he feared the horse would roll over and submerge Lewis, perhaps holding him under the water. He was relieved when that didn't happen but he stared in dismay as the wounded man's body floated away, face down, in the fast-flowing stream. Leaving the remuda, John guided his own horse off the path and into the water. His powerful gelding took the water without concern as John urged him ahead in pursuit of the drowning man. It took longer than John had first imagined and a discouraging number of leaping thrusts, but finally the big gelding pulled up beside Lewis. John pushed his left foot deeply into the stirrup for support, took the reins and the saddle horn in his right hand and leaned far over, reaching for Lewis.

With the water pushing the injured and drowning man in an erratic fashion and the horse beginning to feel the excitement of the situation, it wasn't until the third attempt that John managed to take a full grip on the back of Lewis's shirt. With a heave of his strong arm, he lifted the drowning man up and over his legs. He lay Lewis there, with his head hanging down the animal's off-side.

John turned his gelding onto the edge of the stream and was soon back on firm ground. Pushing into a solid run, heedless of the brush that was whipping both the horse and himself, he rode back to the waiting and frantic group. He pulled to a stop on the trail's grassy berm and lowered Lewis to the ground, as the other men reached to help. Gertie, Lewis' wife, screamed, "He's dead. he's gone and drowned."

Jess, one of the old neighbors who had decided to accompany the travelers, was a quiet man. He had been almost silent and unnoticed along the trip until that moment. But his time had come. Not a big man and considered too old to be put into uniform, he had spent two years as a civilian medic. Although drownings were not a common problem to the army, still, he had gathered just enough knowledge to feel comfortable stepping forward and taking control.

"He ain't no way dead. Not yet he ain't anyway. Stand back and be quiet, all of you."

With that, he dropped to his knees and ripped Lewis's shirt open, scattering the traditional top three buttons into the grass and tearing the cloth downward from there. He then slid the young man onto the edge of the berm so that his head was considerably lower than his body.

Jess forced Lewis's mouth open and flattened his tongue, making sure he would be able to take in life-giving air, if, in fact, he didn't up and die first. To no one in particular, he said, "Someone hold his head." Clara, Jess' own wife, knelt and took a firm grip on Lewis's hair, turning his head sideways, with his mouth nearly buried in the grass.

With great hopes but little finesse, Jess then gave a series of slow, but solid pushes on the distended belly, forcing water to rise and gurgle out of Lewis's mouth. He repeated this rather rough treatment until Lewis finally choked and spasmed.

"You did it Jess. You did it. He's alive."

"That's jest the water he swallowed, is all. Depends now how much he breathed into his lungs. Cain't do much about that. Up to the Lord to save him from here."

Clara looked quickly at her husband. "He's trying to breathe. Don't push any more. Let's see if he can do it on his own."

Jess straightened and squatted back onto his heels, studying Lewis, ready to administer more help if needed. Lewis coughed again, spewing up water and phlegm. He seemed to take a quick breath and then a deeper breath. He had not yet opened his eyes. With his next breath, he choked, shuddered and then rolled onto his side, vomiting another volume of water into the grass. He appeared to relax and breathe more evenly. As the eyes of the entire group were focused on him, Lewis coughed again, breathed deeply, and then opened his eyes, with his face still buried in the grass. He lay still, with only his one arm moving, as he reached to wipe the phlegm from his mouth and the water from his eyes. A great sigh escaped his lips as he rolled onto his side and tried to sit up.

With a scream, Gertie dropped to her knees and threw her arms around her husband.

In the flush of activity, no one had noticed Hammond ride away. The first sign of his absence came with the sounds of a rifle shot. With little doubt about what the shot meant, no one said anything. But every eye was turned back to the stream, and the sounds of breaking branches, as Hammond fought his way through the brush, back to the trail. It took a few moments for him to appear. When he came into sight, he had a saddle balanced over one knee and a bridle draped over his shoulder.

Lewis and his stubborn refusal to see the gelding for what it was had caused Hammond to reach the end of his patience. The single shot clarified the situation. There was no need for lengthy explanations. As he was so apt to do, Hammond soon dismissed the entire affair. They had bigger things to think about. They were going to Texas. No more time to waste.

Hammond rode up to the group and dropped the saddle into the back of Lewis's wagon, followed by the bridle. Only then did he look to see if his son-in-law was among the living. When he saw Lewis sitting upright, with Gertie helping as he struggled to stand, he said, "Get aboard your wagons, all of you. We've wasted enough time for this one day."

As they made their way back to the wagons, Dusty, walking beside the still dazed Lewis, grinned and said, "Son, If'n I'd known you was that all fired thirsty, I'd of passed you my canteen. No need to drink the whole stream."

No one responded to the comment.

He had thought to lighten the moment. He wasn't at all sure that his efforts had born the desired fruit.

Chapter 26

After the excitement and the long delay of the morning, no one mentioned lunch. But at mid-afternoon Hammond hollered, "Pull 'em up John. We'll take a break. You men see to the teams. Ladies, I'd appreciate if you could get some coffee going. Lay out some of those breakfast leftovers too or whatever comes easy to hand. Can't take the time to cook fresh."

With the necessary tasks dealt with, everyone gathered around the fire with their coffee mugs in their hands. Everyone, that is, except John, who stayed with the remuda. He would have enjoyed a coffee but, after the happenings of the morning, he thought it best to hang back.

Lewis had spent the first couple of hours after his near drowning laying in the back of the wagon. He had a piercing headache and the bleeding where his head hit the rock took a long time to stop. Gertie had finally found a clean rag large enough to wrap around the wound, tying it off on his forehead, like a girl's oversized ribbon. She didn't say anything, afraid her anger and fear might take control of her tongue.

The closeness of death had put a deep melancholy into Lewis's spirit. He, too, was silent.

Gertie, after it was seen that Lewis was going to survive the ordeal and knowing all along that his position regarding the unruly gelding was irrational, had sunk into a barely controlled anger. That a useless horse had come so close to leaving her a child raising widow and it was her husband's stubbornness that had caused it all. She couldn't think of a single friendly thing to say to the man. When she failed to respond to anything Lewis said, he remained quiet, sinking further into remorse and melancholy.

When he finally rejoined Gertie on the wagon seat, she told him, with no friendless in her voice, all that had happened while he was unconscious. He was deeply ashamed with the realization that he had been wrong about the gelding. Then, to hear that it was John who had ridden to his rescue and that it was Jess and Clara, a couple he thought of as mere small-acreage farmers, a good bit below his own self-appointed status in the world, who had known what to do about his near drowning, left him with more than just the simple headache. Those facts left him embarrassed and humiliated and thankful, all at once. He had no idea how to respond.

To think that his life had been saved by a black man, a man he had referred to in derogatory terms several times and spoken disparagingly of many times. It was almost too much for his mind to deal with. He was thankful when the lunch break was pushed into mid-afternoon. He couldn't yet face the others. He wasn't sure if he would ever be able to.

As her father called the group to a halt, Gertie turned to Lewis.

"What are you going to do? I know you don't want to but you're going to have to say something. You played the fool, but I ain't never heard of anyone dying from being a fool. And it ain't no permanent thing. Unless you make it that way. But you can't just let it lay."

There was still no sign of friendliness or forgiveness in her voice or attitude.

Lewis had no immediate answer. The two troubled people sat on the wagon seat, a cold distance between them, for several minutes before Lewis said, "I suppose I've got it to do. Ain't going to get any easier."

He slowly and carefully stepped to the ground, holding tightly to the handle screwed into the side of the wagon. Each move he made seemed to move the hammer inside his head, clanging and banging against his skull.

Once his feet felt secure on the ground, he moved to the rear of the wagon and lifted the two children down. With a deep breath or two, and with Gertie holding tightly to his arm, giving him balance, they moved towards the fire. Every eye was on them as they got nearer but no one said anything. Even the children were remaining quiet.

Hattie broke the spell by saying, "Coffee's hot." With that she lifted one of the two metal pots it took to prepare adequate coffee for the group, the flame heated handle thickly wrapped in a folded cloth, and walked among the gathering, filling held-out mugs as she went. After she filled Lewis's mug, she looked deep into his eyes. Lewis almost felt as if she was trying to see if there was anything in the depths of the man.

With the coffee mugs filled and with sliced bread and farm-made cheese, thin-carved off the big orange round purchased in Memphis, passed around, Lewis nervously cleared his throat. Finally, he began his painful, poorly thought-out speech, still a little unclear what all he was intending to say.

"Folks, not much I can say but thank you. Thank you and I'm sorry. Sorry and embarrassed that this ever happened and that I was the cause of it. I had warning enough. But I was so sure. So sure, that I couldn't bring myself to listen to older, more experienced horsemen. I'm asking for your forgiveness for all of that. And again, to offer my deep gratitude for what y'all did."

After an uncomfortable pause, he said, "But I don't see John here."

Hammond said, "He's up ahead a ways. Taking in the shade of that brush up there. With the remuda."

Lewis walked to the fire, picked up the coffee pot and a clean mug, holding it with his finger coiled through the handle. Hattie, immediately understanding his intent, folded a clean cloth napkin around a slice of bread and an ample help-ing of cheese, and placed it in Lewis's other hand. With Gertie still helping him balance, offsetting the dizziness from the whack on the head, he started out to walk the hundred yards to where John stood with the horses.

Something within him changed in that hun-dred-yard walk. Lewis wasn't quite sure what it was. But whatever it was, he was prepared to admit, at least to himself, that it was a growing humility and an acknowledgment that he had a lot to learn yet, about horses and men, both. And perhaps, about himself.

He walked directly to John and held out the cof-fee mug. John said nothing as he took it. Lewis mo-tioned with the nearly empty coffee pot and John held out the mug. The two men were looking into each other's eyes. Lewis glanced down just in time to prevent overflowing the mug. Lewis looked back up at John, offered him the napkin covered lunch, and simply said, "Thank you, John."

John said nothing at all, afraid to utter a word.

Lewis finally put his thoughts together to say, "I was wrong about the gelding, John. I expect I was wrong about you too. Only ever knew one way of life and thinking. Hard to overcome that. I expect it's going to take me awhile. But again, I'm saying 'thank you'. You have anything you want to teach me about horses, John, I'd be pleased to listen."

Although the thought crossed Lewis's mind that a firm handshake might be in order the two men part-ed with a simple nod. And with no word from John.

Chapter 27

No one could be sure if it was the nearness of losing one of their number or simply that the trail seemed long and the villages few. But a quietness, a serenity almost, had settled over their camps.

Hammond, a naturally peaceful and contented man, although occasionally boisterous, accepting of life as it was delivered to him, was not unhappy with the situation. He was finding a similar quietness welling up in himself, as they drew further from their homes and deeper into the relative wilderness of the Arkansas frontier. The quietness of the group gave him space for his own contentment.

It wasn't that Arkansas lacked for farms or settlements. The farms were there in abundance. But the villages were small and widely spaced along their route. Most of the farm buildings seemed to be set far back from the trail. They seldom saw any sign of life. There were, of course, other travelers on the road. Whether by the choice of the others or by happenstance, the groups were plodding along at the pace of their slowest animals, usually the cattle or a milk cow. Only seldom did they come in sight of each other.

Hammond suffered no illusions on the matter of moving and resettling. He knew there would be nothing easy about making their way in Texas. He wasn't at all sure the younger ones understood what starting again would entail but they would soon learn. Truthfully, he was making the move for his children and their children after them. He and Rosa had lost much in the war. Their only son, of course, being their greatest loss. But even with the burning of the home his grandfather had built and with the loss of years of farm production, the two of them could have salvaged enough to live out their lives with a degree of comfort and satisfaction. But he felt strongly that a parent should do at least something to open the way for his children. That was going to be difficult in Tennessee for years to come. The decision to move had been made with his eyes wide open and he wasn't going back on that now. Still, sometimes, in his melancholy, he retreated into a quietness of mind that allowed him to reflect on some 'what if's'.

Sitting the back of a horse hour after hour didn't offer much mental stimulation. Playing mind games with himself seemed harmless enough until the occasional penetrating sadness lifted its ugly head up. At those times he would try to strike up a conversation with one of the other men, just to seek a distraction.

Once, Hammond found himself studying John, at the front of the group, caring for the remuda, and leading them to Texas. In truth, they were simply following the trail but John was at the front of the pack, so it wasn't totally wrong to call him the leader.

He compared his thoughts about John to himself, analyzing the two of them, comparing: John, Black, freed slave, riding a horse and saddle given to him as wages for a job well done, with nothing else in the world he could truly call his own. Sitting tall in the saddle, his head held up and his eyes forward. Seeming to study everything around him. He was going to Texas. Still learning what freedom meant, in its many shapes, but moving forward while he learned.

Hammond understood that John had no idea what he would be doing when he arrived in that fabled land but he seemed to accept that fact and move on, mile by mile. No complaints voiced. Seldom a change in his daily temperament.

Hammond thought about himself; white, born free, prosperous until the war, wife, three daughters, four grandchildren still with considerable coin stashed away for a new start, great hopes for the future.

How had a melancholy settled over Hammond while John never seemed to change, day by day?

He wondered if the situation was considerably different for John, rising from nothing at all, not even freedom, to something, and then to hoping, praying, for more. He doubted if John could give any clear answer on exactly what 'more' was.

For Hammond, it was having much and then falling from something to almost nothing and hoping to again work his way back to something. He amused himself with this additional introspection during the long hours of their travels.

Their forward progress was limited to the sustainable speed of their slowest member. That slowest member was their milk cow. Even though she was a young, strong animal, her continuously re-filling udder was sometimes a burden to her. The calf growing inside her, her second, would be another few months before seeing the light of day. She couldn't do more than ten miles on a good day. Even that required at least one day of rest each week and, a few times, an early stop in the afternoon. Hammond suspected they were pushing the animal to the limits of her endurance but they would need her in Texas. He had no assurance there would be milk cows available for purchase in the rapidly growing state.

After the first week of travel, way back in Tennessee, they had decided that a weekly day of rest was called for. Logically, they chose Sundays. The cattle and the children, especially, seemed to gather strength from the rest time and the delayed arrival wouldn't amount to much, over time.

If the distance scratched on the hand-drawn map was anywhere close to accurate, they had about forty-five to fifty days of travel from when they offloaded from the barge and put the Mississippi behind them, to when they should arrive at Fort

Worth, Texas. Call it two months. That was a lot of nights sleeping in the open. A lot of boring days for the children. A lot of hot days. A lot of rainy days. A lot of steps for the milk cow.

The alternating storms and spring heat would offer occasions enough for people to get on each other's nerves. They could, logically, expect illness along the way. It was Hammond's continuing prayer that the travelers would be spared serious health problems. And Lewis's near drowning was all the accident he cared to contemplate.

Still, nothing was ever accomplished without some cost. The group could live up to the challenge only because they believed in what lay at the end of the trip. He prayed they would not be disappointed.

Arkansas appeared to hold an abundance of flowing water that had to be crossed. There were also more trails, leading off into the forest, than seemed sensible. They had nothing else to judge by, so when the trail divided, they maintained their southwest direction, unless the dirt of that trail showed no recent wagon tracks. Only once did they have to turn the entire train around and make a correction. That mistake cost them enough time that when they got back to the fork in the road, they went into camp early and called it a rest time.

John used the break to go upstream for a bath. He gave ample notice of his intentions. He wasn't about to invite more trouble down on his head. Since the first bathing incident, the others had been careful to announce their bath times too.

Most times, John made sure to stay close to the

horses so there would be no cause for accusation.

The sight of the Ouachita Mountains, at first, sheltered from their eyes by the towering forest around them but finally coming into full view, surprised them. Dusty rode up to Hammond and asked, "That map of yours mention anything about mountains?"

Hammond drew the paper from his vest pocket and unfolded it. The two men studied it as they rode along. Dusty, leaning as far as he could to see the map more closely, pointed to some writing captured within a small circle.

"What's that say? Can't read it from here."

Hammond held the map to the side and turned it to the sun.

"Pretty small scribble. Can't say as I ever bothered with it before. But now that I look, it seems plain enough. 'Mountains'. Just the one word. Doesn't say anything else."

He gazed off into the distance before commenting, "Don't look too tall from here. I'm guessing maybe two to three thousand feet. I hear the mountains far to the west are two miles high and more. Snowcapped all the year round, many of them. Must be some sight. Probably never get to see them though. Long way still from Texas. Further than we plan to go."

"Well, these are right in front of us and looking almighty rugged to me. Rocks and forest and steep grades. I sure hope someone found a trail around that rock pile."

Hammond nodded in agreement and folded

the map.

"Wherever the trail is, if others can ride it so can we."

And they did. Some steep grades, a few upland fed streams, frothing and boiling around and over the rocky stream bottoms, too fast flowing to carelessly trust man or horse to. Caution was called for. They made sure the children were safely held inside the wagons as they proceeded through the marked fords, privately expressing their thanks each time their wheels were rolling on the dry trail again, on the other side.

Even after all the ups and downs since leaving the big river, it didn't seem as if the land had gained much in altitude. As far as they climbed up one grade, they seemed to drop down an equal amount on the other side, with no gain. Jess, riding beside Hammond commented on it.

"Low country all through here, seems to me. I somehow thought we'd be gaining some altitude as we moved inland, away from the big river. Why, I'm guessing we're not more three or four hundred feet above sea level. Of course, might could be I've got that some wrong. Just seems to me, is all."

Hammond couldn't find a reasonable response, so he let it go.

The road widened as they moved westward as if it was marking out the easier way, ushering them along to Texas. But they knew they were not there yet. Nor would they be for a good many days.

With the peaks of the mountains now only visible on the northern horizon, above the mixed hardwood trees that covered their slopes and the borders of the many miles of trail, they began seeing more settlement. Now, most of the off-side two track trails led into the small clearings hacked from the forest. Rough rail fences and hewn-log houses and barns were more often seen. A few folks who noticed their passing stood in house or barn doorways, or glanced up from their gardening, waving their greetings.

Only once did Rosa lean closer to Hammond to be heard above the noise of the rolling wagons.

"It's a long way between these homesteads. They're very beautiful with the green grass and the forest all around but lonesome. I'm not too sure that would suit me. I rather enjoy seeing and talking with folks from time to time. I enjoy getting to town on occasion too."

"We'll pick our settling place with great care, my dear. And since it don't much matter to me, you'll have full say."

"Full say?"

"Well, pretty much."

Rosa pushed her hand through the crook of her husband's arm as he held the reins, leaned her head on his shoulder and chuckled like she used to back in happier days. Before the war. Before their losses. Before Jerry.

Hammond knew it wouldn't last. The reality of their losses was too heavy a burden for Rosa to simply cast off. But, for just a moment, he relished the sound of her youthful happiness. He silently prayed that her heart was, for a moment, as light as her voice.

They no longer had to search out the trail. The wideness of the surface and the increased traffic confirmed that they were, indeed, on the main road. And, to the benefit of the animals, the road was much more level than it had been close to the mountains.

Hardwood forests were giving way to pine-clad, rolling hills. Farms started to get larger and more established. Here and there they saw cotton growing. Even with slavery being abolished a full year past, most of the workers were Black.

Melody, now riding the wagon seat beside her mother mentioned the Black workers. Rosa responded, "Well, honey, even being freed, they have to make a living, the same as we do. I don't suppose they enjoy the hoeing and picking of cotton but I'm sure they enjoy eating and sleeping under cover. And if you would care to notice, there are a good many white workers among them, men and women both. And some pretty young children with hoes in hand. Everyone must make a living. We do what's possible to accomplish that. Your father worked right along with the hired folks when he was young and well into the years after we were married.

"Think back. Did you ever see a time when we didn't always have responsibilities on the farm? Even with your great grandparents and your grandparents leaving what could be called a prosperous heritage for us, we still worked. I, myself cared for the chickens and milked two cows, twice a day, plus making butter and separating the cream for selling in town. I fed what milk the family didn't need to the hogs, holding some back for the fattening chickens. I did that until your older brother and sisters became big and strong enough to take over the milking. You've done your own share of milking and butter making."

Melody laughed and teasingly said, "You never gave up your chickens, Ma."

"I like chickens. For more than just eggs and Sunday dinners. They have real personalities. They're fun to watch. And there's something settling, something peaceful about being around them. We'll be happy to have the chickens when we get settled again."

"What do you suppose we'll find in Texas, Ma?"

Rosa smiled at her youngest daughter, enjoying her inquisitiveness.

"Well, I expect it will be much the same, only different. From what I could find in a couple of books, it's much flatter than Tennessee. It's hotter and dryer. Not much winter. But occasionally the winter winds kick up a fuss. Supposed to be good soil around Fort Worth. Grass and cattle to the south and west. Of course, we won't know if those books held accurate information until we get there. I'm sure we'll find somewhere we like before we settle. And I expect we'll all have enough to do."

Melody seemed to contemplate on this for a few moments before saying, "I've been wondering about meeting other folks. I don't think I'd like to live far out, away from people. I'm hoping there'll be some of the things we had back home. You know, the town visits, a church close enough, maybe a big picnic for everyone to come too. Or even a dance from time to time."

Rosa looked over at this growing daughter and leaned back to find a more comfortable sitting position. Life and maturity happened on a fixed timetable whether the parents were prepared for that in their children, or not. Neither Hammond nor Rosa had ever fought that maturing, nor tried to slow it down. They were pleased with their children and tried to show it.

"I'm thinking what you're really wondering is if you'll find a young man to your liking. I would imagine that a newly opening and fast-growing country like Texas will have far more young men than young women. But you have no need to rush. You've got some growing and learning to do before that time comes.

"It doesn't hurt a young lady to do a bit of dreaming about pretty dresses and dancing with a handsome prince. And sometimes those dreams become true. But the dreams can't be allowed to get in the way of the work that drives it all."

With a chuckle, Rosa passed the reins to her daughter.

"And speaking of work, if you would like to take these leathers and pull the wagon to a stop, I'll step off and walk for some time. My posterior is crying out for mercy."

Melody took the reins and whoa'd the team before saying, "Really mother. I didn't need to know that."

Chapter 28

The hills had given way to slightly rolling, flat land. The hardwood forests were pushed aside, making way for pine trees. The grasslands between the spaced-out pines provided grazing for beef animals. The farms appeared to be larger, the crops more diverse. Although it was early in the year, and not always easy to identify the immature growth, evidence of corn, root crops, watermelons, and other vined crops, along with oats, a few acres of wheat and more and more cotton, were pointed out from one rider to another, as they moved along.

When the outlying buildings of Hope fell into view, everyone took a deep breath, seeing the first real signs of settled civilization in many a mile. Hammond, riding beside Dusty, with Jess on his off-side, said, "Interesting. There's no mention of a town on the map."

Dusty, ready to stop, and knowing his wife was more than ready for at least one night in a hotel bed, offered, "Well, map or no. That's a sight for these sore eyes. If it's as good as it looks from here, I'm thinking we should re-provision and take a rest. For the animals and ourselves too. Maybe look up a hotel and a hot café meal or two. Might even find a bath for the ladies, with honest to goodness hot water."

Hammond agreed, making the decision to stop, for at least one night, perhaps more. The animals needed rest. The people too.

He rightly concluded that Dusty was, even without knowing it, speaking for the group. He rode ahead and hailed John.

"Find somewhere to put up for the night John. Maybe a couple of nights."

Wordlessly, John nodded.

When Hammond had rejoined Dusty, they rode in silence for a few moments. Dusty then glanced over at Hammond and said, "Seems strange giving that responsibility to a black man. A man who probably never made a serious decision in his life until he was freed."

Hammond was slow to answer, thinking up a suitable response. They had ridden together long enough on this trip to understand that Dusty meant no criticism, of John or Hammond, either one. He was simply expressing a died-in-the-wool thought. A thought taken for granted for so long that no one really ever considered an alternative.

Hammond finally found comfort in what he perceived to be the simple truth.

"My friend, although he don't know it himself,

that black man could lead an army, given opportunity. It's crazy how much raw talent the slave owners held down when it could have been put to the benefit of the owners themselves. Don't you ever be afraid to listen to John. Especially on horses. Jessie Macintyre spoke highly of the man when it came to horses and, as far as I'm concerned, John has confirmed Jessie's opinion since taking on the care of the remuda on this trip. We'll wait and see where he points us to for the night before we judge."

"Oh, I ain't judging or criticizing, just say'n it's strange, is all. Feels strange, at least to me."

Hammond felt it best to drop the conversation.

On the western outskirts of the little town, John turned the remuda into a partially treed parkland. There were, perhaps, twenty acres stretched between the road and a small stream of water that wound its way through the bush. The land appeared to be open and unfenced. If anyone objected to their presence, they could move on to another spot.

The riders with the cattle entered, with the wagons following. Hammond and Dusty looking on from the roadway, nodded to each other and rode in.

In the wake of the many days of practice and experience, it took only a few minutes to lay out and set up the camp. Hammond called his two sons-in-law over.

"Lewis, Charles, take out that rope in the back of our wagon and string up a corral in those trees. There's enough grass there to hold the horses and cattle both. Water the teams before you corral them. John will see to watering the riding stock. Then, we'll clean ourselves up and walk into town."

After washing the road dust from hands and faces, the ladies went first to the big general store. The men stayed in camp long enough to go among the horses, checking their feet and shoes. The few animals with loose shoes, or with shoes that needed replacing were sorted out and led down to the blacksmith shop, at the edge of the small town. It wasn't worth getting out their own tools for such a small job. The few coins the blacksmith would charge would be an acceptable expense.

The purchases at the general store were set aside, ready to be placed on the loading dock at the rear of the building. The wagons would be driven there in the morning for loading, before heading out on the road again.

As the dinner hour approached, the decision was made to go as a group to the largest of the two restaurants they could see from the walkway in front of the general store. John reluctantly joined them after Hammond's insistence.

The group filed in and took seats, four at a time, around square tables. The last to enter the establishment were Hammond and Rosa, urging John ahead of them, his hat twisting in his big hands.

Immediately, the young lady serving tables scooted into the kitchen. Just as quickly the cook, a large, florid faced man, appeared.

"Y'all are welcome but your man will have to eat outside. I'll feed him but he ain't welcome in here where other folks are taking their meals.

Hammond took a quick study of the man and forced a friendly smile before saying, "John is not my man. John is my friend and our traveling companion. He'll eat with us or you lose all our business."

"There's a door stoop around back that's convenient to the kitchen. He can take a seat out there. I'll send his dinner out to him."

Hammond, expressing a change of approach, flashed a cunning smile at the cook and looked across to John.

"John, you drag a chair out onto the front veranda."

Then addressing the cook again, he said, "Mr., your girl there can ask these other folks what they wish to eat. But you load up three big plates of that roast steer meat I can see sett'n on the stove top. Don't be sparing on the meat. I'll stand right here until you get 'er done."

The cook didn't like it but he turned back into the kitchen. The serving girl returned shortly with three overloaded plates. Hammond smiled at her. Rosa, standing beside her husband still wasn't quite sure what his plan was.

"Thank you, young lady. Now, you follow me, and bring that grub with you."

With that, he turned and grabbed a chair in each hand and walked to the door. Rosa, now understanding, stepped ahead and held the door open. At the end of the big, covered veranda Hammond placed a chair on each side of John. Rosa sat on one and

Hammond the other. He grinned up at the waitress.

"Lay one of those plates on each of our laps please. Then you bring out some cutlery and a table napkin or two. And we'll be wanting coffee soon enough. Maybe a piece of pie later, should you have any."

Within seconds, the cutlery was there and the three of them began to eat. Almost at once, the door opened again and Lewis arrived, followed by Gertie and the two children. Lewis had a chair in each hand, like Hammond had done. Gertie held the door while every one of the travelers dragged a chair onto the veranda, forming a big, oval group with John seated in the center, at the far end. A light chuckling sound could be heard among the group as they smiled and winked at John.

A dozen or so folks, looking on from the street shook their heads. A few smiled and pointed at the sight.

It took several trips for the waitress but before long, everyone had a meal in front of them. The florid faced cook and owner brought the last two out himself. Although he took a long study, first of John, and then at the group, he simply gave a slight shake of his head and returned to his cooking.

Dusty, ever one to remember his thankfulness for everything in life, now turned to remembering the food.

"Folks, I'm thinking this fare will taste all the better if we were to stop and give thanks."

There was a murmur of agreement.

Not having a voice that could compare with

Hammond's bellow, Dusty had to stand and speak right out. He passed his plate to his wife and raised his arms to heaven. To Dusty, giving thanks was not a matter to be taken lightly.

"Lord God of heaven," he hollered, "Author of all that is good and supplier of all of life's needs."

At the first raising of his voice, folks stopped on the street and on the sidewalk opposite. Several heads were poked out of store doorways. Three or four horsemen pulled to a halt and looked on. Dusty continued until all the needful points were covered. He finished with, "And thank you Lord that we have had the help and friendship of John to see us safely through the miles. There are some Lord, who don't wish to eat with Coloreds. It would be our wish that you might open their hearts and show them the error of their ways. Amen."

Amidst the silence that followed, Dusty regained his seat and relieved his wife of the overflowing plate. Slowly, the street came back to life but many eyes remained on the strange group crowding the veranda.

Two of the horsemen that had stopped in the street pulled up to the tie-rail and stepped to the ground. They tied off and mounted the stairs to enter the restaurant. To no one in particular but loud enough to be heard among the visitors, the man in the lead said, "You slave lovers best keep that boy outa my way, and preferably outa my sight. Be best for everyone if'n you was to get gone outa town jest as soon as ye can."

Hammond and John both would have tried to

stop him, if they could have reached him, but Lewis was seated right at the doorway, with John at the other end of the oval gathering. Fearlessly, and perhaps foolishly, he stood and turned to the man.

Lewis wasn't a large man but anyone taking a careful look would see that his shirt was well filled out and his arms bulged with muscles. Hanging onto great self-confidence, which at one time, before his near-tragic experience in the creek, would have rightly been termed as pride or self-righteousness, he couldn't remember ever being intimidated by anyone. Everyone in the Texas-bound group knew that about the young man.

Although he had been unusually quiet since his near drowning, Lewis held a lifelong, barely suppressed anger, a rough and ready trait, seen only occasionally. Someone challenging him would be wise to take note of his muscular physique as well as the Colt Dragoon .44 side arm he had picked up in the aftermath of the war. He was rarely seen without the weapon holstered and hanging from his belt.

"You keep a civil tongue in your mouth there, fella. John is a friend of ours and a better man than I think you are or ever will be. Now, get along with you and don't bother us."

"And what if I don't?"

With no warning at all Lewis backhanded the man across the face. The deceptively slim Lewis surprised the rider with the quickness and force of the blow. All that was keeping the antagonist from falling to his knees was his frantic grip on the nearby doorjamb. Calmly, Lewis watched the man as he shook his head and stood up straight.

Lewis gave him a moment to walk away. When that didn't immediately happen, he felt the back of Lewis's other hand, knocking the dazed man off the veranda floor and down the steps.

His friend picked him up from the dust of the road and quietly said, "That's a big bite you've chawed off there Shawn. You may not have noticed but there's a whole passel of them sitting there. I think it best we just ride on."

Lewis and the others were pleased when they decided to do just that. Mounting their horses, the troublemakers were soon riding back to the east.

When Lewis took his seat again, there was not a sound from among the group, until John finally spoke up.

"I's be caus'n trouble fo' you folks. Dis been happ'n before. I's be thank'n you fo' speaking fo' me but it be bes if'n I stay in de camp de nex' time."

Hammond jumped in quickly with, "Until we get to Fort Worth, at least, John, you're one of us. What we do, you're welcome to join. We'll see to that, although I'm not sure if Lewis had just the right solution to that situation. But the man was a loudmouth. We'd have to acknowledge that. It's dealt with and behind us now. Just the same, we'll keep a careful watch until we're well away in the morning.

"What you do, John, after Fort Worth is up to you. If you choose to stay with us, we'll try to find a place for you.

"Now, everyone, eat up. There's pie and coffee on the way."

Chapter 29

After a short discussion, the group decided they would forgo the hotel beds and the hot baths. A one-night stay in Hope, Arkansas, was deemed to be sufficient for their needs and their desires.

After leaving the overnight camp, where the ladies substituted a warm water wash in the backs of their wagons in place of the wished-for hot bath, it was a short, two day's drive to the Red River crossing.

When they came in sight of the muddy Red, Hammond gathered everyone close enough to be heard clearly.

"From what I was told back in Hope, we need to be careful around this river. There's a well-marked trail crossing, like we've seen many times in the past few weeks, but those others were smaller and less dangerous streams. Stay close and stick to the crossing. Keep the kids in the wagons. The sandy bottom, apparently, is unpredictable and quicksand is not unusual. John will lead off with the horses. We'll hold the cattle back until John is safely on the other side. Only then will you boys push the cattle through. We'll let just the one wagon cross at a time. When you drive into the water, don't stop. Keep the horses pulling, whatever you have to do. The men will sit their saddles with ropes handy in case any wagon needs help.

"We'll camp at the first good opportunity on the other side. Is that all understood?"

Lewis, starting to come out of the melancholy he imposed on himself after nearly drowning, said, "Let's get 'er done."

John took that as the final word and they were soon on the move.

The loose horses and the cattle all crossed with no trouble. There was some floundering as a couple of the teams balked at the depth of the water and the shifting sand beneath their feet but at no time did they have to swim. The water never came above the floor boards of the wagons, so the stored goods and bedding remained dry. They had no encounters with the dreaded quicksand.

They all heaved a great sigh of relief as they pulled their dripping wagons and animals onto dry ground on the other side of the Red.

After a single night of camping within sight of the Red, they set out again. Following the well laid-out trail, they rode up to a crudely lettered sign, written in black paint, nailed to a post on the side of the road. Hammond was riding ahead of the group. He pulled up and waited for the others. With his booming voice he hollered, "What does that sign say, John?" Hammond was smiling so broadly that he could hardly talk.

John took a long study of the sign before shouting back, with a smile almost as broad as Hammonds, "Ne'r learned ta make out no letters Boss, but I'm gues'n that jes might be say'n Texas."

"And you'd be exactly right. You can always tell your grandchildren that you were the first of us to enter Texas. Drive 'em on young man, we got a ways to go yet. But at least we're in Texas."

There were a few 'hooray's' and a couple of shouts of joy but they died down quickly and the entourage moved on. Within a few minutes, even the last wagon had entered that long-awaited promised land.

With their goal virtually in sight, Hammond couldn't resist pondering again on their futures in Texas. That led naturally to considering where he had come from, his and his parent's past, and the more recent past that impacted Rosa and himself and the girls so profoundly. That pondering led to thoughts of the future and the changes it would bring.

Were they up to facing those changes? Were they big enough inwardly? Were their minds and hearts up to the challenge?

Perhaps, even if there were some questions that could have been honestly directed to a few of the travelers when they left their old lives behind, those questions had been answered along the trail. That long and wearying trail. For there had been changes, growth, in each one. The growth might not show up right away but it would show when the time of need came.

Even men and women who didn't recognize the growth within themselves would come to recognize it by and by. Everyone had grown, matured, facing each day's challenges and lying down at night knowing they had finished the day's work and earned their rest.

He ran through some of the names. Melody, his lovely daughter. Driving the team hour after hour, day after day, and never a complaint as her hands became rough and raw. Even her fright over the bathing incident seemed a lifetime ago. She had clearly grown and matured.

Rosa was just Rosa. Strong, dependable, always able to cope. Making a point always to lend her encouragement and strength to her daughters. Perhaps Rosa had changed the least. Perhaps she needed less changing. Perhaps she had always been the strong one for her children and for their marriage. Except for Jerry. She leaned heavily on Hammond to carry her over the loss of her son.

Charles? Well, Charles was the quiet one. The thinker. The planner. Minnie had chosen well when she said, 'yes' to his proposal of marriage. But even Charles was growing. Hammond could see it in the way he set up their camp, in the way he showed his love for the children, in the way he groomed and cared for his team.

Lewis? In some ways, Lewis would always be Lewis. Strong, sometimes in inappropriate ways and times, but stepping up when the need was upon him. Dependable, never shirking his duty, although he had been raised in a life of some privilege, with others standing in for him from time to time. That reliance on others was gone. Along with that reliance, most of his arrogance and pride had turned into a more pleasant humility and thankfulness, all stemming from the incident in the creek water and the unpredictable gelding.

Yes, Lewis had changed for the better. He had faced some trials his family protected him from in his youth and found that he was up to the challenge. He would be all right in this new land.

John? Well, John had learned to be silent, almost stoic, during his slave years. It was the way of survival. But none of that hid his intelligence or his strengths. His release from slave thinking had started at the Macintyre Horse Ranch. But it had grown day by day since. Still quiet and speaking only when spoken to, it was difficult to get to the depth of John. But those depths were there. Hammond could see it in him. He had watched the black man grow before them all, as the weeks had gone by. None of that meant John wouldn't face great challenges but it meant he had a better than average probability of rising to those challenges and being victorious.

From the crossing of the Red to where they were hoping to call home, put about another three weeks of slow plodding ahead of them. They passed more and more traffic. They started to see cattle running loose, a thing they had never seen in Tennessee. They held their animals closely bunched against the temptation to join their much wilder, roaming cousins.

Since the end of the war there seemed to be endless movement of both people and cattle in the Fort Worth area. The Hammond Gates entourage's arrival didn't do much more than bring a few curious faces to doorways and cause a horseman or two to tip their hats in greeting as they passed by.

As they rolled through the main street in search of a campground, they couldn't help noticing a goodly number of Black faces. A few appeared to be going about some business or other, but most were standing in groups, or sitting on the edge of the raised boardwalk, their feet shuffling aimlessly in the dust of the street.

Fort Worth had been larger before the war but the population dwindled as that conflict raged on. Many of the young men had been away at the battlefront. As happened everywhere, and on both sides of the conflict, considerable numbers of those young men did not return home. Hardships abounded. Businesses dried up. Young fathers and brothers were lost to families. Internal conflicts rose up between die-hard secessionists and those who supported the Union. The hard feelings were lasting well into the post-war period.

The value of the local money was questioned and, finally, at the end of the war, it became almost useless and store owners refused to take it. Cattle markets were down. Texas had fallen on hard times.

Pre-war Texas and the Fort Worth area held nearly one-third of their population as enslaved Blacks. As was happening all over the south, the freeing of these working slaves was putting a serious strain on those farms and businesses that relied on their labor.

But in spite of all the problems faced by the great state of Texas, it still offered what Hammond and his fellow travelers were looking for. Hope for the future. That hope came in the form of land. Land, and opportunity to accomplish what they wanted and needed. Millions of acres of land. Land that was open for settlement.

The big ranches were mostly in the south, or the west, but there was good farmland around Fort Worth.

That success in their ventures would be accomplished through hard work and risk was accepted as a fact. But Hammond and his fellow travelers had never shied from hard work. They wouldn't shy from it in Texas either.

Without any instructions from Hammond, John pushed the arriving remuda towards an old barn on the southern edge of the city, with a large set of corrals behind it. There was no sign of recent use. The grass was knee high in the corrals.

The complex may have been a livery stable at one time. Perhaps before the drop in population. But now it appeared to be unused, abandoned. If there had ever been a painted sign over the big doors, it had long since weathered off.

Lewis quickly rode forward and tied his animal to the corral railing. He then dragged a sagging gate through the long grass. John soon had the horses locked down.

Dusty had the gate to a small corral pulled open. John swung wide and helped Charles guide the cattle inside.

Hammond pulled his wagon along the shaded side of the old building and stepped to the ground. The other wagons pulled up behind and beside him until they were parked two abreast for the length of the old building.

"Place looks abandoned John. Any water in that corral?"

No'sir, Boss. Old wood trough. Might hold de water if'n we be haul'n it ta here from de pump. I see de pump at de front dere."

With all the animals needing water, the men were some time in getting ready to go to town. The troughs in the two corrals leaked water almost as fast as they could dump it in. Hammond was philosophical about the problem.

"I expect the old wood will soak up and close the gaps, by and by."

While the men were busy with that chore, the women sorted out the supplies, getting ready for the evening meal.

The discussion earlier in the day had revolved around the choice of camping and cooking, or hotels and cafes. Conscious of the dwindling stash of coins in their pockets and the problems presented by traveling with a black man, camping and cooking were voted for unanimously.

A decent distance from the wooden wall of the old stable, Jess dug out a fire pit, laying the sods aside to be replaced when they were ready to move on.

Rosa called to her grandchildren.

"You little people can be a big help. How would you like to go around the building and gather all the old wood you can find? Keep an eye out for snakes."

The kids, who had been fighting boredom for weeks, were soon in a competition to see who could find the most wood.

Later, with dinner done and the camp cleaned up and readied for the darkness of night, everyone but John went for a stroll through town.

John had noticed a young black man watching the camp intently while leaning against a roof post on the boardwalk across the road. When the others walked out, the young man took the opportunity to cross the street and approach the camp.

"Saw y'all rid'n in. Rider m'self. Y'all goin' ta ranch'n?"

John was unsure how to answer, so he kept his response brief.

"Ah'm goin ta look fer da rid'n job. D'othors, dey be de farmers. Good folks. Work'n hard."

The visitor offered his name without holding out his hand.

"Caleb, dey be nam'n me. Ain't never know my papa nor my mama. Jes d'other slaves. Don' know who done de nam'n. Ner know any second name. Might be I calls myself by some other name, come by 'n by."

John smiled a bit at the man. Although Caleb looked to be two or three years older than John was himself, he had the feeling that he thought of himself as much younger. Perhaps it was the sight of John leading the arrivals to the campground or perhaps it was that John was riding and was clearly a competent horseman. He said nothing of this to Caleb.

"Ah'm John. Jest John."

The two men studied each other for a bit, wondering where the conversation was going. Finally, Caleb asked, "Y'all camp'n wit de whites?"

"Been travl'n fer nearly de whole of two months. D'all of us together. Car'n fer de horses. Help'n around de camp. Des be de good folks, he said again."

After another silence, while John wondered why the young man was hanging around, John asked, "Where all you be liv'n Caleb?"

Caleb was slow answering but he finally said, "I be sleep'n in dis here ol' stable. Hay in de loft make de good'nuf bed, if'n you don' mind de mice."

John turned and studied the old building, wondering if it was due to fall down on top of whoever was sleeping inside.

"De Boss man o' de build'n don' kir if'n you be liv'n der?"

"I be ask'n roun'. De Boss man o' dis here stable, he join up to de army. Ner be seen no mo'. A'm tink'n he be dead. Dead 'n gone. De townfo'k, dey don' kir I sleep here."

When Caleb saw Hammond leading the group back from town, he slipped around the back corner of the building and disappeared.

The next morning, sitting around the breakfast fire with their last cups of coffee, waiting for the full of the sun to lighten the day, Hammond spoke to John.

"Well, John. You're here. You're in Texas. You were a big help on the trail and each of us wants to thank you. We're going looking for farmland this morning. We picked up some advice and directions in town yesterday.

"I know it's not farming that you have your eye set on but I want you to know that if you can't find other work, you will always be welcome to come and get your hands dirty in this good soil, along with me or any of the others here.

"We've talked and we want to thank you for the work you did and wish you well. I'm hoping to see you from time to time, no matter where you find work."

Even after being free for over a year and having worked with Jessie Macintyre, John was still having trouble with the idea of a white man thanking him for the work he did. And offering his lasting friendship. He responded to Hammond's words with a simple, "Thank you, Boss. I be enjoy de trip, an de work wit de ho'ses. I be look'n fer de rid'n job dis morn'n."

As the wagons and riders spread out to explore the land to the north and west of Fort Worth, Rosa was sitting relaxed on the wagon seat while Melody handled the leathers. Hammond rode his big gelding close enough to the wagon to carry on a conversation with his wife and daughter.

The first question came from Melody.

"What's going to become of John, father?"

"Well, I expect John will do just fine for himself. Eventually. But that's still a good question to ask.

Rosa took up the query.

"It might be my imagination but I seemed to see him grow as we traveled. He certainly needed no help with the horses. And when Lewis was doing his best to act like an ass, John stepped right in and did what had to be done, without waiting to be told."

Melody was shocked.

"Mother, how you talk."

Hammond laughed his raucous laugh. He could easily be heard by the following wagons.

"Little girl. I don't necessarily approve but you must recognize by now that your mother speaks her mind. Then too, when she's right, she's right. There's just no denying that."

After a short, contemplative silence, while she struggled with her thoughts of right and wrong, Melody came back with, "Anyway, we were talking about John, not my brother-in-law."

"Right again, little girl. I believe what your mother saw in our Black friend, we all noticed, too. Hours of slow riding, on a wagon seat or a saddle, either one, leaves a lot of time to think and imagine. A couple of times, I tried to imagine John's position.

His, and thousands of other freed Blacks. But the hard truth is that, even having Blacks living around me all my life, I just can't get my mind to where I can understand. I've never lived a single day without freedom. Until a year ago John had never lived a single day with freedom. How am I supposed to understand that?

"For twenty years, John wasn't allowed a single private thought or action. At least until his owner was smart enough to put him in charge of the care of the farm's last two horses. Then, all of a sudden, with no familiarity with freedom or thinking for himself, and without being able to read or write, he was sent off on a very long and difficult task. You know that story. Now, I grant you, he had considerable help along the way but the fact is, he got the job done.

"John is first, a horseman. That ability came along with him when he was freed. Everything else since then he has had to learn. I expect he will be learning things about living free, among whites, for a long time yet. Things we all knew as children, John is just now learning.

"Your mother is correct, Melody. John grew on our trip. Grew inside. Grew as a freed man. He still doesn't quite know who or what he is but he's growing into that understanding. He still has trouble being accepted by white folks, and he may never totally get over that, but he certainly knows he can work alongside anyone, and do his job. And be appreciated. Appreciated for the work done, if not for the man doing it. The rest will take time.

"His confidence will grow. There'll be some along the way who will try to hold him down. But he'll find a way through that. I'm not so sure about many of the other Blacks I saw sitting idle in the sun, in Fort Worth and along the way from Tennessee. Might be hard times ahead for most of them."

Chapter 30

The land hunters had no sooner left on their pursuit of the future when Caleb sauntered around the back of the barn. He stood on the bottom rail of the corral and studied the horses as John saddled his gelding.

"What you be up to dis morn'n John?"

John looked at the desperately thin young man, wondering when he ate last. He wondered too, if Caleb was truly a rider or if he had said that only to impress John.

"Goin' ride 'roun' some dis morn'n. Look 'n see what dis Fort Worth place be look lac. Maybe so, I see de cows 'n I ask fer de job."

Seeing that the gelding was rigged out and ready to go, Caleb stepped off the rail and opened the gate. John swung aboard and thanked him as he rode out.

"I be back later. De folks dey be back too, by 'n by. I expect dey goin' camp here fo' de while. If'n you be close by here maybe-so you keep de eye on de animals. May be a cup o' coffee left in de pot."

John rode west at a slow trot until he found himself on the bank of a river. He followed along and came to a narrow bridge. He crossed and headed west. He didn't know what good ranching country looked like. This was all pretty flat. But there was grass everywhere so he guessed cattle would like it. He figured cattle didn't much care about the scenery.

Everywhere he had ever been before, whether Carolina, Tennessee or Arkansas, was hilly and tree-covered with ample flowing water most places. This was, clearly, a drier land.

He rode past a few shacks where he saw folks hoeing in the brownish soil. In two places, the farmers stopped, leaned on their hoes and watched him ride past. Only one man waved a hesitant greeting. John lifted his hand in acknowledgment but didn't stop. Farming held no attraction for him.

When his stomach growled at noon, John kept riding. He had brought nothing with him except the canteen of water. He hadn't truly appreciated the canteen Jessie Macintyre had given him before that day. Until then, there had been water available almost any time he wanted to bend over a running stream and scoop it up. In this dry country, even in the few short hours he had been riding, he found the canteen a most welcome addition to his riding kit.

It wasn't until he was several miles west of the town that he started seeing cattle in significant numbers. He stepped up the pace of his riding and watched carefully, looking for any ranch buildings. But he found that buildings or signs of settlement of any sort were few. He was getting ready to re-trace his steps to Fort Worth when he finally saw a trace of smoke rising from the chimney on a small, batten-sided house. He slowed his horse to a care-ful walk. As he approached the outfit, he saw a man watching him from the doorway of a small barn. The two men kept their eyes on one another until they were within speaking distance.

John pulled the gelding to a stop and lifted his battered hat, holding it in front of his chest. The watching man, although deeply sunburnt, was white. He was obviously suspicious of John's intent. A small brown and white dog growled at John's horse but made no threat to come closer.

"Ah's be look'n fer de work, Boss. Be de rider 'n de ho'se man. Knows 'bout ho'ses. Some bout de cows. I's be work'n hard fer you, Boss."

He didn't know what else to say so he sat qui-etly while he waited for a response. It wasn't long in coming.

"Never had me no Colored rider. Don't know as I would want one now. But it don't really make no never mind. I can't hardly keep myself busy, or well fed, either one, around this gunny sack spread. Sorry, no work here. Fact is, you'll have to ride south some ways to find the bigger cattle spreads. Everyone here is still trying to put their lives back together after the war. Having Bluecoats riding about everywhere a man might like to be isn't help-ing either. Be glad to see the end of those boys.

"Best I can do for you is offer water for your horse and wish you luck."

John dismounted and led his horse to the trough at the side of the barn. As the animal drank, he stepped to the pump and worked the lever until the trough was threatening to overflow. He then turned to the rancher, who had hardly moved the whole time of John's visit, and said, "I's tank'n you, Boss."

With that, he swung aboard the gelding and turned for Fort Worth. He was a hundred yards away before he thought to snug his floppy hat back over his curly hair.

When John arrived back at the old barn in Fort Worth, Caleb was sitting in the shade whittling on a piece of barn wood. He watched John dismount to open the gate and run his horse in without rising from the long grass. John unsaddled and carried his rig to the corral fence, balancing it on the top rail.

"Water trough be full. Be you carry de bucket from de pump?"

"Dat be me, a'right. Ne'r seen no other feller be a'doin it. Mos de water, she leak onta de groun."

John thought of Caleb's answer and looked again at the whittler.

"You eat today?"

"Drank de coffee. Washed de pot."

"Be der a food house srv'n de Blacks?"

Caleb pointed with his opened knife blade, "Small place at de end o' de town."

"We's gon' walk dere soon's I wash de hands."

John didn't know what chili was but a bowl each

and a plate of bread between the two men wouldn't cut too deeply into his saved wages. The first mouthful of the chili-pepper laden dish had John gasping for breath. Caleb laughed and kept on spooning in his first food of the day.

Later, with both men sitting on the grass in the shade, they watched Hammond and the others slowly roll through the town. As the wagons came closer Caleb quietly rose to his feet and disappeared around the end of the old building. John stood and opened the corral gate. He then held the team as Hammond gave his wife unnecessary help stepping off the wagon.

The team was soon stripped of its harness. The animals found their own way to the open gate and the water trough inside. The harness was draped over the fence rail beside John's saddle.

The others were doing the same with their teams and riding horses. Then the never-ending pumping and hauling of water commenced. John managed to convince himself that the old trough was leaking less than it had been.

Hammond was the first to speak.

"Did you find a job John?"

"No Boss. Didn't find no one need'n no help. Maybe so tomorrow I's be go d'other way. Across de river and more ta de south."

"Well, you'll find what you need John. You just have to keep looking. The good news for us is that we think we found land we like. And enough for all of us. We'll be going back in the morning to take a more careful look, just to make sure.

"The ladies will soon have dinner ready, John. Will you join us?"

"I's gone ta de eat'n house in town Boss. Be good fer till morn'n now. Maybe drink a coffee if'n you got lots by 'n by."

The tired crew was soon ready for bed. After checking over their animals and refilling the two water troughs, they went to their bedrolls. John rolled his blankets out beside the corral. If he didn't quickly find a job, he may take a look at the hay in the loft. It was bound to be softer than Texas ground.

Chapter 31

The morning breakfast and coffee drinking lagged on until the sun was well past the dawn.

John and Caleb walked back down to the chili house. John again paid, this time for the least costly breakfast item available. Like the bowl of chili that he had never eaten before, he had never heard of a plate of chopped and stirred vegetables, fried in oil and topped with a single fried egg. He looked at it for a while before finally picking up his fork. He discovered that the unfamiliar red vegetable was, in fact, the same red chili that had spiced up his evening meal. The first bite had his eyes watering and his throat constricting as if his body was asking questions of his common sense.

The two men finished their plates in silence, along with a glass of water each and several cups of coffee. John considered the cost and the fact that he seemed to have attracted an expensive follower in Caleb. He decided that the sought after job had to come soon or all his saved up wages from the Mac-intyre would be in the hands of the Mexican cook.

Leaning back in their chairs, Caleb said, "You ready now, to tak de look at de big barn? I be want'n ta show you somet'ing. Now, maybe so you be ready."

The two men sauntered back to the barn. The wagons were gone and the breakfast fire was safely out. John still planned to saddle up and search out a ranch job but he would take a quick look at the barn with Caleb first.

Caleb led John around the building and into the small door at the rear. With that being the only opening, except for a row of small, filthy windows, that would pass almost no light at all, the vast interior remained mostly draped in darkness and cobwebs. Once inside, Caleb stood silently for perhaps thirty seconds, giving John time to see as much as he could in the semi-light.

"Wat yo want'n fo me ta see?"

"I's be want'n yo ta see dis here ol' barn full o' de hos's, wit each one pay'n John 'n 'ol' Caleb de rent money fer ta kir fer dem. An' de big fence ta de outside too."

John said nothing as Caleb led him further into the building. He looked into each stall as he passed. Even in the dimness, he could see that there was little damage in the old building. It was just as the owner had left it when he rode off to the war. The place could be used the way it was, except for some much-needed shovel work.

Each side of the wide dirt-floored aisle was lined

with stalls and mangers. Several water buckets still sat in the cradles formed out of rough-sawn wood. There was uneaten hay in several of the mangers. Some of it was turning a bit moldy.

At the end of the aisle, on one side, was a single, larger pen. John could picture it holding eight or ten horses. Or perhaps a dozen cows and calves. For a short stay, anyway. A quick glance at the un-shoveled remains on the pen floor confirmed that cattle had been held there at one time.

About two-thirds of the way down the aisle, the loft floor stopped, opening the barn to the full height of the roof. John hadn't yet climbed the ladder to the loft, but Caleb assured him that the loft was almost half full of hay, none of it moldy or rotting.

At the far end of the building, a small door led into what had at one time been an office of sorts and a sleeping room. There was nothing left in the room but an old chair and a bunk with one leg broken off. The mouse riddled remains of a straw-filled tick mattress hung lifelessly over the edge of the rope undergirding. John shook his head. He glanced behind him to where Caleb stood waiting, in the doorway.

"We sleep better dan dat even on the slave fa'm."

Back in the aisle, Caleb pushed another small door open and led John into what was obviously the tack room. There were harnesses and miscellaneous leather straps hanging from pegs inserted into the wall. Three dried out saddles were still carefully laid over the stand built for them. After three or four years in the Texas heat, they would take some oiling and work to make them usable again but it could be done.

Another dozen empty racks stood ready to receive more saddles.

Caleb stood wordlessly, figuring John didn't need any explanations. After a full minute, he pushed yet another door open, this one led into a lean-to shed, built onto the side of the building. The lean-to was inside what could be either open-ended hay storage or a wagon shed.

Inside the larger shed stood a full blacksmith shop and shoeing rig. A big door on each end of the small structure would allow for horses to be brought inside.

The forge still had half-burned coal in it, with several bags of nugget coal waiting for use, stored against the outside wall. A wooden box lay off to the side with all manner of metal tools lying in dust-covered silence. More tools hung from pegs on the wall. The anvil, too big to steal or easily tote away, stood at the ready, bolted to the top of a large tree stump.

Again, Caleb said nothing.

When he figured enough time had elapsed, he turned back to the main barn. John followed, his mind whirring with unfamiliar thoughts. Thoughts of caring for the horses and rigs of others. Thoughts of being paid to do the work.

When Caleb stopped and stood silently, John continued walking to the rear of the building, where they had entered. In the dimness, he had a problem figuring out the latch on the big, swinging doors but he finally worked it apart. With his strong shoulder pressed against the wood, he pushed. The hinges squealed and the long grass outside impeded the movement but, soon, the door was open. He then reached for the second door and swung it wide. Light poured in. It was almost as if some kind of life ascended on the long-abandoned structure.

The two recently freed Black men stood shoulder to shoulder, looking down the center aisle of the barn, wondering.

Nothing was said as they closed and latched the big doors. Outside, walking to the corral, John remained quiet but, clearly, he was thinking. Caleb was wise enough to keep his mouth shut, giving John time to ponder the possibilities.

As it was still early enough in the day, John saddled up and again crossed the river, and then journeyed west and a bit south. He could cover perhaps fifteen miles of grass country and still get back in daylight. If there were no ranches needing help in that distance, he would have to ask someone for advice. But who? Who would advise a black man, when there were thousands of them, as well as large numbers of semi-lost veterans roaming the country?

Chapter 32

John's second day on the job hunt was a duplication of the first. He returned late in the evening with slumped shoulders, sitting slack on his bone-weary gelding. Lewis watched his arrival and went to open the corral gate. Wordlessly, he waited for John's report.

"No job yet, Boss."

"Well, perhaps something will show up soon. I talked to a few bartenders in a couple of the saloons along the main street. Told them you were here, waiting to find riding and ranch work. Left them your name. Told them about our trip west and how well you handled the horses. Can't never tell. Could help. Might be a rancher come along looking for a man."

"Thank you, Boss."

The evening dragged on with folks drinking coffee, fitting wagons out for sleeping, putting kids to bed. Hammond walked over to where John was sitting, after returning from his nightly trip with Caleb to the Mexican cantina.

"Let's go for a bit of a walk John."

When they were out of earshot of the others he said, "I have a short-term proposition for you John, maybe for two or three months.

"We've found the land we're looking for. We'll be moving out there in the morning right after we finish up at the land office. We'll camp in the wagons and tents while we get ourselves established. But the cattle and loose horses would be a nuisance to us until we get some fences and corrals built.

"No one seems to care that we've been using this old building and the corrals. If you would stay here for a few weeks and care for our animals, we would pay you the going rate for livery care. That way you would be earning some money and getting a feel for the land and the people. There could even be a rancher or two come along looking for a rider."

The two men stood silently while John tried to sort this all out. It was true that he had allowed his mind to expand over the year or so that he had been free from slavery but to be paid for caring for someone's animals was a wide step in his mind. Almost like being in some kind of business. Like the Mexican cook that kept him fed day by day, with food that he was becoming accustomed to, was in business.

Of course, he had been paid wages on the Macintyre Horse Ranch for working with the animals. And when he found a ranch job he would be paid. This would be almost the same.

As John hesitated, Hammond decided that it might help if they talked about the money.

"I've spoken with the others, John. We've agreed to share the cost. If you would feed and water the animals in the corrals and exercise the horses from time to time, we'll pay you forty dollars each month. That's close to double what a rancher will pay you for riding work. You'll have a wage and enough to feed yourself.

"You might even buy some camp fixings and decide to prepare your own meals."

John gravely shook his head before grinning up at Hammond.

"No, Boss. I's do de cook'n on de ride from Carolina. I's goin' let de Mexican do de cook'n fer me. Be better dat way."

Hammond grinned before saying, "Can't say I blame you John. I've done enough of my own camp cooking to know my meals were just barely edible."

After a short pause, Hammond completed his thoughts on the old barn.

"If someone comes along and claims the building or the hay from the loft, we'll pay them for the hay and the use of the yard. That way there will be no trouble for you. What do you think? Can you see yourself working for us for a couple of months?"

John was at the end of his knowledge or understanding of business. The idea of caring for the animals was no issue to him. But the idea of him being paid for that service, with no rancher or Boss involved, was struggling to be born. Could this be the opportunity to add a bit to his meager savings while he waited for the much-coveted ranching job? While he was still trying to sort it all out, the words seemed to pop out of his mouth as if they had a mind of their own.

"I kir fo de animals, Boss. It be lak you say."

The Tennessee settlers got a late start the next morning. It took far longer for the men to settle up their claims with the land office than they had allowed for. When that bit of paperwork was finally behind them, they trotted their horses back to the big barn.

Waving a handful of papers and with a bigger than life grin on his face, Hammond hollered out, "All done ladies. Get yourselves onto those wagons. We're going to our new homes."

The teams were harnessed and hitched into place in a matter of minutes. With a final goodbye wave and several 'farewells', the wagons rolled out. John stood watching, still wondering exactly what he had gotten himself into. As he stood there, Caleb slunk around the rear of the barn and joined him.

Although Caleb didn't ask, John explained the situation to him. He ended with, "You be stay 'n hep wit de animals, I be pay'n you wit de two meals each day, morn'n 'n even'n."

Caleb answered with a grin.

"When we start wit dis job, John?"

"We's a'ready ta start dis here minute. We's goin fill de leak'n water troughs ag'in. Den we's goin' ride de horses an git 'em some runnin'. You bes' git a saddle from de tack room."

It was a long day of riding and filling ungrateful water troughs. They turned the small bunch of cattle loose and herded them around the area for an hour. The cattle needed to stretch their legs and the horses had to get used to herding duties. The settlers had taken the milk cow with them.

Caleb had proven to be as good as his word. He was a rider. John could see that when Caleb first stepped into a stirrup and took his seat on the dried-out saddle.

With the horses exercised and a night's sleep behind the two Black men, John faced the task of getting the stable ready for use. He could not have said that he had thought it over deeply. It was simply that if he was caring for Hammond's animals, why not care for others? It all seemed simple enough. The barn was there and empty. If the building's owner showed up, they would work it all out somehow.

After thinking it over again on the walk back from breakfast, he strolled directly to the back of the old building.

"We's goin' clean out de barn."

With that, he opened the big doors and picked up a shovel. The outdoor animals had been fed earlier. Now it was time to dung out the barn stalls.

Deciding he needed even more light, John opened the big front doors. As the light poured in, he could see some tools leaning against the rear wall in one of the stalls. There were two more shovels, a scraper or rake of some sort, looking like it was made in the blacksmith shop, a heavy broom, and propped up on its spoked, iron wheel, leaning against the wall, a heavy and crude wheelbarrow. John immediately decided that the one-wheeled machine would make a usable tool for toting out the stall scrapings.

It took most of the day to clean out the barn. The two men then scrubbed the dust and grime off their bodies and clothing as best they could and walked over to the Mexican cantina.

After a dinner of some kind of spiced rice and chunky meat, they saddled and rode horses for an hour. The black clouds, tumbling and rolling in from the west warned of a storm's arrival. With the probability of a night of lightning and thunder, John had checked and re-checked the corrals securing the horses and cattle.

Later, taking in the last couple of hours of the day, sitting on a wooden bench spotted outside the big front doors of the barn, while they let the chilies and beef settle, they watched another group of immigrants slowly work their way through town. There were groups arriving almost daily. Each bunch was a little different from the others, making the study of them an interesting evening pastime.

The newest group was headed up by a big, rough-looking man, sitting tall on a black horse. John could see from a distance that the man was heavily armed and appeared to be ready for any trouble that might raise its head. His suspicious eyes were casting in all directions as he slowly made his way along the main street, at the head of two wagons, and several riders driving bunched-up horses, and a few cattle.

As the rider searched out the way ahead, his eyes fell first on the big barn and the animals in the two outside corrals. They then picked out the two Black men sitting on the bench. John watched intently as he knew he, himself, was being analyzed. His study of the man turned to a bit of anxiety as the fellow nudged his horse towards the barn.

The two stable keepers sat in questioning silence as the man approached. With his turn towards the barn doors, as usual, Caleb found a way to slink quietly out of sight.

When the rider was within easy talking distance he pulled to a stop and pushed his hat to the back of his head. He stood in the stirrups and adjusted his canvas pants as if he was ready to stop after a long day of riding.

"Hostler man around?"

John was faced with a whole new situation. What to say? How to react?

"Jest me dis place, Boss."

The response was a few moments in coming. Almost in wonder at the concept, the rider carelessly pointed a tired arm at the barn'

"You runn'n the livery?"

Well, what was the right answer? Was he running a livery or only caring for the animals in the corrals? John was a quick enough thinker but his mind had never traveled this trail before. Again, with no clear idea of where the talk was going, he said, "Ye'sir Boss, jest me ta dis place. Jes' Ol' John."

The slower moving wagons caught up to the rider and sagged to a stop, waiting for instructions, while their leader thought the situation over. A few other riders drove the loose stock up to the side of the building, holding them there.

Finally, casting a worried eye at the building storm and wishing to bring the long day to an end, and to get shelter for the animals as well as the folks waiting behind him, he said, "Tank McGraw here. Traveling down from Missouri. Need shelter and feed for a few days. Teams, saddle animals and a few cattle. Storm coming in. Like to get the wagons under shelter. Got women and kids to care for. You got room here?"

John, thinking of all the stalls they had cleaned that day and of the big lean-to shed that sheltered the blacksmith shop, as well as the now empty hay storage space, nodded his head with a smile.

"Yassir, Boss, be lots a room. Wagons go under de big roof off to da side. Stalls inside fer de animals. Got de hay. No oats. Water in de pump. No cook'n fires be made close to de barn."

Tank McGraw stepped to the ground, dropped his reins, and walked to the big doors. With a slow study of the stalls, noting the cleanliness, he spoke over his shoulder to John.

"What are you charging for stalling the animals? Feed and water, sheltering the wagons."

John stood and walked closer to his first customer, thinking of what Hammond Gates had already paid him.

"I be feed'n 'n water'n and check'n de feet. Giv'n clean 'n rubdown fer de horses. Twenty-five cents each animal for de day, horses and cattle, both,

Boss. De wagons be no trouble. Dey be no money paid fo' dem."

Without looking at the black man he was doing business with, Tank McGraw turned to the riders who had gathered to the side of the wagons.

"Run those loose animals in here. Put the cattle in the big pen right here. Run one wagon right through the lean-to. Back the other in against the first. Bring the teams here and stall them."

John stood aside and watched as the barn filled with weary animals. He held the gate open as the cattle were driven into the big pen and then shut and latched them in securely.

Driving the first wagon under the shed roof was no problem but John marveled at the ease which with the woman commanding the second wagon lined her unit up and backed the team, putting the wagon where she wanted it on the first try.

The men unhitched the teams and led them to the barn. When John pointed out the tack room, saddles, bridles and harness soon took up most of the saddle racks and wooden pegs driven into the walls. The whole matter was dealt with quickly with little talk from the tired riders.

John was counting animals and figuring in his head. Without thinking of the many reasons he had for hating his time in slavery and the man who had owned him, he silently thanked Jedediah Akins for teaching him how to make purchases and count money. He couldn't write or make out reading but he could do sums. And this sum came to a very attractive number. It would never make him rich but it would more than match what he could expect as a rider on a ranch. His silent thoughts were interrupted.

"Eating place close by John?"

"Yes'sir, Boss. down ta de end o' de street. Call de Cantina. Mexican cook. Good food. Lots a de hot spice but lots a de food too."

With a simple nod of thanks, Tank McGraw led out. The others followed, like chicks following a hen. John figured there was no doubt who was in command of these immigrants.

The McGraw bunch were there for three days, riding out the storm and heavy rains, and making inquiries about available land. When John figured the money due in his head, Tank wasn't sure. John could see his lips moving slightly. He waited while the big man did his silent figuring. Finally, in frustration, Tank called his oldest daughter, a blond-headed girl of about fifteen years.

"Lil. You've spent most of your life in school, seems like. Can you figure this?"

He told her the count of animals and the agreed-too price. The girl heaved a deep sigh and said, "Oh daddy, that's so simple."

She named the same number John had come up with. Disguising perhaps just a hint of shame, the big man paid over the coin. He topped the payment up with a compliment.

"You did good, John. The animals look great, cleaned and well fed. I appreciate you cleaning and oiling the harness too. Perhaps we'll see you again."

"Thank you, Boss. Ah hopes y'all find jest the

right land fer te live on."

As the riders and wagons were lost in the distance and the traffic of Fort Worth, Caleb walked up behind John. He continued in the habit of staying out of the way when white folks were around. It was clear that the man didn't trust whites but he had never offered any explanation.

That he had been a slave was obvious enough but there must be more. John had tried to get the story from him. Caleb wasn't talking. But John suspected he had seen hard times in the past. He suspected Caleb was frightened of something, too. Just what that could be, John had no idea.

Chapter 33

The open barn doors seemed to act as an invitation. The livery customers kept coming, sometimes a lone horseman. Sometimes an immigrant group. One full month went by with the livery at least half full every day. No one complained about the cost and many thanked John for the good service.

When it came right down to running a livery business, Caleb shied away from any indication of ownership or partnership. Since it had been Caleb's original idea, John was careful to clear the air between them before figuring he could claim the business as his own.

Caleb settled for a job working in the livery. His small wages were topped up with the two meals each day that John had originally promised him. Caleb couldn't hide his delight as John counted a few coins into his outstretched hand at the end of the first month. John figured this might be the first real money the man had seen in some time, perhaps ever.

A few weeks after opening the barn doors for business, a man limped up to the front of the livery, seriously favoring one leg. The man's torn shirt, hanging loose over a thick neck, his broad, beefy shoulders, and his waist and hips slimmed down by the many miles traveled, and too many missed meals, plus the bush of a beard almost hiding his identity, made him an easy man to notice. And remember.

His dirty, floppy, rain-damaged hat hid the man's eyes. Through the beard, John could see his mouth working as if he was saying words only to himself.

He was walking beside a worn-out mule pulling a rickety wagon. There was no bowed cover over the wagon, simply an oiled canvas groundsheet pulled tight and tied across the top, protecting whatever was stowed beneath.

John stayed in his chair at the door while the man dropped the mule's lead rope and walked up. He didn't speak or ask a question, figuring the man would state his needs without the question.

Instead of asking for shelter, the limping man said, "Blacksmith. Make anything a body might need, be it made from iron. Shoeing. No one better. Heard there was a smithy shed in back here. Not being used. Could rent it from you. Or work for you. All the time saying what should suit you best."

John had seen some folks down on their luck before that time but this man could match any of them for tired. Wordlessly, he stood and motioned towards the shed, stepping that way, with the man following. The mule stood with drooped head as if it had no intention of going anywhere except, perhaps, the water trough that John kept filled beside the big doors. Within twenty steps, the two men approached the smithy door. John pushed it open and stepped aside. The blacksmith took one step into the space and stopped. Silently, he studied the layout. John could see his shoulders slump, not in resignation but as if to say, 'finally'.

Turning back to look at John, the smithy was clearly studying on the situation. John's appearance and businesslike manner projected the fact that he had come a considerable way towards putting slavery and servitude behind him. The smithy could see more self-confidence in the black man than he felt in himself.

"I'll rent the setup from you if you can wait for the rent until I make some money. Just got barely enough left to buy a small supply of iron and a few shoes. Nothing much left over."

John did some quick figuring before saying, "You don' rent de shop. You do your own business. You pay twenty cents, each dollar you make."

The smithy stuck out his hand. "Grant Wagner. That's a deal."

John met the handshake. "I jes' be John".

As the two men stood there, Caleb made one of his rare appearances. John, figuring the blacksmith had been on short rations for a while said, "We's jest going for de evening feed'n. Dis man be Caleb. He be work'n with de animals, lak me. Sleep ta de loft. Mexican man run de cantina. Food be good. Cost be not too much."

"Well, could be I have a two-bit piece held over for just such a purpose. And I could surely eat. Care if I join you?"

A few more weeks went past with animals coming and going. John had been concerned that the situation might be too good to be true. Although he paid Caleb according to their original agreement, the mysterious ex-slave still showed no interest in ownership or making decisions, even though the original idea for running a livery had come from him. The business was John's and his alone. That left him with more coin in the coffee can but also with more cares burdening his broad shoulders.

One of his concerns seemed to be coming alive when he heard a holler from the front of the barn as he was working over a horse in a back stall. He straightened up to look over the side of the stall and didn't like what he saw. Standing in the big doorway was a man with a shiny star on his shirt. John knew what that star would stand for, although he had never had occasion to be involved with the law. The short stint with the sheriff back at the Rev. Grimsley's small home was the single, short-lived exception. The very thought of further dealings with the law frightened him. But he knew he couldn't ignore the call so he stepped out of the stall and made his way forward.

"Morn'n Boss."

"Are you the one calling himself John?"

"Dat be me Boss. John."

"I've had a complaint filed against you John. Another livery man from the other end of town says you don't have any right to be using this property. Says you're taking up a lot of business that should be coming to him. Rightly, what he's concerned about is the smithy being open and working. His barn is still well used but your man here has cut a deep groove into the smith work at the other livery."

There was a short pause as the sheriff studied the black man standing before him. He finally asked, "Who owns this building now John. It can't be you. Been against the law for Blacks to own property."

John had no ready answer. He had known this day would come but he had never been sure how he would deal with it. He was still holding Hammond Gate's animals in the corrals. Could he somehow use Hammond's name to sort this out? He finally decided that would be a poor solution. The fact that Hammond and his party were using the corrals would be indisputable. But, in reality, Hammond was just one of John's many customers. He had to learn to stand on his own feet and this was another opportunity to prove to himself that he could do that.

"No Boss. Dis ol' building jes be empty. Folks I rode here wit' from Tennessee, dey camp in the yard for a bit. No one come fer de barn. I don' know who own de building.

"I's car'n fer de animals fer de folks Ol' John travel wit from Tennessee. Dat's dem in de corrals to de outside. Dey leave dem here while dey work'n on de new farms. Barn jest be empty. I be clean'n out and kir fer de animals fer folks. Still don't nev'r hear from no owner of de build'n."

The sheriff kind of smiled although he was trying to hide it.

"Just moved in did you, John? Well, you're not the first to simply move in and settle down. Been a lot of that in Texas. Most ranchers don't own the land they claim. Taken as a right, you might say.

"I knew the man who owned this land and barn. He put on a uniform about four years ago and rode off to do his duty, as he saw it. Hasn't been heard from since. I expect he's not coming back. Why don't you walk down to the town office? Talk with Elizabeth Talon down there. Liz, she might know a way for you to work this out. I'll come back in a couple of days. Find out what's been done."

As usual, Caleb was nowhere to be seen during the sheriff's visit. But Grant was in his smithy shop. With all the noise he was making, he was unaware of the sheriff's visit. After the lawman left, John walked to the smithy door and waited for Grant to notice him. The smith rolled a rod of iron in the flaming coals while he turned the bellows pump with his other hand. Lifting the metal and studying the color for temperature, he turned to the big anvil. There, with much light, but skilled hammering, rolling the hot iron over the pointed end of the anvil, he slowly but carefully formed a big letter 'B' into it. He then dropped the half-formed branding iron into the tub of water kept for that purpose and straightened his back with a hand on each hip. Only then did he notice John standing there. He said nothing, just waiting for John to speak.

It took a moment for John to ask his personal

question but, finally he said, "Be you able to make out de readn'n an de writ'n?"

"Can I read and write? Well, yes, I can John. Is there something you need to sort out?"

John told him about the sheriff's visit and the problem with the unowned barn. He then repeated what the law man said about seeing the woman at the town hall. He finished with, "Maybe so you come wit Ol' John. We go dis place, see dis Miss Liz lady. See can we stay wit de barn."

Grant was untying his leather apron before John had finished with the telling. He checked the forge to assure himself that it was safely damped down and put his hand on John's shoulder, turning him to the outside.

"Let's go now, my friend. I'll just wash up a bit and pull a razor across my chin. Then we'll see this Miss Liz."

They reached the town office after a four-block walk and found it empty except for a prim lady seated behind a much-used desk. When she looked up at their entrance, Grant took the lead.

Anyone seeing only the gaunt, bearded man who had first approached John, leading his worn-out wagon and mule, would not recognize the well fed, cleanly shaved and barbered man standing beside John. He might not be regarded as truly handsome but that the ladies of a more mature age noticed him could not be denied.

"Would you be Miss Liz, ma'am?"

"Well, except that I don't care to emphasize the Miss part, I will have to admit to being the one you're seeking."

While John stood on one worried foot and then the other, Grant told the story in brief. He finished with, "What can we do to sort this out and get permission for John to keep running his business in that old barn?"

Liz studied the two men with a grin and a question.

"Am I to presume that John is unable to speak for himself?"

"No ma'am, not at all. It's just that he asked me to come along and help. Perhaps you can understand that."

"Yes, perhaps I can."

She slowly turned her eyes away from the smithy and studied John.

"I think there might be a solution John. The law makers have just recently removed the old prohibition that restricted Black's from owning property. That old barn is not the only unclaimed building in Fort Worth. There are empty properties all over town, with the owners gone or missing. The town fathers would like to clear up some of those ownership questions. It's a matter of taxes more than anything. Unowned properties are difficult to collect taxes on."

She stood and walked to a cabinet. She opened a large, hard covered record book lying on top. After several flipped pages she stopped and studied the records, then turned back to the men.

"There are four years of back taxes owing on that property. The town would settle for one year just to clean up the mess."

She named a dollar amount before saying, "If you can pay out that amount John, I can sign the property to you, and you can own it. Are you able to do that?"

John explained the need to go back to the barn to dig out his cache of carefully saved wealth. Grant offered to wait at the town hall until he returned. Miss Liz offered no objection to either man's offer.

Within one-half hour, Grant was reading the paperwork and witnessing John's X, alongside Liz's own witness signature. A totally bewildered John was soon on his way back to the livery with a folded piece of paper in his pocket. A paper that gave the legal description of the property the old barn sat on and certification that the new owner was John. Liz had at first objected to the title being in a single name.

"What's your family name John."

"Got's no other name Miss. John be all. Jes' John."

That wasn't entirely true but with the horrors of slavery and the confusion brought on by freedom, John saw no solid purpose in using the name assigned to his family. He hadn't needed to up until then. After thinking about it, Liz made the title out to Mr. John, as if that was the owner's last or family name. No one was about to object.

The paper gave him ownership of the land and buildings. Grant studied John on the way back to the barn and chuckled with one of his rare laughs.

"John, I don't believe I've ever seen a man so startled. You walked to that office hoping for some kind of a solution and you return owning the land and building. I'm happy for you. And myself too if you'll let me stay on."

The sheriff never came back. John expected that the news of his purchase had gone from City Hall to the Sheriff's office without delay. In truth, it had traveled much further than that but John, in his simple understanding of life, had no idea that he had become well known, simply by folk's generous use of their free time in visiting and gossiping.

A few days later, John and Caleb were in the loft spreading and stacking a new load of hay as the farmer forked it up off his hay wagon. The same farmer would be bringing three more loads, readying the livery for the winter months.

Caleb was clearly distracted and perhaps worried. John tried again to get the man's story but Caleb wouldn't talk.

The next day Caleb was nowhere to be found. He was usually up and washing at the pump when John found his way out of the tiny office where he had been sleeping on the repaired bunk. But that morning John found himself alone. Nor was the man seen again around Fort Worth. Not for many weeks. John and Grant both had their theories on Caleb's story with no way to prove the accuracy of either one.

Hammond Gates and the other men returned in mid-September for their horses and cattle. When they heard John's story, there were congratulations and handshakes all around.

Business remained good enough for John to add some trade horses and a buggy. Folks wishing to save a few miles on horseback, or to ride out with a young lady on some private venture, could rent the buggy. The horses were for either renting by the day or for sale and trade.

The first and most frequent customer for the buggy was the blacksmith, although John couldn't bring himself to ask for the rent money. He was often seen driving into the countryside with Miss Liz from the town office. John never asked and Grant chose not to discuss the matter.

There was no shortage of white men who resented a black man owning property and a business. John managed to escape most of the racial issues by avoiding being seen, except at his own livery and the Mexican cantina. Only rarely did he venture further into town and then only when he needed something for the business.

And so, the months went by and it was soon approaching a full year that John had first arrived in Texas. But he had never allowed his desire to be a cowboy and cattleman die out. He longed to be astride a horse, riding cow country where he could sense and feel the freedom of space and the open range.

Caleb returned as secretly as he had left. Although he was permitted access to the loft for sleeping, there was no offer of a job. John didn't mind being busy. And he didn't object to hard work. He had known nothing but work all his life. And he surely liked not having to share his meager income with anyone. Livery stables were not noted for gathering riches.

Chapter 34

Tyler Tubbs, owner of the Triple T Ranch, which Tubbs himself referred to simply as the 'the T', rolled his big, high sided wagon up to the open doors of the stable. John heard the jingle of trace chains and stepped to the door opening.

"Morn'n Boss."

Tubbs responded as if the listener just might be deaf.

"Morn'n," he hollered. "Lost a shoe. Heard there was a smithy here."

The face behind the fully loaded voice was weighed down with sun reddened skin, more wrinkles than a man could count, and a big grin. It was topped off with a grease-smeared, grey bowler hat. Tubbs called it his town hat. It was the kind of head covering that could start saloon fights if worn by a greenhorn. But a sober second look at the wagon master's big hands, his flinty, no-nonsense eyes and his much-broken nose, would warn off all but the most foolhardy challengers. And that's assuming the challenger first failed to notice the big .44 Colt with the badly scratched and abused wooden grips, nestled in an oversized holster on Tubb's left hip, situated for a right-hand cross draw. The rancher found the weapon came more easily to hand that way when he was sitting either a wagon seat or a saddle.

"Yassir, Boss, jest inta de big shed. Name be Grant. He do de good work."

Tubbs hollered 'thank you' with a half wave as he pulled the team away from the door and stopped again at the shed entrance. Stiffly, he swung to the ground and disappeared into the smithy, his horse-bowed legs showing the passage of time and his many hours a-saddle. John went back to his work.

In less than a minute, Grant swung the larger doors open on both ends of his smithy.

"Bring him right on in."

Tubbs walked back out and unhitched one of the big Clydesdales, a beautiful light bay animal with four white stockings and lightly feathered hoofs. Grant stood aside as the big brute was led into the forge-warmed shed. The layout of the space allowed the animal to be led straight through the shoeing shed, in one door and out the other, after the work was completed. There was no need to coerce the horse into backing out.

Tubbs stood and watched for a short while, visiting over the noise of the shop, and then went in search of John. He walked down the center aisle in the dimly lit barn until he saw the Black livery man in a stall, brushing down one of his trade horses.

"Smithy tells me your name's John. I'm Tubbs, Tyler Tubbs. Triple T ranch, over to the big bend of the Brazos."

Tubbs laughed at his own joke before saying, "Course, the ol' Brazos ain't much more'n twists and bends. Comes mighty near to meeting itself a time or two. Feller might need a sight more information if'n he was sett'n out to visit the T. All the while assuming he didn't have the time, nor the inclination to tour the country, look'n round one bend and then another."

The two men exchanged knowing grins before Tubbs continued his talk. Rancher Tubbs hadn't had a new victim to share his many insights, and his thoughts on life with, for some months. Since his last visit to Fort Worth, to be exact. John became the unwilling recipient of some of his pent-up talk.

"Got a piece of rid'n work needs doin'. Back out to the T. Two, three months for a man as what wants to rush back to the big city. To take in the lights and throw away his wages, don't ya know.

"Steady on, fer a man as what wants to live free, enjoying the openness of the great outdoors. Not tripping over strangers and having nosy, gossiping folks get'n in the way most every which way a man turns.

"Could use, probably, four men.

"Don't get to town more'n twice to the year. Jest come in fer supplies. And that's only when the cook, that would be Mrs. Tubbs, is threatening to fry up some bacon grease and sawdust from around the firewood pile, less'n I gits to town and comes back with a wagon load of fix'ns.

Mrs. Tubbs, she ain't been to town in a while. Scares her, she says, see'n all these folks to one place. 'Ain't natural', is what she says. 'Land everywhere and all these folks piled one on top of the other'. Don't feel so much different from that my own self.

"Don't really know folks in these parts. Not more than one or two anyway. The banker, who I trust to hold onta my small stash of cash money, what's left after the Confederates went and lost the war, wouldn't be much help a-horseback. And I wouldn't trust lawyer Barnes, who I, unfortunately, have a passing knowledge of, outa my sight. Steal a sheep, that man would, and deny the steal'n, and with him caught lead'n the poor animal away on a rope.

"No, I'm look'n to hire me three, four good men. Riders. Fellas that ain't hon'n to see the lights of the big city every time they takes a bath. T's pretty much sett'n all to itself out there in the hills. Good country. Water close by. Grass about everywhere a man might ride. Well, you get the picture."

John wondered if the man was going to have to stop to catch his breath or if he would just keep on talking. He kept on talking, with barely a hesitation.

"Got a few neighbors. Couple of 'em ain't more than just a good day's ride away. Close enough to figure them as friends. Comanche or two from time to time. Gotta keep our eyes open. Good place for strong men.

"Chance you might know of any such men?"

John's mind was whirling as the two studied each other. He had trouble taking in the rush of words but he felt he caught the most of it.

The reluctant livery operator felt no pull at all to the lights of Fort Worth. And being a property owner and business manager was becoming a shoulder bending burden. He could put it all behind him and never look back, without regret. He was sure of that.

He studied Tubbs intently before deciding that he liked the man. His openness and simplicity appealed to John. He pushed the thought of Comanches aside while he dredged up his original plans, or maybe they were no more than 'hope fors', or perhaps it was just a far-off dream. Dreams left over from when he and Lefty were traveling and talking. Back nigh onto two years ago or more. 'Go to Texas. Get a riding job. Be a cowboy. Ride free.' That was the dream.

"Tell Ol' John what the work is that ya'll needs doi'n, Boss. Might could be I close up de livery and ride out wit' you. That be guess'n you don' mind work'n wit de black man."

The thought of Caleb again came to John.

"Could be 'nother rider listen to yer story. 'Nother Black feller. Good rider."

Tubbs's eyes lit up at the thought of finding two riders before he even got all the way into town.

"Never worked with no black man. Don't much care about yer skin. Care more about the work y'all can do. Ride'n. Gathr'n' ornery brutes out'n the scrub and the hollows and the gullies. Try'n te not get yerselves kilt in the doin' of it. I purely hate hav'n ta bury a good man. Can take up to a good part of a whole work'n day.

"Lotta wild cattle on the loose. Could catch 'em and turn 'em inta cash money if'n I had the men that could handle the job. And that's on top of the "T" herd that's already scattered to who knows where, out in them there hills. Critters we caught and hot-iron branded over the years.

"Got two good men on the payroll now. Jest need the three or four more to round 'er out.

"Mostly me and my son did the catching and branding. Trev, that's my son, he's off on a drive. Him and a small crew of riders. Took a bunch up the line, Nebraska, they call the place. Story is, there's a good market up there. Been gone a while and no news. Hope to see him home soon.

"Anyway, Trev and me, we made a few steers outa some big ol' bulls too. And lots of young ones that didn't understand yet that they were bulls. Now, that there ain't a job fer the delicate of mind ner muscle.

"Ain't been seen, the most of em, fer some time. Like ta lose theirselves in the outback. Gotta be a big bunch of heavy calves runn'n loose by this time. Ready for market, I'm guessing. Or close to it. That's all the while supposing we didn't steer up every last one of them bulls."

Tubbs again laughed at his own joke before repeating, "Pretty much ready fer market, them steers, and some of the calves too, I'm guess'n.

"Plan ta go ta gather'n some wild horses from

outa the back country too. That's after we gits the cattle rounded up. Leastwise, them as what ain't gathered along with the cattle. Break'n 'em fer ridn'. Maybe-so bring'n some ta town fer ta sell te the folks as what needs a saddle animal."

"Any of that appeal to you, John?"

John's answer was a big grin.

"You do da buying of de flour 'n sech that ye came ta town fer. Come back an see Ol' John. I tries to find Caleb. Maybe so, you find other men in town. Maybe find riders, you ask Fernando. He be de cook at de cantina. Across de way dere. Lots a riders be eat'n dat place. Maybe so Caleb and Ol' John come catch de wild ho'ses fer you. You come back by 'n by."

"I'll do that John. Wouldn't that be a hoot for the gossips and loose tongue fools to talk up? The "T" hiring two Black riders and the others be Mex's."

He didn't really sound as if the gossips would dominate much of his thinking.

Laughing out loud, Tubbs walked his bandy-legged walk out of the livery and into the smithy. Grant was just putting his tools away when Tubbs entered the shop.

"All done?"

Grant lifted the re-shod hoof and gave time for Tubbs to study it.

"Good work, Grant. I wish I could do it as well."

"Checked all the others too. Re-clenched a couple of nails on that other bay, outside. You should be good for a long while."

Tubbs led the gentle giant out of the smithy and

back to the wagon. Its mate waited patiently in the shade of the shed roof. When the freshly shod horse was back in place, Tubbs returned to the smithy.

"What do I owe you, Grant."

Grant named the price and Tubbs paid the amount over, adding an extra dime.

"Good work Grant. And that bit will buy you a cool drink as a thanks for gett'n right at it."

Taking a quick look around the corner, towards the big livery doors, and seeing no one, Tubbs turned again to Grant.

"Can I ask you about John?"

Grant made no audible reply. He simply turned his eyes to Tubbs as if to say, 'ask away'.

Tubbs repeated most of his conversation with John. Grant nodded a time or two during the telling. Tubbs closed out his lengthy statement with, "What's your true thought, Grant? Could John and his friend, Caleb, be the men for the job?"

Grant, never a man to rush his way through life, took a longer study of the questioner than he had before. On their first meeting, the main interest had been the big horse's needs. The animal's owner didn't much matter so long as he had the few coins needed to cover the cost. With the questions about John, that had changed.

What else had changed over the months was Grant's thoughts about his Black landlord. Change was grinding only slowly through the country after the war. It was no different for the big smithy.

He had found a liking for John at their very first meeting. Since that time, he had come to not only like the black man but to respect him which is much harder to come by than most folks would own up to. With so much still unsettled around the country, without really thinking about it, the smithy had become somewhat protective of John.

While no one had threatened open violence towards John or set the stable on fire, neither had anyone offered anything resembling friendship. A few white riders had turned away when faced with a Black hostler. But more had stayed and later, spoke their appreciation for the good care their animals received. The smithy wondered how much acceptance had been built on the fact that he, himself, was there. A few times, hearing loud, questioning voices outside, he had walked to the smithy door and simply stood there, his leather apron and smoke smeared face, clearing stating, without speaking aloud, that he would tolerate no foolishness. It was usually enough to end whatever doubts the rider held.

Considering all of those facts as clearly as he could, Grant said, "Friend, you couldn't hire a better man than John. I've talked with the folks he came west with, handling their horses all the way from Tennessee. They sang his praises as a man and as a horseman, both.

"Being busy with the stable, neither of us gets much riding in but I can tell you, John knows horses. Knows them and likes them. And the few times he's had a horse needing care he seemed to know exactly what to do. Never saw anyone beat him on a trade either.

"I don't know as much about Caleb. Comes and goes. Good rider though. I've seen enough to say that. Follows John around like a puppy. Almost seems afraid of something. Has a way of disappearing, time to time. A visit from the sheriff, seeking to rent John's buggy, sent Caleb scooting out the back door. Didn't see him for two days after. You might want to have him face up to what's troubling him before you take him to the back country."

Tubbs thanked the smithy and left on his buying trip. Grant went back to work but it was only a few minutes later that John walked into the little shop. He didn't seem to know how to start the conversation, so Grant helped him out.

"Hear the rancher needs some riders."

"He be want'n four riders fer de ranch far out te de west. Not many folks out dat way, he say. Lots of de wild cattle 'n horses to catch up and bring in. Hid'n in de hills, he say."

"And are you interested in that work John?"

"I goin take de job if'n he offer, an if'n you wants ta buy de barn."

The thought of buying the property hadn't occurred to Grant. He was a little taken back at first mention. Knowing John needed an answer, he said, "Don't know as I can find enough money to buy the barn, John. Anyway, you have a good business going here. I'm pretty sure you're making more money than Tubbs will pay you.

"Are you sure you want to do this? This land and barn are going to be worth some serious money one day soon, sitting right here on the town's main street."

"Yassir, Boss. I be sell'n if'n de job be real. Rancher, he be com'n back, by 'n by ta talk agin. I got's ta find Caleb. Maybe-so be de job fer de bot' of us."

"What do you think the barn is worth John?"

John, who had always been quick with numbers laid out a figure.

"Dat be fo' de barn, de horses an' de buggy."

Grant studied him while his slower mind sorted out what he had in his pocket and in the tin can hidden away in the shop. He came up a bit short.

"Can't put my fingers on that much right now my friend. But I could give you most of it and get the rest to you next time you come to town."

"Dat be a'right. We talk agin, after de rancher, he come back."

Grant nodded his acceptance and said, "You go find Caleb. I'll keep an eye on the stable."

Chapter 35

It turned out that Caleb was sitting in the shade at the back of the barn whittling on a piece of dried-out barn siding. As he often did, he had returned quietly and simply settled in. John was heading to the Mexican cantina in search of the man when he saw him sitting there.

"Why for you sit der, not say you be back? I be goin' look fer you."

Caleb clearly had no answer and John got weary of waiting for the man to talk. There was work needed doing.

"Come in de barn. I's got de work and we gots ta talk some."

With John back to cleaning and currying horses and Caleb listening carefully, John outlined what rancher Tubbs had said.

"You be interested in de work in de lonesome ranch? Work wit de horses and de cows?"

Caleb allowed as how that would suit him fine if

it included a bunk and regular meals.

"You be stay'n here den. Rancher, he be back by 'n by. We's listen agin ta him."

Chapter 36

A couple of hours later, Tubbs hollered his way back into the barn. Walking beside him were two Mexicans. One was a slight, tough-looking man wearing colorful clothing topped off with a large, striped serape, lying over one shoulder and tucked under a braided belt made from a series of multicolored homespun woolen yarns, with a single knot at the front.

Also tucked under the woven belt was his loose-fitting shirt, held tight to his small waist. Over it all was a pistol and holster hanging from a second belt, this one made of leather. John knew nearly nothing of guns and could not guess what kind of weapon it was.

The second man was larger, broad in the shoulders with a flare of belly pushing his shirt outward. He too had a colorful, woven cloth draped over his shoulder and tucked under a braided woolen belt, similar to what his friend was wearing. He wore a pistol that looked to John's untrained eye to be the match for his friend's.

Both men wore tight-fitting pants that flared out, at the bottom, to cover all but the toes of their scuffed riding boots and resting on their large, multi-roweled spurs at the back.

Neither man wore the big, unwieldy sombreros that John had seen on other Mexican riders. They seemed to have taken on the look of the typical western rider with the smaller brimmed Stetson style hat that had exploded in popularity with the westward migration.

The larger of the two held a lit cigarette between his clenched lips. John hesitated and then said, "Best you takes de fire outside de barn."

He was growing past his habit of addressing most others, those he considered as equals, as 'Boss', holding that title in reserve for those who had risen to the point of leadership.

The two men held their stares on each other in a short battle of wills. Tubbs was quick to pick up on the matter and appreciate the contest between two men who were struggling for acceptance in a white world. It was almost a contest for second place in the hierarchy of race. He glanced quickly from one to the other, hiding his grin under his unruly mustache.

John had no intention of allowing smoking anywhere near his barn. He had stared down several white riders before and he wasn't backing down for the Mexican.

Finally, in an unspoken half-acceptance of the hostler's order, the Mexican slowly removed the cigarette from his lips and pinched the fire off the end with his rope and leather-toughened fingers, letting it drop to the dirt floor. With a quick and simple glance downward, the big man toed out the offending tobacco and rubbed it into the dirt. He dropped the remaining portion of the cigarette into his shirt pocket.

John nodded his acceptance, knowing that to ask for more was to cause unnecessary conflict. If slavery had taught him nothing else, it had taught him acceptance. A battle half won was a far sight better than a battle lost.

Tubbs expelled his held breath and said, "John, I need you to meet these men." Motioning towards the smaller of the two, he said, "This here is Alejandro. The other goes by Jorge. Call themselves vaqueros. That's cowboy in American."

Jorge turned with a grim look at his new employer.

"Vaqueros be mucho man with horse and cow. More so than cowboys." He said the word, 'cowboys' with a bit of a sneer.

Wondering what he was getting himself into, Tubbs said, "Well, we'll have to see. Got a couple of pretty good men on the payroll already. Right salty when circumstances call for it. I ain't half bad at the job my own self."

Wishing to move on with the introductions, he said, "John, here is known as a horseman. Don't know this other fella", he added, pointing at Caleb.

The big vaquero was clearly not finished his climb to supremacy of the cowboy ranks. He dismissed the two Black men with a disdainful look and a shrug. John caught all the actions and words and understood immediately what was going on. Always a man of peace whenever possible, he spoke to the two vaqueros.

"I know the horse and a little bit the cow. Maybe you teach Ol' John the rope."

The question had a way of settling everyone down. The smaller of the two men grinned and replied, "I teach. Jorge, he not so good as me with the rope. The lariat."

Tubbs, catching Alejandro's grin roared with laughter. It took a few seconds but both Mexicans finally joined in with grins and shrugs.

Tubbs tried to pull it all together with another question.

"Any of you fellas object to working with a man that's not the same color as yourself? Or sleeping in the same bunkhouse? Can't have ya rid'n all the ways out to the "T" and then hav'n problems. If'n ya got a problem, best ya stays in town."

When no one spoke, Tubbs motioned to Caleb

"I take it John, that this man is interested in signing on for a job of work."

"Yassir Boss. Dis be Caleb."

"Well, Caleb, what's your story? Are you a rider?"

"Never been a animal Caleb cain't set on an ride, Boss."

"Well, that's fine Caleb. But we only have your word for that. You understand that if you can't measure up, I'll pay you off and you can make your way back to town?"

"Dat be fine Boss. I do good work fer you."

"All right, but I'm told that you ran off when the

sheriff came around. What's that all about, young man? Are you running from the law?"

Caleb flashed a lost look at John, not knowing how to answer. He wanted the job but he was still scared. He thought he might have hidden it but, clearly, he hadn't. Again, John took the lead.

"You have to tell de man Caleb. No job until you be honest. I sees you be sceired a' something. Best you jest say what it be."

Caleb glanced around the circle of men before asking, in a quiet voice, "Be der de man catchers out to de ranch?"

John looked at the man in wonder but it was Tubbs that answered.

"Are you asking about slave catchers, Caleb? Ain't no more slave catchers. Ain't been a single one since over a full year ago. Don't understand how you wouldn't know that. I take it you ran away and you been living in fear ever since. Is that how it is?"

Caleb couldn't lift his eyes from the dirt floor. He said nothing. But John did.

"Boss be right, Caleb. You be free man. You and me bot'. No more be slaves. No more be scared of de white man. No more be runn'n away."

Caleb still didn't raise his head but he spoke quietly, "Dat be de trute?"

John and Tubbs answered almost in unison.

"Yes, dat be true.

"That's God's truth, Caleb."

Into the following silence, they all heard the black man sniff and shudder before he turned and headed out the back door.

Chapter 37

It took two more days for Tubbs to complete his buying and for John to sign the property over to Grant. Leaving the wagon parked beside the general store's loading dock, Tubbs brought the big team to the stable for John's care.

Each of the newly hired men did some personal buying, laying in a supply of new pants and shirts and whatever small items they desired to have, knowing there would be no more trips to town for many months. In the privacy of John's small office and sleeping room, he counted out enough coins for Caleb to outfit himself. The two men went together to do their buying. Caleb had no experience at all with the spending of money except for a few coins at the cantina. He would need John's help.

Briefly, John reflected on the fact that he, himself, knew nothing at all about freedom and responsibility, a brief few months before. Now, here he was showing a fellow Black how to fend for himself.

Rosa Hammond had called it personal growth but John knew nothing about that. All he knew was that it caused a strange sensation to rise within him.

The two vaqueros took to hanging around the stable, getting to know the Black riders they would be working with. Alejandro was heard to laugh a few times as he talked with John or Caleb. Jorge acted like he still had something to prove. But he didn't light up a smoke again or test John in any other way.

Alejandro went with John to help him pick out a braided leather lariat. John purchased one at thirty feet in length and one at fifty feet. He would leave it up to rancher Tubbs to supply the ropes that Caleb would use.

Walking back to the stable, Alejandro said, "We will work with the small lariat. You will need much practice before you are ready for the other."

As they waited for the rancher to complete his business, John spent many hours behind the barn following Alejandro's instructions in the use of the braided lariat. After the first few throws, he started catching a fence post with about every second or third throw. Alejandro saddled his horse and told John to watch as he spurred the animal past the corral. With three swirls around his own head and a flick of the wrist, from the back of the running horse, he had the fence post caught firmly.

He grinned as he rode back to the barn, coiling his long lariat.

"Be more trouble when the cow, she be running in the brush. Fence post not run so fast."

John and Caleb, both watching the performance,

knew they would be a while learning that part of their new trade.

The last purchase Tubbs insisted John and Caleb make was for a belt gun and holster.

"Don't put it on here in town. There's still likely to be some hard feeling about Blacks carrying guns. Best we don't push our luck. But, on the trip home, we'll get you some practice in. Man needs a weapon in that back country. Lots of ways for a fella to get in trouble, without you count in the Comanche. Could come the day, you'll be happy to have a weapon close to hand.

"You'll need a saddle gun too, but I have enough back to the spread to outfit y'all. Like to keep the "T" prepared. Man never knows."

The rancher called the four new hands into a group, standing in the aisle of the barn.

"I've need of talking with y'all to once. Just so's we all understand. We cain't have no misunderstandings nor any trouble out to the "T".

"You take my pay, you ride my horses, you sleep in my bunkhouse, you put your feet under Mrs. Tubb's table, that all adds up to you rid'n for the "T" brand. The day should come you can't ride for the "T", or you get lonesome fer town, you let me know. I'll pay you off and wish you luck. No hard feelings. You ever ride against the "T", I'll shoot you dead and leave you where you lay as an example to others. And don't you ever doubt that."

Tubbs had more to say but a sneering Jorge interrupted, "You think you *hombre malo*, you shoot Jorge?"

Before the words were fully out of Jorge's mouth, Tubbs had his pistol pressed against the man's lips, the hammer pulled back. No one really saw the rancher do anything. The weapon just seemed to be there. Tubbs' eyes were bullets almost as deadly as the .44 slugs in the Colt. It stopped the big vaquero cold. The others stood in wonder. Tubbs studied Jorge for a full half minute before he spoke again.

"Rightly, I'm a friendly man, Jorge. I never look for trouble. But it's like I said. You ever go against me; I'll shoot you dead.

"Another thing you need to know. Don't you ever misjudge Mrs. Tubbs. You choose to make a problem, you'd be best off to make it with me. That woman don't have no middle ground. She has weapons stored within reach in her kitchen and around the house. And she ain't shy about hauling them out. Why, I seen her one time, whilst I was watching from the door of the barn. She was standing on the porch, right outside her kitchen door. Standing there big as life, lay'n hot lead at the feet of three Comanche try'n ta sneak up on the house. She didn't shoot ta kill anyone, but those boys ran for their horses and was gone, just the same.

"Reason she didn't shoot to kill is, that's hard, rocky ground out there. Digg'n a hole ain't no bargain. Bein as it would be a grave don't make it no easier."

Dropping the gun back into its holster, he turned his eyes from man to man.

"Any questions?"

There didn't seem to be any.

"OK. If we all understand the situation, let's ride."

It was a long, slow three-day trek back to the Triple T. It looked to John like Tubbs may have almost bought out the general store's entire stock. The high sided wagon was loaded to the top, and covered with an oiled canvas, tightly tied down. A long, two-man crosscut saw and two new scythes were tied on top of the canvas cover.

True to his word, Tubbs introduced the Black riders to handguns after the evening meal was over and the camp put in order, on their first night away from town. Caleb picked up on the weapon fairly quickly but John had a problem. Getting the curved handle firmly settled into his big fist proved to be awkward. But the bigger problem was that his large fingers were not made for triggers and small trigger guards. He missed his targets by embarrassing distances.

Jorge watched for a few minutes and then stepped forward, lifting the gun from John's hand.

"You listen to Jorge. You watch. You learn."

Tubbs stood back, happy to give over the teaching to the big Mexican.

The second day on the trail, they started into the hills. Following the river and the faint marks of previous wagon trips to town, they pulled into the yard of the Triple T just before full dark at the end of the third day. Two men came from the bunkhouse chewing matchsticks, attracted by the rattle of trace chains and the crunch of steel-rimmed wheels grinding on the rocky road. Tubbs' shout came near to drowning out the wagon noise.

"Hello, the T. Anyone here or ya'll run off ta see the elephant?"

Tubbs barely glanced at his two long-time riders, Baylor and Austin, but at the sight of Mrs. Tubbs coming onto the covered porch, a dishtowel hanging from one hand, he dropped to the ground, fast walked to the house, leaped up onto the porch and twirled the woman around in a circle.

She swatted him with the dishrag, laughing, "You put me down, you big oaf. You'll have us both dizzy and falling off'n the porch, you keep that up."

"Wahl, it's jest so danged good ta see ya mother. Been gone a long spell. Ain't had no home cookin' nor anything else as what might keep a feller close ta home, in all that time. Is that a baked pie, I smell comm'n from yer kitchen?"

"You look to the animals and then git yourself down to the crick with a bar of soap and a towel. I'll see what's still in the oven that's fit to eat. Now git along with ya."

Chapter 38

Introducing men of different skin color to the original crew didn't expose any obvious problems. As in any situation, where new men are added to a familiar crew, trust and comradeship would take some time. And experience. Riders need to know they can depend on their riding mates. In a dangerous country, doing dangerous work, there was no room for a man who wasn't up to the task. Each man would soon know the abilities of the others. The system was self-weeding. Men who didn't measure up were soon paid off and taken from the payroll.

Tubbs was sure that if the men managed to get through a few meals and a night or two together in the bunkhouse, they would find a way to work together.

He had employed all-white crews in past days that still had problems between the strong personalities, although they managed to work effectively together. He couldn't see that mixing the races would add significantly to the problems the riders faced on the "T".

After taking on the first breakfast, served up by Mrs. Tubbs, with everyone seated around the big kitchen table, Tubbs, himself stood to his feet to fetch the newly boiled coffee pot, the second of the morning. Walking around the table refilling the big crockery mugs, he started laying out the day's work. He purposely split the new men apart.

"Baylor, I want you should take Alejandro and Caleb with you. Go south, up that big draw, for, perhaps ten miles. Then swing off to the east. Show the new men around the area a bit but don't waste all day in the doing of it. Start a gather. Been nigh on'ta two years since we emptied that country out. Time we did it again.

"Dig out everything you can easily get, cattle and horses both. We'll double back and ride further south when we've done the bulk of the first distance. I want to clean the country out for a full thirty miles. It's head shaking how far a cow critter can wander, given time. Ain't no reason to it. They'll walk right over good grass, looking for who knows what."

"Baylor and Austin, you already know this but I'll say it for the new men.

"This here is a big country, fellas. Got a bit of everything. Big, round top hills, trees to the top and down the other side. Not much grass under them trees but the beef critters find shade up there, so we have to ride them all. Some mighty rough hills, too. Rocky and steep sided. Between those hills lie acres of open grass lands. Water enough, here and there. The cattle will be broken into bunches. Have to ride every foot of that land. Good cattle country but it ain't easy. Baylor and Austin been over it many's the time. You listen to them, you won't go far wrong."

He stopped talking while he took a few steps and placed the coffee pot back on the big wood stove.

"If we ride down the whole country and then start back, we run the serious risk of gathering up an unwieldy number of animals. We'd end up having to split the herd, bringing some in while the others are left to wander again. Best we take it in manageable jumps. That will leave you combing out the country that was already worked, picking up stuff you missed the first time, as you make your way back to the ranch.

"By the time we're done, we should have everything. The crews from the other ranches will be doing the same at their ends. You'll all join up and work the center, by and by. At the end, we'll all go down together a last time to comb each area for a final look. We'll sort out the other brands from the "T" brutes as you work along.

You won't get time to bring each day's gather right to the yard but get them moving along this way. If you leave them on good grass, they should still be there in the morning. You'll be able to re-gather them without too much trouble.

"You can probably get back to the ranch in time for supper and a night in your own sack. At least for the first few days.

"Take along a change of horse each. Switch yer

saddles over, come noon time. Well shucks, you already know that, so I suppose I'm jest rambling.

"Sort the caught-out horses from the cattle and push them along home. Drop the cattle off in a bunch. We'll go back tomorrow and pick them up again.

"We'll corral the horses here. Any wild stuff that gives you trouble, let them go. We'll pick them up later too. Don't waste time on the wild horses. Right now, the money to keep the "T" operating, is in the cattle."

The rancher waited, giving time for questions or a response to the orders. When nothing was said, he turned to the other end of the table.

"Austin, I want you should take Jorge and John and go south, same as Baylor, and then angle to the west. Follow what I just said about the south and east gather. You'll all be working within a few miles of each other.

"We'll keep doing that until we're out a good way and in all directions. I want this country combed for stock.

"I'll stay in the yard or close by anyway. We need some more horse fencing. I'll take to the hills off to the north and start dropping trees, all the time hoping to find enough straight ones to get the job done. We'll take a team up later and gather them in for posts and rails."

Setting out to following orders, the men seemed to understand, without discussion, that keeping their mouths closed until they got better acquainted would be the wisest choice. The words 'nigger' and

'Mex' and other derogatory terms were carefully avoided. Tubbs made it plain he wouldn't stand for it. The older "T" hands were ready with a hard look to bring any such talk to an end.

It was on the third day of the south gather that the teasing, so common among riders, started. The first was when Alejandro said, "Senor Caleb, we are here to put the lariats on the cow. Boss man, he will tell us when he want us to rope the bush. Maybe-so you let me show you a leetle more with the rope."

"And maybe so I will show you better how to ride de horse."

Baylor burst out laughing and soon there were grins all around. Inwardly, Baylor heaved a great sigh of relief.

This was a degree of acceptance of one another that said, without using the actual words, 'you'll do'.

The crew that rode into the rougher hills to the west was hindered a bit by the pride and touchiness of Jorge. John, who had grown well past the slave thinking that would dominate so many freed men for years to come, was not easily intimidated. Owning property and running a livery business for over a year, although he didn't really enjoy the experience, was a great learning and mellowing experience.

Slowly, day by day, John did his work, learning as he rode until, finally, in the second week Jorge started to talk to him as an equal. Austin, who had led more than one crew for the "T" in times past, allowed the men to sort things out for themselves.

As the crews worked further from the ranch, they each took a small wagon along to carry bedding, extra clothing, camp fixings and food. It turned out that Alejandro was a fair to middling cook although the supplies sent along were a good bit short on chilis for his liking.

The west side crew was less fortunate. When asked about cooking, John smiled at Austin.

"Best yo do it yo'self, Boss. I's not much as de cook."

Jorge didn't offer and wasn't asked. Austin finally took on the task. He figured the only thing keeping the others from complaining about what was piled onto their plates was the fear of being assigned to the job themselves.

Looking the situation over as the weeks slowly passed, Tubbs figured they had driven in fewer horses but more cattle than he had figured on. Many of the beef animals already held the Triple T brand. A few held the brands of neighboring ranchers. The neighbors' animals were turned loose and pushed back as they found them. When the calves of the neighboring animals could be identified, they were turned out with the cows. As hungry as he was for beef animals, Tubbs had no intention of claiming another man's calves.

The cattle would be pushed to the big, grassed plain beside the "T" ranch yard. There they would be held until the gather was completed, with Tubbs himself, riding around the gather occasionally, to push back any wanderers.

Clearing the country of animals took the most of

two months. Horses and men, both, were worn to a nub. It required all the saddle animals the "T" could offer to keep the hard-working men mounted.

In the final three weeks, Tubbs pulled the two crews together and had them do a last, full sweep. The crews from the close-by ranches had all worked together to sort out the branded stock and any big, ready to wean calves that were clearly following a branded cow.

In all that time, there had been no race issues between the men that they couldn't work out.

Tubbs hated to leave Mrs. Tubbs alone at the ranch but he did it anyway, just for a few days, long enough to ride to the farthest gathering point. There, together with the neighboring ranchers, they did the final sorting.

Chapter 39

The home corrals were crowded with horses. Most wore the small Triple T brand, although at least half of those hadn't been seen for the past year or more. There were, perhaps, twenty animals that had been running free in the hills, unclaimed and unbranded. They were wild, in a sense, but mingling with the ranch horses had taken a bit of the wild out of them although they still showed little inclination towards accepting confinement.

Four animals, three mares and a dark bay stallion, were showing no sign at all of accepting their captivity. They had caused no undue concern during the drive when they were bunched with other, familiar animals. But in the confines of the high-railed corral, they panicked as if finally understanding their loss of freedom. It was a light grey mare who was the leader.

Their constant rushing from one side of the corral to the other and the bugling of the stallion had the animals in both corrals acting up.

Tubbs, standing outside the corral, looked up at John as he sat a ranch gelding, inside the big corral.

"What do you think John?"

Dat stallion, he be ter'n de fence down. Him or dat grey mare. Might be best you jest turn dem out. De stallion and de mares, all of dem. None never be good work'n horse. Better dey be in de hills mak'n de foals. By 'n by you catch de foals."

Tubbs was slow answering. Studying John while he chewed on a straw of dried grass, his foot on the bottom corral rail, his arms folded in front of him, resting on the top rail. He thumbed his hat brim back and studied the animals. Finally, he answered John.

"I know you're right John but I sure like the looks of that horse. Don't believe I've ever seen an animal with better lines. He could fill our barn with sale-able foals, given time. He'd be a problem though. We can both see that.

"We could probably geld him and make a saddle animal out of him, eventually, once he forgot about the ladies. But that would be a criminal waste of good horseflesh. And then, we already have the yearling foals that were following those mares. So that's something of his, at least."

Another minute went past while the two men thought the situation over. With the light of an idea being born shining from Tubb's eyes, he half turned towards John. Speaking with a grin, he said, "No, we'll not geld him but there's nothing stopping us from claiming him for the T. Him and the mares with him. That will make their get, ours too."

Turning towards the men who were branding cattle, knowing he would need the best ropers on the ranch, he called out, his voice booming, as it usually did, "Alejandro. Jorge." With a beckoning arm, he summoned them to the horse corral.

Raising his voice even higher and taking a step towards the fire he hollered out, "Baylor. Let the cattle go for a bit. Horses com'n your way."

Baylor looked up and nodded.

The Mexican riders had been doing most of the roping for the branding crew. Now they could show their worth with the horses.

"You men reckon you can get a rope on that stallion? I figure to haul him down to the fire. Throw him and brand him. The "T" brand will mark him as ours, him and those three mares that are causing trouble. John will work with you."

It took a wild, hoof stomping half hour and all the rope skills the vaqueros could dig out of their lengthy experience but, finally, the beautiful bay stallion lay on the ground beside the fire, firmly trussed. At the touch of the hot iron, the animal let out a scream of pain and indignation, thrashing against the ropes, and thumping his head against the dust and filth of the branding grounds.

Tubbs figured the pain would last only a short while. The anger and fear of man would follow the horse all his days.

In order to keep the newly branded horses together, Tubbs had the stallion secured in a small, unused corral. He was pushed into the confining space and turned loose.

It was the work of another full hour for the men to get the Triple T brand on the three mares. The stallion was threatening to kick his way to freedom before the ordeal was completed.

Everyone involved, men and horses alike, were exhausted.

Calling the entire crew together and instructing them to spread out, holding the cattle tightly while the four freshly branded renegades were let out of the corral, Tubbs looked the situation over carefully. Finding it to his satisfaction, he said, "John, turn them out. You and Caleb ride them off the property and into the hills. When they're safely off the ranch, let them be, and make your way back here. Lunch will be ready.

Chapter 40

With the cattle sorted and branded, the market animals were held on the big grass flat, to the west of the headquarters buildings. John and Caleb would hold them there.

The breeding stock and the newborns were turned back into the hills.

Tubbs wanted the cows and bulls pushed several miles away, into a grassed valley that had yet to be grazed that spring. He went along with the crew, returning home once the cattle arrived, while the men stayed on to check the area for water holes and see to the animals' wellbeing for a couple of days.

Arriving back at the Triple T, Tubbs dismounted outside the open barn door with the intention of leading his gelding into the dim interior. Immediately, he spotted two animals carrying strange brands stalled close to the door. Another, with the Triple T showing on its left hip, he hadn't seen for some time.

He viewed the T animal with a mixture of hope and concern. Never walking if he could ride, he stepped back into the saddle and kicked his gelding into a fast trot towards the house. As he neared the white-painted yard fence, he leaped from the saddle, the beginnings of rheumatism causing his knees to sag. He caught himself before he fell, staggered a bit and then dropped the reins, leaving the horse to pick at the grass around the bottom of the fence.

He was rushing towards the porch stairs when the kitchen door was flung open. He stopped his forward motion so quickly he came close to tripping.

"Afternoon Pa. We been wondering when you'd get home. You been tak'n a nap under a bush out by the river? Tak'n it easy while all the rest of the world is hard at work?"

"Trev? Why look at ya, son. I hardly knowed you. Look'n good though."

In three long steps Tubbs' son was across the porch and descending the worn wooden stairs two at a time.

What started as a handshake ended up being a firm hug, a most unusual demonstration of emotion from the stiff-necked Tubbs. Finally, the two men parted, and each took a step back.

"Good to see you, Pa. Good to be home too. Ma seems to be fair'n well. Been a long time. The most of a year since I rode out."

Mrs. Tubbs came to the door with a welcoming smile.

"Come in here you two. And call the others.

Dinner's about ready to be put on the table."

"Be right there, Ma. Just have to look after this horse Pa left to wander. You'd think a man his age would know better."

He didn't try very hard to hide his grin as he spoke to his mother.

As Trev picked up the dragging reins, his father burst out, "Why you young punk, hardly past yer wean'n and here you're trying ta…"

The laughter from Trev and his mother drowned out whatever else Tubbs might have intended to say.

Trev led the horse to the water trough and then to the barn. When he came back out, he was followed by two riders. One was Black. His parents were still standing on the porch, waiting.

"Pa, you need to meet Buck and Sol. Ma's already met them. Picked these boys up on the way north with that sale herd. Stuck with me all the way into Nebraska. Held the herd on good Nebraska grass. Stayed together through some almighty miserable winter weather, holding the animals against their temptation to wander. Rode back south together after we got the herd sold and off our hands. Thought perhaps we'd find a place for them on the "T". They've proven up, to my liking. Figured they'd fit in, rid'n this rough country."

Tubbs went from one man to another, shaking hands.

"Good to have you boys here. And thanks for hanging in with the herd. Ain't real fond of cold weather my own self. Gets cold enough here from time to time but it don't last like I hear tell about that north country.

"Set yourselves down ta lunch. We'll find a place for you in the crew, sure enough."

With that, Tubbs ran the iron bar around the triangle hanging from a porch beam. The clanging iron would call John and Caleb to the table.

Chapter 41

There was a bit of awkwardness and newness for John and Caleb, sitting around the big table with the family and the new riders. John had noticed Sol studying him several times during the meal, glancing from Caleb, to himself and back again. Nothing was said but John knew there would be questions from the Black rider from the north when opportunity allowed.

Tubbs, known to his family and crew as a thinking, plotting, planning man, was not secretive. He held little about the affairs or plans of the "T" from the crew and nothing at all from the family. While the men pushed their chairs back and stretched out, as they enjoyed their fresh coffee, he took the opportunity to bring his newly arrived son into the picture with the horses.

"Hired John on mostly to work the horses. Him and Caleb both. Came highly recommended. Met the two of them on the last trip to the big city.

Swung over to the cattle during the roundup," he reported in his usual disjointed fashion. "Round-up was later this spring than usual. Seems no one took the trouble to organize it. Finally, got er done though.

"But you need to keep in mind, Trev, that John and Caleb were brought on mainly to work horses. They're not needed on the summer crew. We plan to keep them in the yard to bring the horses to where they can be sold off, hoping all the time to make a profit for the "T".

"We drove in fourteen branded "T" horses, most-ly geldings. Just the three mares. On top of that, the boys brought in thirty-two unbranded animals. Wild stuff but not particularly unruly, except for four of the beasts. Turned that four back a short while ago. Prettiest stallion I ever did see. Don't know how he hasn't shown up before this time. Three of his harem. Those three had almost full-grown foals trail'n 'em. Good looking animals. We held the young ones back and branded them for the "T". John and Caleb will be throwing the leather on them soon as they have a bit more size to them.

"We gelded the poorest of the two. Left the other colt whole. Might grow into a herd sire for someone, given time. The third is a filly. We'll hold her over for breeding. Should get some good stock from that bunch, by 'n by."

"What are you hoping for the horses, Pa? We don't really need them on the T."

"With the war fading into memory and the land filling up with farmers and cattlemen, they'll be a need for good riding and working stock. John and Caleb are going to gentle-break and train that stock so's anyone can ride 'em, man, woman or child. We get maybe ten readied for market, we'll take them to Fort Worth. Hopefully come home with a saddlebag sagg'n heavy with gold."

Tubbs then enjoyed a good laugh. Trev and his mother, understanding the man and his sense of humor, enjoyed the laugh with him, knowing he wasn't in the habit of riding the open country with saddlebags of gold coin. Not when there was a choice of banks in Fort Worth.

The four riders looked on with quizzical expressions.

"Now, Trev, you get your men settled into the bunkhouse. No reason they couldn't take a break for a day, after your long trail to home. After that, they can relieve John and Caleb with the cattle so's those two can go back to the horses.

The rest of the crew will be rid'n in by 'n by. Then we'll sort out the summer's work. One of the things we'll be doing is building a few more corrals. But that can wait a day or two yet.

"You get those boys settled out, you come back to the porch. Your mother and I will want to hear about your trip north.

It seemed the capacity for coffee was never ending as was the situation on most of the west. Mrs. Tubbs brought a fresh pot and some clean mugs, setting it on an uneven ceramic tile, causing it to rock a bit as she set it down. She took her own seat as Trev poured the steaming brew. He lifted his own mug to his mouth, took a small sip, and deciding it was too hot, set it back down and started to tell about the north country.

"Great cattle country up there, Pa. Wide open. Grass everywhere. Water only where you find it. Can't depend on the streams or even the rivers. Rivers can be wide, but not deep. Need a bit of rain to keep them flowing. Often running towards dry, come to be late in the summer. Have to watch for the gyp water.

"Cold. Almighty cold, come winter. But she's opening up. Wagon loads of far-seeing men, with their women and kids showing up steady, taking up land and putting down roots. What with the rails being built across the territory, I expect they'll be dropping off homesteaders by the thousands in a year or two.

"Already a good smattering of cattlemen making their way into the land. Enough to have a few skirmishes over grazing borders and such. Of course, none of them owns the land they claim. But in their minds, they do. A lot of the cattle are scrubs. More horn than beef. Stuff pushed out of the breaks and the hollows and driven north by smaller, independent drovers. Hardly worth the trouble, as poor as a lot of them are.

"My understanding is that the best of the range animals have already been claimed and branded for the big outfits, down south.

"Like new country everywhere it seems, there's bound to be some head butting from time to time, as things get sorted out. To avoid getting mixed up in any of that, we kept the herd away from the settlements so we had no trouble."

Tubbs listened carefully and then asked, "Am I hearing you say there's a market for a better grade of beef animal?"

"I would say that's the most promising market. There's animals enough up there already to feed the population. And the costs of driving or shipping a good animal is the same as shipping a poor one. But the end price would be different. Makes sense to me that a rancher should want the best. Bulls, at least. Might could breed the herd up, given time, with good bulls."

"Where did you make your sale?"

"Cheyenne. That's in what they're calling Wyoming. Of course, neither Wyoming nor Nebraska are states yet. But that will soon enough come. Cheyenne is a pretty good town. I was told there's near enough four thousand folks there now. Lots of excitement about rail construction. Army is trying to keep the cattlemen from moving further west. Still some Indian trouble out that way. Of course, no one is listening to the army. The voice of free land and grass shouts louder than any army.

"All high country up there. Snow-capped mountains off to the west. Land sits at six thousand feet according to the railway surveyors. Wind blows most of the time."

Trev's mother waited for an opening in the talk and then said, "That's a powerful bunch of beef animals the crew have on the west flats. More than enough to make up a good drive, I should think. Is there still a market up there worth the chase?"

Tubbs nodded at his wife's question and then added to it.

"We couldn't get more than, maybe nine, ten dollars a head for them here. By what you told us you sold the herd for after the drive to this here Cheyenne you talked about, it sounds like it might be worth taking this bunch north."

"No doubt there's money to be made in a drive Pa. It's a bit late in the year to be starting out but we could make Cheyenne before full winter came upon us if we got right to it. And provided all went well on the drive.

"Mind you, like I just said, all that country sits at six thousand feet and more. Being that high and that far north, winter just might come in July.

"I asked a fella when we first got there if it snowed much. He just laughed and shook his head. Said, 'You don't like snow, you won't much enjoy Cheyenne, nor anywhere else in Wyoming.'

"But the clear answer to your question is 'yes', we can improve the price of beef over the Fort Worth price. Probably by a considerable margin. Of course, if we were to get on north of there, to Montana and the gold fields, we could raise the price even more. But it's really late in the year for that. It's another long drive from Cheyenne to the gold fields of Montana or even to the central or eastern grasslands."

Tubbs shot a questioning look at his son.

"You're telling me there's ranchers able to grow cattle that far north? You're funn'n me."

"No Pa, I ain't funn'n you. Like Wyoming and Nebraska, Montana is mostly grass, they tell me. Grass and the Rocky Mountains. Great cattle country but it's early in the game. Not many ranches there yet and not much market, once the gold miners are fed. Of course, the market brutes could be shipped down the Missouri River to the eastern market.

"Our best market might be for bred heifers. Ranchers could grow their herds quickly if enough quality heifers were driven that way."

"As to ranching that far north, and since you're sitting down, and your heart can probably handle another surprise, I'll tell you this. Folks are talking up the grass in Canada, north of Montana and Dakota. Say it's a better country than Wyoming. Millions of acres of grass and nary a cow critter in sight. That's how folks that's been there are telling it. All I have is saloon talk but I heard the same story from several sober men. Got to be at least some truth to the matter.

"Now you will understand, I wasn't up that far. I had no reason to go beyond Cheyenne. And I only stayed in that country to winter the herd. Pointed my nag south just as soon as opportunity allowed."

Tubbs and his wife sat in newly informed silence. Never once in their lives had they seen a map of the north country or considered the merits of the northern land for cattle. That information would require some ruminating on before it settled in their minds.

Without further debate Trev made a quick ride to Fort Worth and came back with a crew of riders. Most were green at trailing but a couple of experienced drovers, along with Trev and the two men who rode home from the last drive could handle the job alright. Within one week the herd was on the trail. Tubbs rode along for the first few miles and then dropped off to the side to watch the animals file past.

The short winter passed quickly, with the crew alternating between herding the yard animals and riding the hills. Trev and most of the crew returned right after Christmas. Their drive to Cheyenne was successful. They immediately began planning for the next spring's drive, this time into Montana.

The short, spring roundup, much smaller and simpler than the one the year before, was completed. The men were back to their yard duties, branding and sorting the herd, readying the market animals for a north drive. Put together with some held-over market steers from the previous spring's gather, plus the bred heifers, there was a sizable group.

John and Caleb were each working with the captured horses when Tubbs rode his gelding up to the corral.

"Come over here, boys."

The two Black cowboys trotted their geldings up to the corral fence. Caleb swung his leg over the animal's neck, resting it comfortably with his knee, hooked over the horn.

With no introduction or reason for the question,

Tubbs said, "How many saleable horses do you think we could put together right at this time?"

John and Caleb sat silently for several seconds before turning their eyes to look at each other as if asking 'what do you think'.

John's lips moved a bit as he mentally figured a number. Finally, he again looked at Caleb but his riding partner had always grabbed up second place when in John's company. Caleb offered no help.

"There's maybe four of de new horses what could be sold as good work'n animals, Boss. That's not say'n they wouldn't benefit from some more time here on the T, but any good rider can get a day's rid'n outa dem. Not quite sure if'n dey be fit fer de ladies yet. But I'm thinking you could spare some of de ranches' animals. May be best for de T, if'n you was to sell off some of de older horses and we, dat's Caleb and me, we was to train up de new ones..."

John had more thoughts on that but Tubbs interrupted him.

"John, that's a great plan. I'd like to take and run ten or twelve saddle animals into Fort Worth in a couple of days. You fellas pick out good solid rides from our old stock. We can spare that many while you get the others trained up. You get that done and the two of you can ride along with Trev. Take the sale animals inta town. Maybe leave them with your blacksmith friend at the livery. He can hold them for sale."

Completely satisfied with his decision, Tubbs turned and trotted his mount back to the barn.

Chapter 42

Caleb jumped down from his saddle and swung the gate open to the big corral beside the livery barn in Fort Worth. Trev and John pushed fourteen horses in and then tied their own animals to the outside of the corral fence.

Stepping to the ground, the two drovers lifted their hats, almost in unison, wiping the sweat from the foreheads with their shirt sleeves. They turned towards the barn in time to see a young man walking towards them.

"Help you fellas?"

Trev answered, "Need to do a piece of business with the boss."

John spoke up with, "Grant be around dis afternoon?"

"He's here. In the smithy. Powerful busy though. He leaves the livery to me."

Trev smiled at the young man while he said, "And I'm sure you do a great job of it too."

As was his common habit, Caleb tried to make himself invisible while Trev and the livery worker studied on each other. John quietly walked towards the front of the barn and the door into the smithy. As his shadow passed across the anvil Grant was working on, the smithy glanced up, taking his eyes from his work for only the briefest moment, before again taking a twist on the hot iron he was forming into a gate hinge. Then, as if a light had been turned on in his memory, his head snapped up, studying the smiling figure blocking the doorway's light. He laid his tools across the anvil and turned fully around.

"John. Is that really you?"

"Dat be me Grant."

The smith wiped his hands on an already dirty rag and reached for John's hand. The two big men shook, smiling at each other, lost for words for a short time. Still clutching John's hand, Grant led his Black friend outside, away from the heat of the forge.

"John, John. I can't tell you how good it is to see you. You're looking well. I'm guessing you've found ranch life to be to your liking. What brings you into the big city today?"

"Brought some horses for y'all ta sell. We put dem inta de big corral. My boss man be talk'n ta yer livery keeper over ta der."

"Well, let's go see what you've got."

As John and Grant approached the corral, Trev stepped forward.

"You must be Grant. I'm Trev Tubbs, Triple

T ranch. John tells me you met my father some months back."

"Indeed, I did. Hired away a friend of mine, one of the best men I've ever known. Did me a favor at the same time. Bought up this barn and business from John after he decided to go to ranching. Now I'm told you have some horses that need selling. Tell me what you've got and what you want done."

The arrangement for the care and sale of the horses took only a few minutes. When that was done, Grant said, "Now, I'm assuming you fellas are planning for a night or two in the hotel before you head back. Perhaps you would agree to be my guests, that's mine and Mrs. Wagner's, in the hotel dining room this evening."

John couldn't hold back his grinning question.

"Der be a Mrs. Grant now?"

"Yes, indeed. I am married, and happily so. You will remember Miss Talon from the city office, John. She's not Miss anymore. Not for these past four months. I'm hoping she's the better for the change. I certainly know I am."

Trev and Caleb didn't know how to respond to that news but John met it with another big smile.

"Nice lady. An' she not be 'Miss' anymore." John said this with a grin and a question in his voice as if needing confirmation of the fact.

"Indeed not."

Trev wanted to free himself from matters that didn't concern him. He needed to find a hotel room and do a bit of shopping that his mother especially asked for.

"We'll go now and get ourselves settled in, Grant. Does six work for dinner for you?"

With that settled and arrangements for the keeping of their saddle animals made, each man threw his bedroll, with a change of clothing rolled up inside, over their shoulders and headed for the hotel. When there was no argument about renting rooms to the two Black men, John took it as a further sign of the big changes taking place in the country. He was also aware that these changes would not be quite so advanced in other places and may not even include all of Fort Worth. But with Blacks now making up over twenty percent of all ranch riders, this working end of the city had been forced into making concessions unheard of, or unimagined, short years before.

Caleb and John felt no need to make any purchases, so they wandered down to the cantina and drank coffee and ate some Mexican sweet rolls the cook had put together. Without making a big fuss over it, Caleb insisted on picking up the tab. With some of his wages weighing heavy in his pocket, he took it as the first opportunity he had to show his gratitude for the many meals John had laid down the coins for.

Walking into the dining room in time to meet Grant and the new Mrs. Wagner, it was obvious, from looks, that the three cowboys had each found and used the hotel bathtub.

Mrs. Wagner blushed and said nothing as her husband extolled on her virtues and was vociferous on the improvements in his life since the two had become one.

The dinner spread before them was adequate to the point of stretching their appetites to near the breaking point. The dinner and the conversation filled a pleasant evening, a total change from a typical ranch day. But morning comes early in a cowboy's life and the men were anxious to wrap up the visit. With handshakes all around and promises to meet again as soon as circumstances allowed, Grant and his bride made their exit but not before the smith pulled John off by himself. Quietly and unobtrusively, Grant reached into his jacket pocket and withdrew a small canvas sack, tied tight at the top with drawstrings. He pressed it into John's hand and curled the big black man's fingers around it with a smile and a 'thank you'.

"That will settle the amount owing on the barn John. And a couple of coins extra for interest. You can count it if you wish."

John, somehow recognizing that to pour out the gold coins for counting, in a land where a man's word was his bond, would be an insult, grinned and said, "Well, I'm tanking yo fo dat Grant."

With that, he dropped the sack into his own pocket and nothing more was said.

The men got an early start home the next morning, riding along with three new cowboys and a cook. Trev had hired the men for the next north drive.

Life on the "T" fell smoothly into the pleasant months of full spring. Trev and his riders from the north worked over the cattle until they felt they had a trail herd worth the trouble and risk of a drive. They held back two hundred heifers from the new gather, planning on offering them as bred heifers or herd replacements the next spring.

With the other riders Trev had hired in Fort Worth, plus the cook, working from the back of a canvas-covered democrat wagon, and a neighbor boy, who was pushing hard into adulthood, acting as remuda hostler, the herd was ready to be pushed off the T and onto the trail north.

Caleb, waiting until the last moment, said, "I be sure lik'n ta see dat new country off der to da north. Maybe so, you use me on dis here drive?"

Trev and his father communicated without words, simply studying each other for a few seconds. With a slight nod from Tubbs, Trev grinned at Caleb.

"Grab your bedroll. We're leaving out of here right this very minute. You'll have to catch up."

With so many herds being pushed up the trail, grazed down grass and dried-up water sources, or markets already satisfied by other drives, was a constant worry. But Tubbs sent them off anyway, praying for the best results.

John worked the horses by himself for the summer while the other riders cared for the cattle.

When Tubbs felt the timing was right, counting the months for the next spring's calving, he turned the younger bulls in with the heifers, as he had done the year before. He would keep them in the yard until fall, before turning them out to graze the hills of the Triple T.

Chapter 43

As 1871 rolled into view, John was twenty-six-years-old and had been free from slavery for the past six of those years. He often thought of his parents and his brothers and sisters. Wondering about them. Missing them. But the single time he had asked Lefty to write a letter for him, addressing it to the pastor of the Black church back in the village beside the Shady Lane Farm, the pastor had written back saying the family had moved north, looking for work. He had neither seen nor heard from them again. The chances of finding where they had gone were very slim.

Beyond his disappointment at the loss of his family, the news left John wondering what had happened on the Shady Lane Farm that would cause his family to look for better options. He would probably never have that curiosity satisfied.

With the work on the "T" caught up, Tubbs spoke to the men who hadn't followed Trev on the drive.

"Neighbor down south a ways. Murphy Blandon by name. Double X Ranch. Small spread. He seems to like it that way. Only carries the two riders year-round. Brings in some help for roundup. Wasn't on the roundup himself but you met his boys out on the grass. After roundup, his three brought-in boys asked for their pay before the sorting and branding was done. Off to see the elephant, I'm guessing. Wants to borrow a crew. Three, four men to do the branding and such. I figure the "T" can spare a few of you men for a couple of weeks. Won't take any longer than that. Any of you want'n a change of scenery for a short bit?"

The men silently studied each other across the breakfast table. It was soon apparent that the men were indifferent. Someone asked if Mrs. Blandon was as good a cook as Mrs. Tubbs. There was light laughter around the group but it was also obvious that, for the men, their stomachs were as important as their pay envelopes. Tubbs, himself, brought it to a head.

"Ain't no one I ever knowed what could rattle the pots and pans like Mrs. Tubbs. But I expect no one would suffer down to the Double X either. Blandon himself looks healthy enough."

It was finally decided that John would go along with Alejandro and Jorge. Caleb had again joined the crew pushing the trail herd north, towards Cheyenne.

With about twenty miles to ride, the men waited until the following morning to pull away from the "T".

Tubbs' guess proved to be about right. The XX work was done up in just short of two weeks. When Alejandro and Jorge rode back into the "T" alone, at first Tubbs looked into the distant trail they had followed. Deciding that John was not coming along, he looked over to where the two Mexican riders were tying their mounts to the corral.

"Don't see John with y'all."

Jorge waited for Alejandro to speak. When that didn't happen, he took a step away from his horse, dragging the saddle with him. He swung the saddle and blanket onto the top rail and then reached to lead the animal into the corral before looking back at Tubbs. Finally, he turned.

"John was offered a horse training job over to the Double X. Sent you a message. Said he was thankful for all you done for him and that he'd be along one day soon to pick up his pay and such. No horse work left here on the "T", so he decided to take up with Blandon."

Tubbs stared at the man as if he couldn't believe the message. He turned to Alejandro as if he might offer some further insight into John's thinking. Finally, accepting the truth of the message, he turned and made a slow walk to the house. It was true, what John said. There was no horse work left on the "T". Not much work at all as far as that went. He would have to think on this. And how better was a man to think than with a cup of coffee to hand, sitting in the shade of his covered front porch?

Chapter 44

As Alejandro explained it to Tubbs, on the XX that morning Blandon had looked across the breakfast table at John. There were just the six of them sitting with their last coffee for the morning. There was Blandon himself and his Missus, along with a fella that called himself Bo, a long, whisper-thin rider that drifted in a year or so before, looking for a job, or at the least, a cup of coffee, and stayed on to become the single steady man on the ranch.

Along with them were the three men borrowed from the T.

"Cattle works about done up for a spell fellas. Bo, working along with me can pretty much keep up for the summer. Alejandro, Jorge, John, I have your pay ready for you. Thanks for the work done. And tell Tubbs that I appreciate letting you boys go for a few days. You're free to ride back just as soon as the mood should strike you.

"But the word around, John, is that if'n a feller

wants to have his horses broke easy, that is, with a combination of kindness and discipline, making it so's a man can get a day's work outa the nags without he has to be spurr'n every minute of the day, it's John you need to have doing the break'n.

"'Never a better horseman in the land.'

"Heard that about you too.

"'No one can train a horse like John.'

"'Stronger than a Texas norther,'" so some are say'n.

"'Train a cutt'n horse till a fella can work cattle with his hands in his pockets if'n he was to choose to do so.'

"'Waste of a good horseman to have him work'n cattle,' that's the news being whispered about.

"'Quiet man worth listening to, comes to horse talk.'

"'Walked away from a good livery business down to Fort Worth to go cowboying.'

"Heard all of that about you and more yet. Any of that true John? Or maybe-so is it all true?"

John sat silently, looking at the table, and the wreck of dirty dishes left over from their just-completed breakfast, not knowing how to answer. Into the uncomfortable silence, Bo, normally not a talker himself, dared to speak.

"Worked together, John and me, for just the few days. Got some things yet to learn about cow critters. Comes to horses though..." He stopped his talk at that point, wondering if he had been right to speak at all.

Mrs. Blandon patted the back of her husband's

hand.

"Let it go, my dear. I expect the talk you heard was right enough but you can see that you're embarrassing John. Time will tell if John will stay on for a while, like you're wanting him to. Wouldn't be long and we'd all see what strengths the Lord has given him. Let it go for now."

John thanked her with his eyes, still not saying anything.

Blandon nodded at his wife's words and said, "I guess what I'm trying to say John is that there's a job here for you if you want to work horses. I keep saddle horses, of course. But I also keep some runners. You haven't seen them yet. They're down in the bottom pasture. Run like the wind those boys will and love every minute of it. Beat most any other animal in a straight out run. Exciting just to be around.

"How'd you like to stay on and work with my runners?"

Tubbs listened to all of this, sorting out the truth through Alejandro's somewhat garbled English. He then thanked Alejandro and went to saddle a horse. On the rare occasion when coffee and quiet didn't solve the questions swirling through Tubbs' mind, there was always riding. He would ride now.

Later that evening, with John's decision to stay with the XX, working with the running horses, behind him, and the day's work done, John and Bo sprawled across their beds in the tiny bunkhouse, visiting out the last hour of the day.

"Seems like as if one of those big ranches would

put you to work John, paying a good bit better than what you'll earn on the Double X. I don't know as you're the best man with horses I ever saw but you're at least right up there with the very best. Ever think of going south to where the big fellas hold their cattle in the multiple thousands and their riders in the dozens and their horses in their hundreds?"

John turned a bit to get a better look at his riding partner.

"Never did. I think I's be better just where I's at. I work, do de best job I can. Save my wages. Maybe-so some day soon I have enough for a small spread jest fer Ol' John. Dat be a good day. Maybe-so it happen. Some day."

"Well John, I hope you make it. Had a dream like that myself one time. Danged ol' war kind of took the hope out of me. But a man can't see into the future. Not too far anyhow. Never know what might come about. For either one of us. Jest got to keep on breathing and working. Breathing and working..."

Later, when the lamp was blown out and Bo was snoring in his bunk a few feet away, John lay awake, with his arms folded above him, his interlaced fingers cupping his head, his mind swirling with all that had been said that day. And with his thoughts trying to make some sense of it all. He re-traced his long ride from the slave farm to where he was now. That made him remember the one time he and Sol had found opportunity for a private talk. Sitting in the shade of a scraggly bush, eating the lunch Mrs. B had packed them, they got to visiting.

In answer to a question from John, Sol had said, "I was never a slave John. Or I guess I was if a child can rightly be called a slave. My folks saw the opportunity to escape and they ran. Pa was killed along the way by the slave hunters but my Mother made it to safety with me and a younger sister. I was old enough to run myself. Mother ran, carrying my sister. I don't remember much about it but I seem to recall hiding and crawling and praying. And along the way, there were folks that helped us. I have no idea who they were.

"Even being free, life wasn't any way easy, what with my Mother having no man to support her, and all. But she made do somehow. Year or so later a fella knocked on our door. We'd seen him around the little town we lived in but didn't know him or his name.

"Being polite, mother asked him in and gave him a cup of tea. She wasn't a coffee drinker. Anyway, coffee was too expensive to buy for a widow woman who made do on housekeeper wages. The visit didn't last longer than it took to drink that cup of tea and I seem to remember the man was uncomfortable sitting up to table with Mother. Three or four other visits followed that one, including a couple where my sister and I were scooted outside, leaving the two of them alone.

"Long and the short of it was that this fella had lost his wife to the fever and was left with three little ones he knew he couldn't raise himself. He had a pretty good income from a factory job.

"Of course, you can see where this story is going. He became my stepfather and life improved for all of us. He turned out to be a good man. Good for Mother and good for all the kids."

John remained silent as the story was being told. Scratching in the grass and dirt at his feet, Sol seemed to be looking for an ending to the talk. He struggled with it for a few seconds before saying, "Not just exactly sure why I told you that story John, as true as it all is. And maybe I'm no example or no one to talk. But the truth is, if we want something in life, like that fella wanted a good wife, we need to do some planning and then step out. Step out to where that want can be found.

"Makes me wonder if you have a want, John. You see most of the aging riders, the ones hanging around the towns telling old stories to anyone who will listen, that's your future. And mine too, if we don't have a want and go after it. Those fellas mostly spent their pay on drink and gambling, laughing at the ones who saved against a cold winter. Well, now their cold winters have come upon them, their pay is spent, and no one will hire them.

"That doesn't paint the kind of picture I see for myself. Now, you might say, 'well, you're just riding the country, chasing another man's cows.' As true as that is, you got to understand. I just took a hankering to see some country. This is no permanent thing. I've got me some land back east. A full quarter section. Hundred and sixty acres of grass and hope for the future. Nice spot. Big ol' oak trees. Stream running through. Little fishing hole, or a swimming hole, whatever a man might see in it. House is kind of old, but livable. Barn built for milking, although I don't see myself going in that direction.

"I'm heading back there after this next trip. Pretty little lady in the next town I've kind of been sweet talking. Got to get back before some other fella turns her head."

After another short silence, he finished with, "Yep, you got to have a want in this life John. Got to have a want."

Much later, after a restless hour lying awake, John started to piece together his 'want'. The picture wasn't at all new. But now it held more detail. A few acres of land, a herd big enough to provide for him and a growing family, a good stable of horses, a woman. The woman's face wouldn't come clear. It couldn't be expected to. But he already had a name picked out for her. A private name. Not necessarily the one her parents had tagged her with but a love name he would place on her for himself. He didn't know when, or how, or where. All he knew was that he had a picture. A want, as Sol had called it. He had saved his earning since his first pay back on the Macintyre Horse Ranch. It wasn't enough. Not yet. But it was a start.

Yes, he had a want. Indeed, he did.

Not the end
To be continued

We have no intention of leaving John lying in a hard bunk on the XX ranch. But it's enough for now. It's been a long trail and a ranch rider needs some rest.

But follow along to book two of Just John,
coming soon.

JUST JOHN
Book two
Northward to Home

Tom Lynch stood in his stirrups and waved his Stetson over his head, trying to gain John's attention. But it was Clayton Burgess who saw the wave and lifted his hat while staring across the herd, in effect asking a question. Tom pointed his hat at John, barely visible through the dust cloud and the rising heat waves off the backs of the sweating cattle. Clayton dipped his hat in understanding. He turned in his saddle. A shrieking whistle sounded through his teeth and over his curled lips, a sound that gained John's attention, but also a sound that Tom feared would one day cause the herd to rise into a run.

When John looked up, Clayton pointed across the backs of twelve hundred dusty, sweating animals. It was only then that the Black rider understood. Waving his own hat, John pulled off to the side, from his flank position, and waited for the tail end of the herd to pass him by.

As the last drag rider, enveloped in dust and sweat and cow stink, rode past him, John kicked his horse into motion, riding wide of the herd and the other crewmen. In a couple of minutes, he pulled up beside Tom, who was sitting with one leg hooked over the horn, while his cigarette smoke rose into the dusty air.

Initially, Tom had refused to take the black man onto the drive crew. He had no faith in any black man's riding ability, or his handling of horses or cattle. It was only when Bill Moodie made himself clear to Tom, 'no John, no Bill,' that the trail driver relented.

Tom had wanted Bill, a well experienced drover and a widely respected man. He nodded his approval with the condition, "I'll give him a few days to prove up. I'll not have a man that leaves his load for others to carry."

Since that day John had shown himself to be the equal of any man on the drive.

"John, you see that pile of rocks over there?"

"Yassir, Boss. What that be for? Why someone take de time ta pile de rocks up out here on dis grass?"

"Have you ever seen a map of the country John? I mean the whole country, top to bottom and side to side."

"No sir, Boss, I ain't never seen no map like dat"

"Where are you from originally John? I'm assuming you were a slave on some farm or plantation."

"Yassir, I be slave down to Sout' Carolina. Big farm. Left from outa der 'n rode dis here old Hound-

Dog horse to Tennessee. Worked on de horse ranch fo more dan one year befo rid'n wit some fok's to Fort Worth. Dat be down to Texas. I be in Fort Worth past one year. Den go ride fo' Mr. Tubbs. He own de "T" ranch down der. Stay der maybe-so more den fo' years. Rancher, he be kep me on fo' to work de cattle 'n de horses. Mostly de horses. Gentle and train fo rid'n and fo' pull'n de wagon. Rancher, he sell de horses down to Fort Worth."

"So how did you get up here? To Montana?"

"I be work'n for nother ranch. Mr. Blandon, he own de XX. Small place wit jest de two riders. Fella named Bo an Ol' John. Boss man Blandon, he raise de runn'n horses. Racehorses, he call dem. Raise cow critters too but mostly he love de horses.

"I be work'n der three years, training de horses and chas'n de cows, time ta time. Den, I be want'n ta see mo' o' de country, Boss. Maybe-so find other way ta make money for ta buy my own ranch some-day. Maybe-so make more dan de ranch job. I ride wit' de herd. Go to place be call Dodge City. Den we take 'nother herd ta place be call Cheyenne. Dat be in Wyoming. Big place. Lots a people, maybe-so near as big as Fort Worth. Too much crowded. Ol' John not want'n ta stay. Ride wit Bill Moodie tak'n 'nother herd to dis Montana place.

"Bill Moodie, he say we go ta de gold mine. Maybe-so we make much money. Mor' dan fo herding de cows."

John chuckled at his last statement while Tom smiled at the remembrance of the story with the unhappy ending that Bill, himself, had told.

"Well John, you've seen more of these United States than I have. I've seen maps of the whole area though. The country is very big. But although it's a big land, it doesn't just keep on going. Mexico hangs tight on the southern border and the oceans wash up to the east and west coasts. On the north is Canada. Some years ago, the surveyors worked their way across this vast land and staked out the borders. They marked that border from east to west for thousands of miles. Sometimes they placed iron peg markers into solid rock. I'm told that's what they did in the high up mountains.

"But on the grasslands," Tom continued, pointing to the large stack of rounded prairie boulders, placed in a rough square about four feet to a side on the ground and rising to a single balanced rock at the top, about four feet above the surrounding grass, "where there is no rock to hold an iron peg securely, they piled up what's called a rock cairn. They might pile the rocks around an iron peg driven into the black loam or they may stand a wooded post up and pile the rock around it.

"What you're looking at there is a rock cairn, marking the border between the United States and Canada. Right now, sitting here, you and I are still in the United States. The herd has moved on, into Canada. And that's where we're going."

"Where we tak' dis herd Boss?"

"We're taking them to Fort McLeod. That's just a little over one hundred miles. We'll be there in less than a week."

"What be dis Fort McLeod place?"

"Fort McLeod is a small village, but it's where the Canadian police make their headquarters. They're called the North-West Mounted Police."

Tom dropped his foot back into the stirrup and nudged his horse into a walk. John rode along beside him, turning just once to look back at the rock cairn. The herd was walking in a tight group, showing no stragglers. John wouldn't be needed for another few minutes.

"The North West Mounted Police, the NWMP, as they're known, were set up by the Canadian federal government to police the western half of the country. They had some American whisky traders to push out. The whiskey trade was causing terrible problems among the Indians. And then, they hoped to hold the Indians to their own recognized territories and get them to stop the waring between the tribes.

"And, of course, they also hoped to have a peaceful situation for when the ranchers and farmers started arriving in larger numbers. That won't happen until the railway is finished. That will take some time yet.

"The Canadian government felt it was better to form up a special police force, rather than send out the army. They've been proved to be correct on that.

The settlements up here are not policed by local sheriffs like they are down south. The NWMP have taken on the task. Done a pretty good job of it too. Gun fights and violence are almost unknown.

Unfortunately, none of that means the Indians are being treated well or fairly but so far, the Mounties have pretty well held it together."

John seemed to think on this information for a few seconds before turning to Tom.

"I's be going back to da job now Boss. Maybe-so we talk again bout dis Canada place."

"Maybe-so we will, John."

To be continued

If you like this, check out: Mac's Way

Raised in poverty in Missouri, Mac is determined to find a better life for himself and the girl who is still a vague vision in his mind. Work on the Santa Fe Trail, and on a Mississippi River boat give him a start, but the years of Civil War leave him broke and footloose in South Texas. There he discovers more cattle running loose than he ever knew existed. Teaming up with two ex-Federal soldiers, he sets out to gather his wealth, one head at a time.

While gathering and driving Longhorns, Mac and his friends meet an interesting collection of characters, including Margo. Mac and Margo and the crew learn about Longhorns, and life, from hard experience before they eventually head west. Outlaws and harrowing river crossings are just two of the challenges they face along their way.

AVAILABLE NOW

About the Author

Reg Quist's pioneer heritage includes sod shacks, prairie fires, home births, and children's graves under the prairie sod, all working together in the lives of people creating their own space in a new land.

Quist's career choice took him into the construction world. From heavy industrial work, to construction camps in the remote northern bush, the author emulated his grandfathers, who were both builders, as well as pioneer farmers and ranchers.

Quist's writing career was late in pushing itself forward, remaining a hobby while family and career took precedence. Only in early retirement, was there time for more serious writing.